THE WATER CYCLE

Novel

Andrew Nyongesa

Mwanaka Media and Publishing Pvt Ltd,
Chitungwiza Zimbabwe

*

Creativity, Wisdom and Beauty

Publisher:
Mmap
Mwanaka Media and Publishing Pvt Ltd
24 Svosve Road, Zengeza 1
Chitungwiza Zimbabwe
mwanaka@yahoo.com
https//mwanakamediaandpublishing.weebly.com

Distributed in and outside N. America by African Books
Collective
orders@africanbookscollective.com
www.africanbookscollective.com

ISBN: 978-0-7974-9439-8
EAN: 9780797494398

© Andrew Nyongesa 2018

DISCLAIMER

All views expressed in this publication are those of the author
and do not necessarily reflect the views of *Mmap*.

AKNOWLEDGEMENT

I wish to thank the following people for their assistance to make this book successful: Mr. Stephen Barasa, my composition writing teacher who taught me empathy as a cornerstone in creative writing. Mr. David Sikulu, my high school teacher of English who guided me to work hard and succeed in life. Dr. John Mugubi (Kenyatta University); he gave me a strong foundation in stylistics. Dr. Kisa Amateshe; he taught me the importance of grammatical rules in writing. Dr. Justus Makokha for his exemplary mentorship and networking that accessed me to serious publishers. My late father, Japheth Nyongesa who taught me the importance of education in life. I thank my wife Esther Mualuko for giving me the peace and moral support to write this book.

DEDICATION

I dedicate this novel to my mother Lena Simiyu Nyongesa. Thank you for raising me well and teaching me the folklores of my people.

GLOSSARY

Bakoki: A Luhya term used to refer to a colleague in the age set.

Bamaina: Men who belong to the ageset, Maina of Bukusu community.

Bayobo: A term used by the Luhya to refer to the Sabaot people who live on Mount Elgon (Mount Masaba).

Enderema: A climbing plant with smooth leaves that grows along rivers in Western Kenya.

Ekhafu: A Bukusu word for cattle.

Enguu: A herb that was used by the Luhya to treat wounds.

Ilitungu: A stringed, musical instrument among the Luhya people of Kenya.

Khuchukhila: A stage in Bukusu (Luhya) circumcision when a father advises the initiate and smears his body with a molten mixture of fermented flour and yeast.

Khutumia Kamaika: A rite that is carried out after marriage in which the groom works himself up in a tantrum to beat his wife as a welcome sign to the challenges of marriage.

Kumuse: A sitting of elders after death of a respected person that aims at counseling the bereaved and appropriate his wealth.

Kwiche: A Luhya word used to accept a challenge in a riddling session.

Mulembe yaya : It is courteous way of treating a sister.

Foreword

As Maya Angelou said, a bird doesn't sing because it has an answer, it sings because it has a song. *The Water Cycle* is yet another song from Andrew Nyongesa's copious literary harp. Through careful management of language in this novel, Nyongesa is able to yield pleasure. The splendour of linguistic manipulation at syntactic and lexical level brings out unsparing instinct for reality to bear on platitudes and pieties of society. The concreteness of texture of language employed evokes and recreates sensory perceptions that subtly depict the projected meaning. The sense of human tragedy dominates the main character, Kisiang'ani. It manifests through hubris and pathos in every milestone of his life. As Robert Frost would say, the author of *The Water Cycle* has "truly been acquainted with the night".

Because he knows the midnight as well as the high noon, because he understands the ordeals as well as the triumphs of the human spirit, in this novel, just like in *The Endless Battle* and *The Blissabyss*, Nyongesa holds deep faith in the spirit of humans, and it is hardly an accident that he couples Literature and power, for he sees Literature as the means of saving power from itself. When power in whatever form leads people like Mauka, Kisiang'ani and Mukesi towards pride, Literature reminds them of their limitations. When power narrows areas of people's concern, Literature reminds them of the richness and diversity of their existence and the need to promote healthy vibrant societies to ameliorate human suffering; to promote a thoughtful, empathetic world order. Where power corrupts, literary art cleanses; for literature establishes the basic human truth which must serve as the touchstone of our judgment.

I congratulate Andrew Nyongesa on being faithful to his personal vision of reality. And in *The Water Cycle*, through the physical, cultural and psychological conflicts in the prime mover, the author remains a champion of the individual mind and sensibility against an unfeeling, narcissistic and intrusive society. In pursuing his perceptions of reality, like Mukesi, the author often sails against the currents of time. This is not popular role, but he soldiers on like a true artist.

John Mugubi, phD
Dean, School of Creative Arts, Film and Media Studies
Kenyatta University, Nairobi.

PROLOGUE

"Gather your shattering pieces and be firm. Dry your emotional springs and be hard." That was his mantra. A man had to be strong. A man had to be lion hearted to protect his wife and children from enemies. Many a time, he exhorted his sons that fears and tears never ought to be familiar with manhood. He was a man whose gifts would spun many generations. He was a man of means; a celebrated proprietor of tens of wives, hundreds of children and thousands of cattle. This was evident in his appearance: bull shoulders, fat cheeks, sinewy muscles and a shiny dark skin. A hale and hearty man. Ever clad in a leopard skin from a beast he had single handedly killed adjacent to his cave. He had sworn in the name of his ancestors to hand it down to hundreds of descendants as an eligible monument of his courage and fearlessness. Every first born son of each generation was entitled to the skin.

He considered it a duty he owed society to kill every stranger he encountered. He did not just have a strong attachment to war but was a seasoned architect of the same. His air was grave and ghost-like. Any encounter with a man who could not respond to his greeting in the language of Mwambu yielded a duel whose consequences were tragic. Such to him, were atrocious intruders into the privacy of the sons of Mwambu and deserved death penalty or severe fines in form of women or cattle, depending on his whims.

In his sage advice to sons, which he seldom gave, he held that other tribes especially Bayobos, were dishonourable characters. He exhorted his sons to instigate scathing brawls whenever they bumped into them, the result of which was wealth: women, cattle or land. He never bickered with a wife.

He never argued with a son. He thundered and they darted in frenzy. Dance to his tune or die.

He was a valiant man. He would not allow this foreigner who was approaching him this misty evening to live. He was on his trap inspection tour on the outskirts of Chebyuk.

He had stood at a desolate place surrounded by little thin trees. Caves and high grasses, peering into a distant west. An intruder was pacing towards him; a thin rascal. He set his pipe of Marijuana ablaze and smoked it with great vehemence. His bloodshot eyes beheld the sun setting in Masolo and a gust of the wind blowing the mist towards Okoro, the distant depression yonder.

The foreigner came closer and the valiant man warmed up for combat. His first act was to tighten his grip on the spear. Secondly, fasten the grasp on the shield. Thirdly, clear his throat of phlegm to draw his opponent's attention. His fourth, was hampered by swearing,

'I'll kill him or get circumcised again. Am I not a descendant of Mango? The courageous man who killed a flying snake?'

"If he's a Muyobo, I'll kill him."

".....how are you!" The man uttered his fourth act in first language to place the identity of the stranger. The stranger stared at the apparition timidly.

He seemed to be on his gathering tour to the forest. In a rising scotching fury, the 'mighty' man warmed himself up for a duel. In a flip of an eyelid, a flying arrow reached him and in a flash hauled his shield to immolate its break neck momentum. The 'valiant' man advanced towards his opponent. A torrent of arrows reached him at short intervals. He dodged and blocked them with the shield. The man hurtled through the high grasses and scything weeds. He slipped down the miry sloppy paths. He dodged high trees and flying arrows while his eyes were on the opponent. Although he was in flight, the stranger was retracting in his presence.

He paused to scheme his assault and the enemy halted too. He took a good stock of him. Thanks to Wele Khakaba, he had no arrow remaining. He vowed to employ every tactic his masculine wit could devise to kill the man. Nay. He could make a fortune from him. He sprang up and dashed at him. His shield firmly gripped in his left. His spear rose shoulder high in a throwing pose. The race intensified. The adversary retracted as fast as though he was waiting for death.

"I'll throw it!' He thundered. The enemy uttered a heart rending shriek and crashed on the ground to evade the spear. There he lay unharmed but under the valiant man's foot.

"Say what you will give me or die!" He growled.

He tapped his victim's tummy with the tip of his spear.

"No! Don't kill me. I'll give you five cows!" He cried.

"I don't want your sick cows!" The 'valiant' man refused.

"I'll give you Chemutai, my eldest daughter," the victim shrieked.

"Quickly!" The man roared.

They walked arm in arm to the victim's home a few yards away from the forest to obtain the day's booty. Although he thought of the possibility of the man having friends at home, he was not the kind of man even a hundred men confronted successfully. He swaggered with a bold defiance up to the scanty hedge of the man's shanty. The captive came out with a wailing naked girl and handed her over to him. A few miserable voices grumbled but died at the horrid sight of the fearless man who received the lass at the hedge. He motioned her to silence and led her to his cave in the vast homestead of Chebyuk to become his twentieth wife. Frowning cliffs cast a thick black darkness on every object around them as the orb of the sun went to bed in Masolo.

That was the 'prominent' man. The warrior of renown who fought resiliently. Bayobos were a nuisance in Mount Masaba but he always picked on one or two to serve as examples to the rest. These were revered principles and manners of Buchacha Milisio, a great ancestor of Kisiang'ani and the above episode, one of his many creations. He was shunned by friend and foe alike because to him people were insects and their blood a fantastic sight.

PART ONE:

Chapter One

Kisiang'ani picked a chair, threw it in front of his hut and slumped on it. He raised his sad face and surveyed their land. Their home stood at the top of a slopping terrain hatched by giant depressions that randomly appropriated the land into huge miserable chunks. One lonely mass stood on the south fronting him. It emerged from Okoro spring far below and agonized its way up to Cheleba at the summit. Its scanty settlement gave the boy a picture of a pretty maiden from whom suitors refrained. Another chunk rose from River Okoro and strove northwards to their home at the tip. Kisiang'ani gazed at the plateau between the blocks and saw dark caves, dark river valleys and strings of winding paths. He could also see minute heads of people scratching their farms.

Farther in the south beyond the rugged terrain, he beheld the plains of Okoro and Lwanda enclosed in the hazy horizon of Masolo. That was the place which was said to harbour emaciated dark people who did not get circumcised. The entire stretch of land from Lwanda, Mulatiwa, Chwele and Kimilili was owned by the sons of Mwambu.

The Bayobos sojourned in the land from Cheleba, Kebee, and Kapsakwanyi all the way to Kipsigon in the west. The remaining stretch of land from Kaboriot, Banandek and Korong'odunyi was inhabited by the Batono, people who resisted the light and fell in love with darkness in Mount Masaba forest.

Kisiang'ani would not understand how a human being could live on mere honey, shy away from traveling and greet no one on his way. The Okiek, as they were called in school, circumcised their boys randomly. They 'cut' a boy who asked for it at any time of the year, unlike his people who did it biennially.

Kisiang'ani was a slim boy of dark complexion. He had a broad face with enormous ears. His knees were bow legged with toes profusely enlarged by jiggers, which compelled his feet to face sideways whenever he walked. He was a disillusioned boy whose attempts to smile were thwarted by the rigours of life. Deprivation was depicted on each lineament of his face. He flounced around with a clouded brow and drooping neck. His attire was one: school uniform- a baggy orange shirt he had acquired from his uncle, Wetuya.

There is no doubt that Kisiangiani was a cross youth, like so many children in Cheleba who were abandoned to fend for themselves immediately they learned to pronounce a syllable. Consequently, it would be absurd to expect an iota of peace in his soul.

The boy was in the lowest and worst of his spirits. Everything around him was repulsive; beginning with his father Mauka. Kisiang'ani was not pleased with Mauka's apathy towards his education. Though this was the honey of Cheleba in the changing times, it surprised the boy that the subject was not licensed in the home.

He stood up and surveyed the home with utmost displeasure. All the two hundred yards to the east extending southward to Okoro springs and stretching a thousand yards to the west was Mauka's territory. There were no worries about land for inheritance. They were only three sons out of the nine children Butilu had borne; the land was their inheritance. It was a haunting ghost of Mauka's life. Butilu had negated her obligation of siring sons to inherit his land. Her insistence on siring girls infuriated him.

Mauka was a surly man with a permanent glare. Ever lonely, he conversed with none in the home but his pipe. He was tall and sinewy with dark complexion. His luxuriant crop of hair was unkempt and rolled on the nape of his neck in dirty strands. Mauka was a good hand at nothing but dissipation. He rose at cock-crow to go in search for bhang and booze. He either inhaled Marijuana steam or smoked it before embarking on the parental responsibility of discipline.

The leopard skin that Kisiang'ani at times spotted under his dark blanket was an indelible mark of his great ancestry. It complicated the possibility of a wife or child questioning his directives. His left hand carried a bottle of snuff and right, a long spear. His countenance bore a frown that evinced little or no consideration for children. Perhaps it would not be wrong to say that Mauka's feelings had been emptied by the invariable rites of the sons of Mwambu and the philosophies of his ancestors as handed down by his father. A child did not ask him for food or clothing; everything was on his farm. In any case he was neither delicately nurtured nor tenderly brought up. He held that society had a leader and the subject. The leader maintained a vertical communication with his subject. He was a chief enemy of discussion and never entertained a belligerent child. Something once directed had to be executed. Formal education, for instance, was white man's shit and no descendant of Buchacha's would step at the school as long as he was alive. Secondly, his oxen would only be released to the farm with his blessing. Kisiang'ani found this absurd.

Meanwhile words reached the young man; a kikuyu called Wamba had been nominated in the big house to represent black people. His mother had told him that he was fourteen seasons, two seasons away from initiation to manhood.

Kisiang'ani disliked this too. The wind was blowing and there seemed to be another initiation far better than the cutting of the foreskin. An initiated man had come to Cheleba, well bred and prosperous. He had wondered aimlessly in Cheleba with omukasa, village elder, encouraging parents to take their children to school. The man was Situma Barasa, his model. He was soft spoken with soft palms that seemed to have never touched a hoe but he was the headmaster of Cheleba Primary School.

In spite of Mauka's threats, Kisiang'ani resolved to go to the 'iron sheets' (school) to be like Situma Barasa. He looked at the agony that his people went through, 'scratching' that rugged terrain all year round. He decided to try another way. Mauka had condemned the disobedience in the strongest terms and fists had proceeded.

"You're not my son!" He had roared.

"Oh, dad, teacher said…"

"Idiot! Eat his b-!" He lashed out obscenities. "You left cattle to go and idle around that foolish, Situma!"

He growled, caning him. His excuses landed on deaf ears as Mauka flogged him. Tears had gashed from his eyes profusely, his body pulsating under excrutiating pain. He hurtled his way over the food, over the cow dung in the yard; thorn apple hedge and tumbled into the green maize. The tumult had risen behind him.

Since then, Kisiang'ani had become as miserable as orphans were in all aspects of life. The boy earnestly wished he were not born. Why a father craved obsolete and extravagant customs at the expense of education, he could not understand. It afforded him unmingled astonishment.

Mauka considered his son's disobedience as domestic treason; a credible symptom of rebellion and eventual failure.

But he was happy because he had indicated to him the concealed feelings of his bosom and his contribution towards the "crazy phenomenon."

But in the whole crisis, his mother remained hopeful in despair. Then he realized that women who were the most despised in Cheleba were the most affectionate and productive. He was touched by his mother's toils to support him, her attempts to generate life in the home, both of which were repugnant to Mauka's nature. The calm enduring way with which she bore his cruelty. Day by day, Mauka directed to her countless obscenities and insults. But her heart was still. She had loved him once and the glow of that first passion he had lit behind her father's kraal always awakened a feeling of submission in her bosom. Indeed every villager; every life in Cheleba had lots of pity for Butilu.

Whatever the boy would say to Butilu, he said not a word to Mauka. She exhorted him to work smart and excel at school. She remained the supreme sharer of all his troubles, joys and aspirations. Kisiang'ani planned his time into alternate allotments of learning and weeding in Chebyuk. His mother showed him this sole means of survival: weeding *erobo*. It was a quarter an acre of land full of weeds, which labourers, were allotted to weed for a few shillings' pay that sustained Kisiang'ani in school

The boy had exceptional aptitude as proved by his academic performance in the first year at school. He had maintained a brilliant record without strain. Kisiang'ani had become the jewel of pubescent girls but he had fallen for Sitawa on account of her boldness, industry and complexion. She was his sole competitor in class and it gave him jitters whenever he lacked fees.

Kisiang'ani stood up and flounced towards the kitchen. Sitting at the door was Nabangala sorting beans. The sun had risen to the centre of the sky and the mist was clearing away from the valley. Trees rustled in a light wind, birds sung on boughs and the tiniest grass was instinct with life.

"Why are you sad," Nabangala asked.

"Father refuses to pay my fees. Should I laugh?"

"Uuum, extreme stubbornness destroyed bird's beak," Nabangala warned.

"Firewood on the rack laughed at his friend in hearthstones."

"Ng'oo," she made a face, "I'll excite you."

"Do."

"Namunaiiiiii…(can I throw a riddle?)."

"Kwicheeee…(throw it)."

"Even if you try and try…"

"You can't catch air," Kisiang'ani answered.

"I leave through this and return through that."

"The sun."

"Namunaiiiiiiiiiii…?"

Kisiang'ani did not reply.

"What!" Nabangala tittered.

He flounced away with a grimace. He had become conscious of Nabangala's criticism in the first riddle. Kisiang'ani now made up his mind to solely step on the path to his ambition. Like a solitary blind man groping, he prepared to stumble on stones and fall in gullies to his destination. His siblings who he had thought backed him up against his callous father wished him failure. Distressing was his sleep and horrific his dreams, dreams that bore constant reference to failure. Nevertheless, he cherished his ambition.

His mother's hut caught his fresh sight. Reddish earthen floor, a wall of red mud hanging between rafters; bedding of large hide adjacent to the cooking stones, roofed by a firewood rack; clouds of soot strands dangled over it.

"What misery!" Kisiang'ani thought, "I won't live such life!" He declared under his breath. The roof was of grass thatch sand-witched with a few maize stalks. "Yes, I shan't live such a life," the boy spoke mentally, "I'll work with my hands, obtain my fees and study. I'll become a teacher like Situma, marry a teacher and put up a home near Masolo."

With a melancholic air, he quickened his pace to Chebyuk. Chebyuk was called 'Up' in Cheleba. If somebody said 'so and so went Up' then you tacitly understood that 'so and so' had gone to Chebyuk. It was the land from Kebee, Kipsigon, Kipsiro all the way to Rikai, the summit of Mount Masaba. Bayobo and Batono owned large tracts of land in this fertile region. When hard times came, the sons of Mwambu went Up in search for contracts. The masters would measure *erobo*; his people would weed it for four tins of potatoes or two white man's coins. That is what Kisiang'ani sought as he wandered where he could to raise his fees.

His ancestors, save for mythical Buchacha (who he doubted whether he lived) were known as far as Bangamek for their skill in using the hoe and rearing cattle. Those unfortunate to be employed in Chebyuk went as far as Kitali on white man's farms to work as tillers and herders. Industrious and honest they were, servants who neither stole the master's cattle nor crops.

But Kisiang'ani fidgeted. Some attributes of his people were piteous. Their poverty made them confuse confidence for pride. The trees rustled in the wind, birds sang upon boughs and the worker ants on the ground toiled on for survival. The grasshopper twanged in search for the day's meal as Kisiang'ani sought *erobo* for his sustenance.

Chapter Two

He was going to be circumcised. What delightful news! Buchacha's great grandson would soon be initiated into manhood. Word went from Cheleba to Rikai. Indeed the offspring of a great man is grand. Cheleba beamed with hilarity and butterflies fluttered merrily exulting in their short life. Everything was bright and cheery. People erected emblems of life everywhere. The Mauka's were the happiest on Mount Masaba to prepare this occasion to initiate a descendant of a 'valiant' man whose name carried granaries of his valiant acts; a man whose character was refined by peril and judgments, by the outcome. Who else but Buchacha epitomized manhood? Here had come a moment to circumcise a son entitled to his leopard skin in Mauka's house. Merry voices and laughter flew over the village. There was clanging of bells, blowing of horns, shouting of children and thumping of feet. They echoed and re-echoed in Cheleba from the earliest of dusk to the latest of dawn. The happy cheers accompanying pots of Busaa transformed Cheleba overnight. Noise and bustle; song and dance painted the entire landscape.

To many souls the rite brings long moments of leisure and pleasure. How many kinsmen scattered in Kitali, Bangamek and the city in their toils for survival are bound back to society in a happy state of love? It is an invariable rite and a man who evades it is a misfit. He is an abomination and will never be buried with a foreskin to defile the land of Mwambu and Sela. He would be circumcised on his death mat before burial. Even *bamia*, the Iteso, who lived among the sons of Mwambu had to lose that skin to save the land from defilement.

Kisiang'ani heard about black people joining *Lecheko* (legislative council). He could not make anything of it until Butilu explained that an African, Wamba Mathuu, had joined the whites in Nairobi to rule. He also heard that other people on the other mountain where Maina Wanalukale lived, were demanding for their land. Kisiang'ani did not understand why these people complained about land when in fact Mauka had more than enough for himself. Why wouldn't they go to Mount Masaba?

Kisiang'ani had a soft spot for the colonialist. Had he not saved his maternal grand father? He had filched him from the claws of famine in Masolo and given him a job. Raised by fate as an orphan, Wekutu, Butilu's father, had barely lived on porridge in Masolo. With the coming of the white man, he had got employed as a herder in Kitali. Hamstrung, the master, gave him a few coins with which he had bought six head of cattle. After leaving the master's farm, he had reared them well. In six seasons, he had raised eighty heads of cattle.

Wekutu's fame had spread like an invention in Sirisia, Nalondo, Namwesi and Sitabicha. This was a man whose Ugali was prepared using milk and his wife, Nanjala took the whole day milking his cows.

Nonetheless, colonialist or no colonialist, Kisiang'ani saw ahead of him the most trying moment of his life. It was a rite that inculcated a high moral in the initiates. It made him look forward with pleasant anticipation of the privileges that awaited the adults (initiated). Perhaps after it, his father would set him free to release oxen on the farm.

Among all the sons of Mwambu, circumcision ceremony was a furnace through which impure gold was refined into pure. It was the hearth on which raw milk was heated into an edible. It was a class for sex education, a house of rebuke and a theatre for presentation of love songs. It was a dais on which the candidate stood to tell the 'whole world' that he was no longer a boy but a mature man. Able to take someone's daughter to protect and provide for. Able to confront the storms of life and prevail. During this occasion, tears and fears were bled out and courage injected in the boy.

In spite of his poverty, Mauka could not be a let-down in this season of merriment when childhood was preparing to painfully pass away from his son. He had offered a fat bull to fulfill the pressing role of a father. Other plans were underway.

Chapter Three

Sitawa's undying desire to go to school came face to face with a dispiriting reaction from her father, Wamalwa. It was fruitless to torture her mind over the 'trifle'. It was never to be tolerated. It was never to be borne and she was depressed. She was anxious about her future. 'What is my future? These animals?' Sitawa asked herself with a profound scrutiny at the herd of cattle around her. Out of the fifteen years she had lived on earth, five she had laboured with her father's cattle without any fruit. Had her father been generous enough, he would have bought her 'a rag' to cover her waist from amorous glances of boys.

Nevertheless, her father deluded her into the belief that herding was profitable in itself. Of the ten children in their family, her father loved her most. His personal attachment to her could not be easily accounted for.

Wamalwa was a tall muscular man with an irrevocable passion for optimism. He had a smile that endured on his face. This light hearted manner did not mean compromise. Nay, he did not condone despair and laziness. Generally, he was a masculine replica of Sitawa. She could not doubt that her father cherished hard work and strength though without the cruelty she saw among men in Cheleba.

A man must work, was his common saying. He was so obsessed with it. He argued that it was a man's tears, something Sitawa did not understand. "If a man cries around, who will encourage his wife and children?" He would say. Wamalwa therefore maintained that tears, fears, laments and pity were unwelcome on the menu of manhood.

As Sitawa roamed in Namwela with cattle, she thought about her father, what he stood for and the outcome. For Wamalwa, energy was for production and not for fighting. Only lay-abouts fought. Consequently, diligence was the truss of riches and as long as a man maintained a tight grip on the hoe and strap, he would grow rich in crops and cattle.

She could see why her father had tens of head of cattle, hundreds of goats and sheep on the vast homestead. It stood on the southern end of Cheleba Primary School. The home proclaimed Wamalwa as a man of honour matched to none except the upstart Situma.

Resting in front his hut this morning, Wamalwa laboured under temporary annoyance and anxiety. He glanced at the 'iron sheets' on the north. Their shiny reflection intimidated the brown of his grass thatch. The rectangular deviant haughtily poised at the summit of the rising landscape. He grasped his staff and smoked his pipe with critical solemnity. It was cold and the sun was rising above the school.

Clad in a dark blanket, Wamalwa moved his gaze to the land in the south. He could see Chwele, Kimilili and Kitali far below. His home stood on a slanting terrain that descended into a gigantic valley. The valley stretched thousands of yards into the distant hazy horizons of Masolo.

"I'm saving my coins, I'll go there," he pointed beyond Kitali, "and buy a moving hut," he broke into a grin but the shiny iron sheet drew his attention again. It dwarfed his joy. In pretext of learning, it had swallowed all his children. It was Wanangali, the monster. It had begun with the 'effeminate' Situma wandering in Cheleba, pleading with men to release their children. Mauka, Wanyenya and other respected elders had refused but Wamalwa had released his worst and reserved the best children. But an ogre was an ogre; give him a finger and he grabs the whole hand. They had compelled him day by day until most of his children went to the iron sheet. Had he not sent his favourite out to herd, she would be there too.

Then would he be a "fertile impotent" and his children, orphans without a father to train them into the ways of their ancestors. What father would rejoice to sire children and abandon them to strangers to nurture into ways he did not embrace. Ponder as he would, Wamalwa could not accept these misleading changes. Today, he vowed in the name of Sindani, never to desert Sitawa in the hands of foreigners.

Meanwhile, Sitawa loitered in the bush grazing. With a glance at the climbing sun, she concluded that it was morning. She was a thin, brown girl with a tattered banana sheath at the pubic area. Only the dangling gourd of milk on her neck covered her budding breasts.

Sitawa wished her father assigned her brothers this tedious job. The wilderness was full of dangers her sex could not stand. There was rape from boys, threat of leopards, elephants, lions and scaring serpents in the rocks.

Two seasons ago, her grandfather, Wekhanya had confronted a leopard. He had secured its fore limbs and wrestled the whole day without victory on either side. Her father, Wamalwa had appeared at the scene. In an acute feat, he had driven his spear in the beast; it had died then. As bad luck would have it, its fur had infected Wekhanya with a queer disease; he had died three days later.

This was sufficient evidence she hung on to disobey her good father. But many hindrances stood ahead. A mere teenager and worse still a girl, other options except rebellion could do. A mother's curse to her was tolerable but a father's lament was unbearable.

There was a cool breeze blowing over her body this morning. She solaced herself with the thought of Situma, the man who would remain a legend forever. He spoke through the nose as white men did. He pissed milk and shat biscuits. His airs were greatly affected by the softening effects of novelties. He could buy the whole Mount Masaba in a stroke of a pen and Sitawa yearned for such a husband. A husband who ploughed with his pen, sowed with his pen and weeded with his pen.

She wandered with animals to river Okoro. She raised her eyes and saw children smartly dressed. They were clad in blue tunics, white blouses and feet shod in funny things. What lovely attire! What was her frayed semblance in contrast with the beauty she saw! She glimpsed at the scanty sheaths around her groin and cursed the day she was born.

She did not see why she wandered in the bush as her friends dressed well and learnt the language of the white man.

Sitawa had heard words about the white man. He spoke using the nose, he had no toes on his feet and travelled around in a moving hut- only Situma possessed one in Cheleba. He sent black people to the iron sheets and taught them how to speak using the nose. Those as fluent as Situma were made teachers or flown to the sky, their home will be where the world came to an end.

In the recesses of her heart, Sitawa longed for this new knowledge that relieved Situma from the banal toil of scooping the slopes of Mount Masaba as the only means of survival. She had seen the struggles of her people; expansive acres of maize smitten by hail stones, into threads of sisal; hundreds of cattle raided by Bayobos and thousands waned by diseases and drought. She could not trust farming alone; Sitawa desired a change.

As the sun went to sleep, she drank the last sips of milk from her gourd. She spent the whole day on it. The bright orange haze of the sinking sun sprayed the Tororo plug when she drove the animals home. As she approached home, she could see her mother near the cooking stones. Around her were her elder sisters singing a song that she soloed:

Simbi:	*Pilingali yauma*	*The wedding is lively*
	Pilingali yauma	*The wedding is lively*
Daughters:	*U,wu yauma huu*	*oh, it is lively*
Simbi:	*Yaumila Mwitukhu*	*It is lively in the mansion*
	Yaumila mwitukhu	*It is lively in the mansion*
Daughters:	*Uwu yauma huu*	*Oh it is lively*
Simbi:	*Nendumukhana*	*Had I been a girl*
	Nendumukhana	*Had I been a girl*
Daughters:	*Uwu yauma huu.*	*Oh it is lively*
Simbi:	*Senje burende*	*I would not get married*
	Senje burende	*I would not get married*
Daughters:	*Uwu yauma huu.*	*Oh, it is lively*
Simbi:	*Noliango wenywe*	*When you are at home*
	Noliango wenywe	*When you are at home*
Daughters:	*uwu yauma huu*	*Oh it is lively*
Simbi:	*Beyela lisafu*	*They wipe with leaves*
	Beyela lisafu	*They wipe with leaves*
Daughters:	*Uwu yauma huu*	*Oh it is lively*

She no sooner entered the cattle shed than there was a great making of faces and sarcastic peals of laughter from Mamai and Mating'i, her older siblings.

"A girl who herds!" Shouted Mamai, "you'll be our servant," Mating'i added. They chortled.

"You have done well daughter, who is that mocking you?" Simbi said with a gracious smile.

"Mamai….oh, chei!" Cried Sitawa.

"Sit down ma'am," pleaded Simbi

"I…..I…I shall…never herd….again…!" stammered Sitawa.

She broke down and wept hysterically. Simbi, her caring mother, implored her to relax.

"I'll tell your father tomorrow."

Her anger subsided as Simbi cast the first signal to open the story telling session, "Long long time ago…"

They all prepared their ears for enjoyment.

Chapter Four

Kisiang'ani had been effectively drilled in preparation for the ceremony through what was called *prakitisi* (rehearsals). It began as early as April. He was taught how to put on the clung and strike the hammer on it. The hammer was a steel rod with a hollow cylindrical base. It was grasped by the fore finger and thumb and struck on the clung to produce a clanging sound. It was during *prakitisi* that Kisiang'ani was taught the science of making beads. He picked them, dried and stringed them. He wore them across the chest from left to right side of the neck and vice versa. Kisiang'ani was introduced to the whistle. It was blown to produce a shrill sound to the rhythm of the song. He was then encouraged to jangle the bells at a pace consistent to the beat of the song.

Beads flung methodically across the back with a chirping sound as the clanging bells supplied the beat to harmonize the dance. Boys and girls left home at the infancy of the night to go and sing circumcision songs to prepare Kisiang'ani for his initiation. There were veteran heroes of Cheleba who sometimes struck the bells with such stamina that they shattered into pieces. Such candidates were revered and graduated from the season with a trail of girls after them. Wamalwa, Sitawa's father, had such a repute.

Having done with prakitisi, Kisiang'ani was ready to begin the first stage of initiation the following day. All his dreams nowadays bore constant reference to circumcision. Around him was bright and pleasant. The sunlight, the flowers and air proclaimed warmth and amity. Mauka who always had a grimace now afforded a smile.

The following morning saw the launching of *Khuchukhila*, in the home. Mauka rose at sun-up and after taking his yester supper, he looked prepared to give some instructions to his son. He was in high spirits but controlled his emotions to approach the crucial moment with a coolness that characterized true manhood. He summoned his son and gave him the preface of the rite.

"Do not worry son," Mauka said in a happy frame of mind, "the knife is not painful." He then dismissed his son.

As the sun rose to the centre of the sky, neighbours started strolling into the compound to witness the ceremony of initiation of Kisiang'ani, a son of great ancestry. Sitawa had got word and she would not miss it.

Cheery crowds arrived in the home and found Mauka pacing up and down in a state of anxiety and ecstasy. Kisiang'ani was given a cooking pot to go straight and fetch water at the river. Meanwhile, Butilu was busy preparing busaa, local brew, to serve men attendants of the ceremony. She was grinding yeast on the grinding stones to add in the fried fermented flour.

Kisiang'ani reached the river and drew water in the pot. He hoisted it onto his head and trudged up the rising terrain without looking back. This was the last time Kisiang'ani was carrying water on his head and obeying errands of that nature. He would never be sent to fetch water at the river or choose to do it hence forth. What would women do? He would soon be a man.

He arrived in front of his father's hut and cautiously unloaded the pot from his head. There was another pot on the ground in which Mauka ordered him to pour the water. That is what he meant. Any careless gush that resulted in spills had ill consequences- he would be circumcised bit by bit and how painful it would be.

Inside the pot was ground yeast churned with fermented maize flour. A crowd of people with curious faces stood around the pot as Mauka churned the mixture in preparation for the next stage.

He stirred and coalesced the mixture. Then, raising his eyes onto his son's, he insulted him vehemently for five minutes. Kisiang'ani clanged his bells without a flicker of the eyelid. Mauka motioned him to stop clanging bells and be alert.

"As a man you just come thus, without a flicker of an eye lid," Mauka thundered. Everything was dead quiet. Silence was a curious audience of the event.

"Your mother's cowardice ends now," he roared, "if you cower from the knife, you inherited your uncle's blood!"
He gashed a handful of molten mixture from the pot and flung it at his chest.

"Buchacha never cowered! Neither did I!"

The ball struck his chest with a thud and sprayed in random jets. They lay siege to his eyes and in a reflex the eyelids flickered to ward off the awful intrusion. Mauka smacked him.

"That's feminine fear!" He snarled.

He slapped him again. Kisiang'ani evinced no sign of joy, forthwith. Beads of tears gleamed on his eyes.

"Take cowardice to your mother! You don't cry here!" Thundered Mauka.

Wambilianga soloed a circumcision chant to wind up the stage. Men raised their staffs high and sang:

Soloist: Oh, oo, oh!   *Oh, oo, oh!*

Crowd: *Ooh! Oh, oh!*   *Ooh! Oh, oh!*
Soloist: *Musinde nolire Ebunyolo*   *If you fear go to Ebunyolo*

Crowd: *Aaoh! Aoh, oo!*   *Aaoh! Aoh, oo!*

Maratani then smeared him with the molten mixture from head, forehead, chest, down to the calf and toes. Wambilianga soloed a song and the home was thrown into frenzy. Uproarious was the mirth of the crowd as it responded to the enthusiastic chants in the extreme of wildest joy. They chanted stamping their feet and dancing. They went round and round with all their strengths.

Kisiang'ani forgot his sorrows. He disposed his sulks and exulted in the bliss of the momentary excitement. He hopped back and forth, resonated his back methodically and jangled his bells with dexterity; prancing round and round to the pace of the song. He gripped his whistle firmly between his lips. It groaned with the melancholy of the song. His beads swung across the back sweeping off the cold stuff.

Wambilianga stood in front of him to teach him new styles. He had to imitate everything. Down down they went, up up they rose; shaking their shoulders and arms to the beat of the song.

Kisiang'ani then blew the whistle to signify that he had left the home to invite friends and relatives to attend a ceremony that marked his transition to adulthood. As the hot sun sucked the moisture from the stuff, he turned to a bipedal white antelope, clanging bells.

Being the first day, they called on those relatives in proximity. Upon arrival, the singers would stamp their feet to the beat of the song. Kisiang'ani would prance with his chest a few inches from the ground, his bells jangling to the throb of the soloists' voice. He would vibrate his chest with all the beauty his mind could lay hands on.

The soloists' voice swirled with such passion that no son of Mwambu would hear and remain the same. They were songs that thrilled gaily and dismally; reproaching deviants, admonishing hyenas; pulling down the fort of vice and setting up the foundation to a hedge of virtues in line with the customs of the sons of Mwambu.

And the mobile crew behind him reached out for their voices and attacked the songs at the highest pitch of their lungs. Volleys of insults were directed at the man Situma Barasa. They sung about him as a stupid man whose daughters never touched the hoe. He was a woman as he carried a pot on his head while his wives watched, he was a weakling who cooked for his family; a hermit who greeted nobody. How excited Mauka was with these pieces.

"These are true sons of Mwambu," he muttered, "they are not ruined like my son!" He added. Mauka could not bring himself to the belief that a descendant of Buchacha would waste as a vagabond at Chebyuk? To afford a bowl of white man's refuse at the iron sheets. Why would his son not sit down and nurture what Buchacha left behind?

"A scavenger indeed!" He muttered and took an emphatic pinch of snuff as a tribute to the deviance of his son.

He saw his son in a very delicate situation; at the precipice of loss. Kisiang'ani had stood at the gate of the damp ways of the white man; the man who had massacred his ancestors in the plains at Chetambe without reason. What about his kinsmen? Heaps upon heaps, had lain dead, never to live again. Dead for sharing the air the man was breathing. Mauka could not forget it. The white man had stricken innocent souls by thunder and lightning. They had fled with their spears and shields to evade the consumptive flame but it had advanced like Wanangali and drowned them in river Nzoia.

Did his son know this? Did Butilu tell him these stories?

"It is women to tell these stories," he muttered, "to nurture the Buchacha heart in him!"

How he yearned to reach out and right the wrongs in Kisiang'ani's soul. He desired to plough down the tares that Situma had sown to groom a man as valiant as Buchacha. He wished his son understood the bad side of the ways of the white man. He would take him to Kitali to witness his cruelty.

Mauka wiped some stray grains of snuff from his upper lip and swore to start a crush program during the ceremony as his deliberate determination to crack down on alien values in his son. Nobody else suffered his pain. When one suffers an internal haemorrhage, it is only painful to him.

Who else knew how Buchacha had been forced at a withering age to shamefully leave his home and die as a fugitive in Masolo. The white man supported by Bayobo mercenaries had frustrated the old man. Did Kisiang'ani know this? He was a victim of ignorance.

And the young men sang around Cheleba. Pretty girls with amorous gestures gyrated their waists provocatively. In each home, the father was given a chance to counsel the candidate after an ear piercing ululation and lively dance from the mother as sign of hospitality. The candidate had to tolerate vehement insults and spittle in severe cases with automaton rapidity. Arguments, complaints and protests were the worst tendencies to manifest then.

Having passed the test of humility and obedience, Kisiang'ani would be presented with a goat or heifer and the dance would set off for another home.

The following day was the day Kisiang'ani lived to recall. It was no easy day for him. It was a dry day with a dry bracing coldness; the paths were hard and grass crisp. They sprinted all the way from Cheleba to Kitali to invite his maternal uncle. They chanted sweet songs, he danced the rumba; he jangled his bells. Having borne the clangs for three days, his wrists vibrated with streaks of pain.

Wetuya, for that was the uncle's name, was a haggard looking shabbily clad man with ridges of privation on his face. He felt his poverty; he manifested it through his subdued tone of voice. But he had doled out a fat bull for slaughter as custom stipulated. He was a man; his wife Nelima would testify. Though short of stature, he confronted gangs of Bayobos and solitarily threw them out of his home.

After the usual dancing and singing, Kisiang'ani stood still, clanging his bells with glaring eyes upon his uncle. Wetuya emitting an odour of busaa mingled with Marijuana, he gashed a handful of dung from the rumen and bending his fierce eyes on the nephew, hurled it on his chest.

"You just stand the knife thus without a flicker of an eyelid!" He snarled.

"I am your uncle and I stood the knife! Wekutu never ran away from it. If you cower from it then you inherited your father's blood!" The man mumbled and flung another mound of dung. No one dared admonish him for the low tone of voice. They knew him. Wetuya was not the kind of man who gripped his spear and let the enemy go unscathed. He had never lost a duel. Villagers shied away from provoking his anger.

He stepped forward and grabbed one of Kisiang'ani's bells as if to snatch it from him. Kisiang'ani seized it in a single jerk and was greeted with a roar of applause. He had known them as customary exams designed to screen him perfectly. There before his uncle, he had proved that Mauka had not forced him into initiation but he had voluntarily stood forward to enter into the furnace to be refined into an adult.

Wambilianga soloed the chant and milling voices sang it with a passion that clouded the home with a mysterious power. He knocked his bells, his soul ecstatically yielding to a bombardment of strange passion for something. He wept. Tears streamed as the chant roared around him. His heart craved circumcision.

Kisiang'ani got an insight into the nature of the rite. It went beyond the cutting of the foreskin and bound one to the blessings and curses of his ancestors.

The men at the sacrifices examined it to see whether the boy would 'stand the knife'.

"He will," Maratani announced and joy flew over the revellers.

An enormous chunk of meat was hewn from the neck, belly and testicles; holed at the top-end and lowered into his neck. It hung over his chest and the meat dangled above his stomach with the testicles upon his penis. His body emitted an awful stench of raw meat, yeast and fresh dung as he was led into a lonely hut for supper.

After the scanty meal, darkness closed in and a clap of thunder warned them of the approaching storm. The crowd had taken busaa and they laughed at nothing and everything. Some still carried calabashes full of liquor.

Wambilianga set a song in motion, staggering here and there with a lamp; his voice hoarse and fierce. The crowd sung it passionately and danced with a vigour that reflected the meals that Wetuya had generously offered them. After a few feats of dance, Wambilianga motioned him to leave and he jogged along the middle of the crowd wearily and drearily enough towards Cheleba. He had to be circumcised the following day.

The crew reeled along, young women and young men tipsy, staggering on miry sloppy paths. They bumped into trees and wild animals; boozing, insulting, shouting, singing and dancing. The girls swayed their hips while harmonizing the songs with soprano and alto. Wambilianga paved the way with the lantern and Kisiang'ani followed jangling all the way home. His meat and the untidy pair of shorts were the only cover against the pelting fall of rain and the cold draughts of the night. Busaa inspirited the jovial revellers to bid defiance to the ferocious attack of nature. They arrived home at three in the morning, in a stampede. Butilu emerged from the kitchen like an arrow and pierced the cold air with a screeching ululation. The home was thrown astir. A crowd of relatives who had arrived from 'all corners of the world' spilled to the front of Butilu's hut to join the spirited dance.

Round and round the crowd ran, up and up Kisiang'ani rose; down and down he bent and kaka the clangs sounded, his back resonating to the beat of the song. His meat swept the ground, his father's land. Everything was at the peak. There were multitudinous roars, Kisiang'ani's vibration of the back at right angles to the ground and prancing into the revolving crowd to create space.

What a dance! It was the kind that could provoke an elderly to defy the limits of menopause and enjoy their honey moon. In short, there was not a more pleasurable season among the sons of Mwambu than circumcision.

There was Mauka with a bright look, there was Wamalwa with a brighter face. There were relatives in the home. It was a moment to know your cousin's cousin's cousin and your aunt's nephew's cousin.

Mauka swaggered towards the candidate with airs of the most important person on the occasion. His lion gait manifested his significance. He approached his son and roared,

"The morning is here! Don't tremble in your knees with your mother's cowardice!" He removed the meat from the neck and purred, "A man you just match that way! Without a flicker of an eye!" He retreated and handed the meat over to his sister, Repa. She darted into the kitchen with it, her mouth salivating.

Mauka then scooped bull dung from the rumen of the slain bull and hurled it at Kisiang'ani's chest. Wambilianga soloed the circumcision chant and the crowd sang in once more.

"You must leave bad manners today!' Mauka snarled descending a fiery slap at Kisiang'ani. Tears of bitterness lingered on his glaring eyes as a ball of phlegm reached his face. They were an intoxication of busaa. Kisiang'ani struggled with the temptation to hate his father. He suspected revenge but he had no room for questions; custom had to be fulfilled.

He was a stooge before his kinsmen. They would pee in his mouth as long as it was reasonable enough to be counted as a means of inculcating discipline in him.

As Mauka was still thinking of another way of persecution, Wamalwa appeared at the scene and took the boy to a special hut. Well acquainted with custom, he realized that Mauka had gone overboard.

Inside the hut, Kisiang'ani was served with half roast, salt less chips of meat and ugali. He was warned against washing hands before the meal and tearing the meat with canines. Any disobedience would yield the penalty of bit by bit circumcision. He swallowed the chips in haste amid a terrible odour of cow dung.

Kisiang'ani was transferred into another hut where he met old men who mastered the customs of his people.

"Remove your shorts!" roared Matumbai of stern face.

He hesitated; he threw it down. Matumbai grabbed the organ and pushed the foreskin backwards.

"Ugh! How impotent you are!" He exclaimed.

The skin could not go beyond the head.

"Ugh, Pooh!" Spat Wetala.
Wamalwa remained calm and collected.

"You mean you have never taken a girl to the bush?" Asked Matumbai.

He struck his staff on the ground.

"They're symptoms of impotence!" Mauka roared with a vibrating bass.

"Tomorrow he'll pay for his impotence!" Warned Matumbai

"Papa, it's not a serious problem," said Wamalwa, "Wambaya's assistant will finish it before the knife."

"After this, ensure you lay a girl," asserted Matumbai. "Don't just louse around, sleep with a woman or you'll die without children and bring shame on your ancestors!"

"You'll then not be buried normally," Wetala added, "another door will be faked at the back of your hut to pass your corpse to the grave, right?"

Kisiang'ani nodded with automaton rapidity.

"And if you don't get a girl to assists you hatch, go to your paternal aunt, she'll assist you," Wetala advised

"Oh no, is that custom?" Wamalwa doubted

"Wamalwa, why does the paternal aunt take the meat with the bull's penis from the boy?" Asked Matumbai.

"I think that applies in rare cases where the boy has disability or…,"explained Wamalwa.

"Wamalwa, a female monitor lizard told its male counterpart to enquire to understand these things. I encourage you to enquire; you are getting lost!" Asserted Mauka.

Kisiang'ani was driven to the field again; it was 4 am. The moon was suffocated by dark clouds. It was a fine dry night, faint dark though.

Young men and men drank heartily and laughed at anything. The youth paired up in preparation for the imminent dance and other passionate issues they knew better. There were chorus demands for hot water by the straw shaking men in Mauka's hut. Butilu with her fellow women ran round and round to add hot water in the pot of busaa.

With Kisiang'ani's reappearance on the ground, there ensued a germination of joy and Wambilianga who had assumed the professional name master soloed a moving song. The milling crowd brought their lungs into full use and there arose one might roar of noise and bustle. There was screaming of women, banging of doors and rolling of obscenities. There was order and confusion; disobedience in obedience. Freedom adorned every shoulder. Virtuous insults flew in the air. There was a moral fornication for young adults as long as the maiden remained a virgin. There was a space for moral adultery as long as the owner got you not. It was night devoted to feasting, wooing, seducing and caressing. The cheerful light of blazing fires, the clowns in the theatre and the cheery audience made the Maukas historic.

Vehicles were manufactured to shift Kisiang'ani into adulthood. A vehicle was an even number of boys and girls who held one another at the shoulder and ran round and round the candidate. After a few rotations, it would break loose and disappear in pairs. A boy would take the girl somewhere for a date.

Kisiang'ani grew tired and tears glistened on his eyes. Wetala stood before him with a lantern taunting him with obscenities.

"Your mother's b-!" He insulted, whenever the boy flipped his eyelid. Kisiang'ani was astounded. How could he sleep with his aunt? What crime had his mother committed?

The rays of Venus spattered upon them. Cock crows ensued and Wambilianga led the customary song.

Wambilianga: *Okhabona surwe wekana, musinde*
              Do not Venus and retreat
Crowd: *Aah! Aah! Okhabona surwe wekana. Aah! Aah!*
              Don't see Venus and cower.

Kisiang'ani was taken to the place of the mud on river Okoro. Rituals had been performed here to conjure up the spirit of circumcision. He threw his pair of shorts on the ground and there he was, nude.

"That thing is big," a tipsy man croaked.

"Ugh, stop," angry voices hushed him.

"Has it ever fitted its bolt?" The man teased again. The crowd flew into fits of laughter.

Kisiang'ani leapt into the icy mud and stood as erect as teak. Nyongesa flung a ball of freezing mud on his chest and growled.

"A man you just come that way! As you stand the knife all birds keep quiet. The woman you are going to marry will see you today. So never flip an eyelid. Never raise the heel and she is yours!"

He then daubed his body with mud. The depression between the forehead and the nose was filled with mud. Kisiang'ani resembled the flying snake that Mango killed. A big ball of mud was planted on his head; a special grass was stabbed on it to face skywards like an aerial.

Kisiang'ani was a serpent as he strutted home naked with a gait of a boy scout, going to raise a flag of her majesty's queen of England. A voice set the circumcision chant in motion- that age-old song that was composed during Mango's times- and the squad sang with enthusiasm.

A kilometre away from home, a woman crossed ahead and forward flew stones and staffs. Unspeakable insults followed suit.

"We shall break your cunt!" Wambilianga barked.

"Take it to your father!" A tipsy man snarled.

Three men ran after her, hurling what they could find at her. Kisiang'ani pitied the woman. Her kind were the worst creatures to cross ahead. Queen or princess, it never mattered. They were capable of anything…they staggered a few yards ahead and he was halted. Wambilianga repeated the monotonous advice.

"You just stand that way without a flicker of an eye!"

It was the surgeon's moment to steal a glance at the foreskin to choose the suitable style at the critical moment.

The mighty battalion sang. As it approached home, they thinned out and the voices fainted into the morning cold. Not the faintest rustle interrupted the tranquil in the home. He lumbered in the middle of the curious crowd, solitarily and wearily. He staggered towards the circumcision ground only to meet his sole guide: his harsh father, Mauka. He was clad in a leopard skin, a spear in his right and snuff in his left.

"You are my first born, named after my father, Kisiang'ani Kurima and you must not shame us. All these people watch to see how you face this enemy. Life is fire and you must be strong to stand its tests!"

Mauka led him to the last spot, a sisal sack with dry soil spread over it. In a streak, he felt the rapture of his virginity after a single backward push. A forward pull of the skin succeeded and commenced sharp stabs of pain with the shrill of a whistle to mark the end of his childhood.

Women ululated and men sang a war song while thumping their feet.

Yaya khwera Omurwa
Aah khwera Omurwa
Papa khwera Omurwa
Aah, khwera Omurwa

Sister we have killed Omurwa
Aaah we have killed Omurwa
Father we have killed Omurwa
Aah, we have killed Omurwa

It was tempestuous. What a state of happiness!

Chapter Five

Simbi was a short, plump woman with the gift of the gab. Her calves, arms and cheeks like hips were gross and smooth. She was brown of complexion. She talked less to outsiders but more within Wamalwa's territory. She was a fountain spring of the folklore of the sons of Mwambu and Sela.

She was an oral artist, a reserve of narratives and sayings. Nurtured on Musimbi's lap of opulence and married in the affluent Wamalwas, she distinguished herself as a mother with a super memory that burrowed deep into incidents of distant pasts. Episodes of the famine of vehicles, the big war, and the construction of the snake came tumbling in the ears of her audience.

All her children watched her as she blew into hearthstones. They expected a morsel of wisdom from her lips. She had already begun the story.

"Mila and the ogre," suggested Mating'i.

"Hippo and fire," said Mamai

"Mamai! Mamai! What are you doing in the kitchen?" Called Wamalwa.

Mamai dashed out and joined his father in the lawn. He had lit a fire under the mango tree. With Wanyonyi, they conversed like adults around it.

It was taboo for a boy to keep the company of women in the kitchen. Although the young Mamai disliked the stringent rule, he had proved its importance through a shameful instance.

At nine years of age, Simbi had entrusted him in the hands of his older sister, Mating'i. They had shared the bedding. Mating'i became 'generous'. She presented to him the rights of marriage night by night. The boy had lived like a married man until fate spilled guts.

It began when Wanyonyi, his elder brother, wanted to know if he had ever lain a girl. Mamai had insisted that he had a world of experience.

"With who?" Wanyonyi had asked.

"Mating'i!" He had blurted.

"Bad manners!" Wanyonyi had roared and struck. Strokes of the cane had come pouring on him. Embarrassment had followed with Wanyonyi reporting the scandal to Simbi. Mating'i had been beaten and suspended from the home for two days; henceforth Mamai was banished from Mating'i's privacy.

Indeed the few instances he stepped in the kitchen, rekindled the shameful scandal. His sisters often sat carelessly when their wrappers stirred, he would see everything from the smooth thighs to the centre of their femoral system. This is what prompted Mamai to obey his father's voice whenever it summoned him to leave the kitchen. Simbi could not be deterred by Wamalwa's possession of sons. She would proceed,

"There lived a beautiful girl called Sela. The story of her beauty visited every home in the world. But Sela loved pleasure. She loved song and dance; she adored ilitungu. She would surrender her soul to any man who knew how to play it."

"One day, Mwambu, her elder brother, went for a stroll. When he reached the river, he saw Sela picking enderema; he got elated. He knew that in the evening he would have a meal he had missed for a very long time. At supper time, Mwambu bounced in, braced to enjoy enderema only to find the usual cowpeas.

"Where is the enderema I saw you picking?" Thundered Mwambu.

"I didn't go to the river today," replied Sela.

"You're a liar!" Roared Mwambu and slapped her.

"If it were me I'd have slapped her also," interrupted Mating'i.

"Bad manners! A woman shouldn't fight a man." Advised Simbi.

Sela wept and returned to the kitchen. She did not blame her brother; he rarely beat her. She resolved to visit the river to unearth the root of her troubles.

She rose at sun rise and headed for the river. She found a dark fat girl, exactly like her picking enderema. Sela was extremely shocked. She had met her own ghost.

Reliving her fate the previous night, she decided to greet the girl.

"Mulembe yaya (How are you, sister?)."

"Mulembe swa."

"I am Sela," she introduced.

"I am also Sela," the stranger said.

They embraced, both surprised.

Sela told the stranger the experience she had had the previous evening. Sela Two agreed that he had seen a man pass by with a gaze that suggested that he knew her. She proceeded to welcome her to their home but warned her that she was the only human being in a family of monsters. When they reached home, Sela Two said that the man eaters had gone hunting and would return with song and dance.

"When they come," instructed Sela Two, "don't come out however sweet the songs are."

"I won't," affirmed Sela One.

"I'll dig a pit in the compound and hide you there," Sela Two suggested and continued, "and don't be tempted by the moving songs, please."

"I won't, sister," insisted Sela One.

"After the evening meal, Sela, sister to ogres, dug a deep pit behind the store and hid Sela One there. She covered the mouth with banana leaves. The ogres arrived, lively. The home was thrown astir with merry songs and dances accompanied by crotchet beats of the drums. They thumped their feet, shook their shoulders and clapped their hands; the result was a moving kamabeka dance. Their voices mixed well to produce a harmonious song. They sniffed their noses around and caught a visitor's scent in the home. They sang a song to express it:

Sela mukeni muya kaunya muno
Sela mukeni muya kaunya muno
Sela mukeni muya kaunya muno
Sela mukeni muya kaunya muno

Sela we've smelt a visitor's scent
Sela we've smelt a visitor's scent
Sela we've smelt a visitor's scent
Sela we've smelt a visitor's scent

Sela Two was astonished at their sensitivity and sang another moving song to dissuade them that there was no visitor on the compound. She named them one by one:

Okanakhundia papa okanakhundia
Okanakhundia Wamukobe okanakhundia
Okanakhundia Wamalabe okanakhundia

Want to swallow me dad want to swallow me
Want to swallow me Wamukobe want to swallow me
Want to swallow me Wamukobe want to swallow me
Want to swallow me brothers, where do I find a visitor?

And Simbi said, "Like mine, Sela Two's voice was sweet but it did not convince the monsters. They enlivened their dance and thumped their feet with an amazing passion. What vigour! They plucked their matungus skillfully; Sela One inside the pit died of pleasure. She swayed her body to the slightest change of rhythm. She forgot all her fears. She forgot warnings. Those sweet voices that soothed her passion would not kill her. It was Sela Two's sheer jealousy to deny her a moment of happiness. She danced, danced and danced. She climbed up the pit, threw away the banana leaves and joined the frisky dance."

"Mama, didn't they eat him?" Interrupted Sitawa.

"The ogres rejoiced to see the food and danced more vigorously," replied Simbi.

Sela we've smelt the visitor's scent
Sela we've smelt the visitor's scent
What we said was true
Sela we smelt the visitor's scent.

The ogres then began licking Sela One; the foolish girl thought they were attracted to her. They stopped licking her and tore her skin. They stopped singing and scrambled over the parts of her body. She whimpered and called Sela One to no avail. Nobody could save her from the hands of these man eaters. They ate all her flesh, deserted the bones in front of the store and went to sleep.

The following morning, Sela Two woke up and seeing her friend's bones wept at her foolishness. How could she risk her life for a dance? She went to the bush and plucked a branch from the tree, Lufufu. She arranged the bones in position and lashed them. Sela came back to life. Sela Two warned her never to be lured by song. She vowed to obey.

"Whenever the monsters came and sung their song, Sela Two would sing her song and they would apologize

Ndomakhandio luweni ndomakhandio
Ndomakhandio Kichwa ndomakhandio

I'm just joking Luweni I'm just joking.
I'm just joking Kichwa I'm just joking.

Sela One would not come out of the pit. Days went on. One day Sela One said,

"Come with me so that you live with human beings. It's hard to stay with ogres."

"She must have become very happy." Mating'i interrupted.

"True," affirmed Simbi and proceeded, "Sela Two agreed on condition that nobody called her ogre."

They reached home and Mwambu was very elated to welcome them. He found it very hard to distinguish between them but his sister had a gap in the teeth that Sela Two lacked. After few days, he married Sela Two vowing never to call her ogre. But my daughters, beer can make the tethered cow dance. One day, after drinking busaa, local brew,

Mwambu stood up and shouted, "These are the disadvantages of being born among ogres!"

Sela Two picked a rope, ran to the banana farm and hanged herself.

"Why did she kill herself," asked Sitawa.

"Men don't keep all their promises."

"Even they seduce us using small things," Mating'i added.

"That is why it's good for me to go to school," Sitawa raised her complaint.

"Who will look after cattle?" Asked Simbi

"I go to school tomorrow!" Asserted Sitawa and matched out in a chorus of sobs.

Simbi reached out for her daughter and holding her in her arms, she soothingly dispelled her agitation by caresses. She tried to dissuade her from the determination without avail. Her firmness stunned her. The way she could not see the impending dangers, her father's reaction of course, reminded Simbi the haunting power of ambition in the girl.

Simbi had no other option other than persuade Wamalwa to let Sitawa go to the iron sheets. That night she appeared before her husband with the request but he remained adamant. Did Simbi know what she was asking for? Was she not asking for a co-wife to look after his cattle?

"Let me hear no more of the matter," Wamalwa spoke with finality. Why would the white man take all that was his? Nothing worthy of mention about the subject occurred in the home that night.

Sitawa wept that night. She cursed love and courted hatred. How harmful love was. It threatened to sacrifice her future. Her groans disturbed Mating'i's sleep and she rose up to clear the mess.

"Disobey him!" She roared, "Why should you cry here like a starving gecko? You rise up tomorrow and go to school!"

Sitawa's despair abated upon hearing her sister's voice, "Your desire is good! You're not going to kill anybody, are you? Act! Stop bleating here like a she goat!"

Sitawa beheld a lasting solution to her problem. She had to act. She slept anxiously and rose up at five, in the morning. She packed maize and cabbages on a donkey with Mating'i's assistance and trudged to Chwele and sell them to buy books and uniform. It was her first time to disobey Wamalwa.

Wamalwa did not doubt that her daughter had a future in the world. Sindani, his father had had a super memory. He could memorize all the cases and the seasons in which they took place. Consequently, no plaintiff or defendant lied before the council of elders about seasons while he was alive. With such noble ancestry, he was certain that his children, especially Sitawa, would succeed. But how, was the question he could not answer.

The wind was blowing and even Wamalwa knew that values were changing. Situma's rise into prominence attested to that fact. Secretly, the old man knew that it paid no dividends to oppose such truths. But he feared for the age-old customs of his people. Would these aliens who spoke through the nose raise his children in the ways of the tribe?

As the new day greeted him, Wamalwa had resolved to call his daughter to warn her against the dangers of alienation before releasing her. But when he opened the daughters hut, Sitawa had gone...gone...

"Papa, let her go or she'll kill herself like Sela Two," asserted Mating'i.

The old man gazed at her daughter and loved her maturity. Mating'i would make a good mother too. He thought as he led the cattle out of the shed. He had to look after them now.

"Where did she go?" Asked the old man.

"Chwele," replied Mating'I, "to sell her cabbages and go to school."

"Who will look after cattle?" Asked Wamalwa, apprehensively.

Chapter Six

Kisiang'ani crossed over the river and enrolled on the list of men amid ululations and chants. Men stamped their feet with staffs held high. They roared war songs. Another man had been born in Cheleba. His aunt Repa charged forth with a cooking stick bathed in busaa and presented it to him.

There were screams of joy, shouts of delight; hums of cheerfulness and shuffles of hundreds of feet around him. Tipsy men bayed, bulls bellowed in the yard; children cried and grasses wept under the devastating weight of the dew. Curious looks, masculine and feminine, gazed at his genital area. Some had already settled under trees to discuss the little scandals of the night with relish.

As stabs of pain jabbed him, Kisiang'ani pondered over the man Omurwa who his people claimed to have assassinated after each circumcision ceremony. The legend had diverse theories of origin. There were those who claimed that barwa referred to the Maasai and Nandi raiders who were a big threat to existence of other tribes from Kitali along the Great Valley to the city in the time of Buchacha.

A closer enquiry into the legend from elders like Wekutu, his late grand father, held that Omurwa was an accomplished Iteso soldier who lived near Masolo. In those anarchical times when the sons of Mwambu strongly resisted the entry of the Iteso into their land, Omurwa was so severe that they lost hundreds of men in each battle.

The sons of Mwambu had sat down and devised a plot to destroy him. They had selected a brown, plump girl and sent her to him as an appeasement. Having found a brown woman a rarity in Amagoro, Omurwa spent days and nights with her.

During one of those forenoon moments, the sons of Mwambu made a surprise attack and Omurwa was assassinated. Jets of blood had sprayed from his manhood with mixed screams of delight and distress. The song was composed under inspiration of the assassination.

With Nabangala's assistance, Kisiang'ani cautiously sat on a chair and sighed with relief.

"The worst is over now!" He thought. He raised his face and saw Sitawa in the crowd. He avoided her eyes.

He gazed at his blood. It dripped on the ground to seal an eternal covenant with his ancestors. He was now a man. How delighted he was by the thought. Forthwith, he would be rendered an ear in a gathering of men. Moreover, he would be entrusted with responsibilities. He would release family oxen on the farm in the absence of Mauka. The decision to marry, the decision to go to the iron sheets and other adult privileges were on his hands.

"You have stood well," said Sitawa, dropping a coin on a plate in front of Kisiang'ani.

"Eeeh," he mumbled and cursed mentally, 'What hell had brought her?'

How embarrassing that such a beautiful girl should see him thus. Furthermore, it was a bitter experience for his wounded pain ridden instrument of manhood to erect, that the presence of Sitawa at this critical moment would stimulate just that!

Kisiang'ani entertained a loving hate not only for Sitawa but also pretty girls. There was no enemy but beauty at that time. He realized why the newly circumcised made batons with which they whacked any girl in sight.

His aunt Repa appeared at the scene and scrapped the mud from his head. She clawed a lumpsome and it tumbled with a jingle of coins. Little had Kisiang'ani known that the elated crowd had stuck coins in his muddy head. Not one was Kisiang'ani's, they were customarily a recompense for Repa's service during the ceremony. She chucked them into her brassiere and disappeared into the hut.

Wambilianga led Kisiang'ani into esimba, his new hut. With guidance, the boy staggered backwards, like a serpent, around the hut before entering it. He was wrapped in a blanket, which he tightly gripped above his groin.

They entered the hut and sat on a hide. His knees jutted above the floor. His blood trickled on. It oozed from the bottom of the organ's glans and spilled onto the murky floor. It formed a stream at the centre of the hut. Kisiang'ani felt drowsy; Mauka overcame his apathy and sought a solution to the problem.

He picked the head of his manhood and examined it. Many blood vessels had been cut during the quick minor surgery and had to be knotted if Kisiang'ani were to live. Mauka summoned Wambaya to deal with the situation. Wambaya tried to locate the cut vessels in vain. The oozing blood hindered him.

He picked lantana leaves and wiped away the blood from the wound. Kisiang'ani winced with pain. He could see numerous sand particles in the wound. He wished they used some other powder to reduce friction during the operation. Acute bouts of pain thudded through his head at every move of Wambaya's hand.

He spotted the first blood vessel and clipped it with his nails. Kisiang'ani writhed and groaned. His mouth twisted. His groin jerked backwards to evade Wambaya's callous hand. Wambaya remained indifferent. His finger skillfully picked the first blood vessel and knotted it tautly with a sisal string. Kisiang'ani gnashed his teeth and tightened his grasp on his hand as a murderous sting reached his brain with a savage throb.

The boy sobbed in pain. His heart pounded at the pulse of the smarting streaks of pain.

"You've got to be a man!" Wambaya said wiping the bloody wound again. He got another blood vessel and secured it with his fingernails. Stings of pain succeeded; what torture! They overpowered him. He raised his right hand, placed it on Wambaya and mumbled, " just…leave…me…"

"No! They must make you a man!" Mauka shouted and struck his staff on the ground.

Kisiang'ani surrendered to the torture. All his body was a ground work of pain as Wambaya sought, clipped and knotted the six blood vessels. Indeed he was Omurwa, wallowing in anguish after three days of pleasure. Streams of blood flowed and covered his hide. A breeze of cold air blew in to fan up the stings. They smiled and jabbed him at the isukuti beat. Kisiang'ani had never felt this in his life.

Mauka swaggered in with a bandage and wrapped it around the untidy wound. Wambaya, his assistant and Mauka sat fronting him. Mauka flung a blanket on his head and another session began.

Wambaya sipped busaa, spattered it on Kisiang'ani and said, "I'm Wambaya your circumciser, listen to my counsel!" He paused, swallowed a lamp of phlegm and proceeded, "Lay a girl before you fetch firewood for her. If it's somebody's wife do the same. Enjoy her warmth before you assist her split firewood. Otherwise her husband will find you. Think about my words."

He drank from his tin again and spattered a mouthful.

"Respect your parents. Your father is your father; never lay your hand on him, however provocative he may be. You are circumcised now; it's the uncircumcised that beat their fathers. Keep his company from now on and avoid your mother's. The kitchen is not your place; build you own hut. Never again should you sleep under the same roof with your mother. Woe to you if you marry your wife and sleep under the same roof with your father."

"Now you are a man. When you visit your brother and find him, you can talk into the night but when he is not there don't talk to his wife into the night. She's your brother's wife. When she wrongs you don't touch her. Let your brother beat her."

"Crying stops today! You're a man. If you come home and find your parents sleeping on empty stomachs, don't call them names. Work hard as a man and find something for them to eat. Wherever you go, remember home. Build your own house to avoid the shame of sleeping in your father's house."

He sipped another mouthful and stole a glance at Mauka to signify his end, "Never climb on animals! You're circumcised. It is the uncircumcised who climb on animals."

"It should never reach my ear that you have climbed on a fellow man. Such deviants should not be allowed to live and defile Mango's land. Itch yourself where your hand reaches. Don't burden yourself with things you can't afford. Son, the door which is open is yours and that which is shut isn't yours." Wambaya finished his counsel and welcomed Mauka to proceed.

Mauka sipped busaa from the tin and spattered it on his son, "Bad manners leave you today! You have today deserted sandals of rudeness and shod sandals of gentleness. You have abandoned your mother's clothes and put on mine! Base natures must die and discipline birthed. When I beat your mother, do not come near; when I want to beat you run away." Mauka finished his counsel.

Wambaya was given his dues: three cocks and ten shillings and off he left to go and make merry, the only use for which the money was meant.

Kisiang'ani's wound set forth on the long journey of healing, the summit of which was attained on the third day. His penis was so inflated that it had not a single spot from which to grasp. The bulging meat had protruded out of the minute holes of the bandage. A pool of pus seethed at the bottom of the distended head. Streaks of pain jabbed from there at a mere touch. He sobbed in the cauldron of affliction like the sons of Mwambu in the face of the British canon at Chetambe Fort.

Three nights he had spent without a wink of an eye and any thought of Sitawa called for heel knocks using a baton to purge down the steams of passion that endangered his wound.

Nabangala brought warm water and he spent the whole day removing the embedded bandage thread by thread. Mauka had gone to gather; enguu, the medicinal herb renowned for its efficient treatment of chronic wounds.

Enguu was gathered by first whistling a certain tune that wooed it. Mauka plucked the dry leaves and ground them into powder. No sooner had Kisiang'ani washed his bloated wound red than Mauka stormed in and sprayed the dust on it. Jerks of pain struck him. Pangs succeeded in mighty waves that proceeded from his groin, stomach and head. The random stings made him wince, gnash his teeth, sob in choruses and shed torrents of tears. They were tears of torment and anguish.

Kisiang'ani staggered onto his two feet and gyrated his waist in arcs at the rhythmical thudding of the pain. He groaned holding his penis with both hands. The wound had escalated into the preamble of the groin; he could not evade touching it. The stings twirled. They set his pubic ablaze; a mixture of blood and pus trickled down his fingers. Mauka nodded, full of delight.

"Ha! Ha! Ha! You must be a man!" He laughed, "And bad manners shall leave you!"

Kisiang'ani glared at him and thought it was an evil spirit in the guise of a man. His hoarse bass was a replica of a sisieno chortling in abyss.

"That's the cost of becoming a man!" Mauka repeated. Kisiang'ani's endurance had been stretched to the summit. The flood of pain overpowered him and down rolled tears. He shouted and sprinted, nude, holding his wedding tackle.

"Don't!" Mauka barked. He tried to bar him but he had already done some yards. He had forgotten the pain. Mauka reached out for his son. He motioned him to sit down. The boy wept with fragments of sorrowful syllables.

"No….no……papa! Buy me the white man's medicine ……now……or …..I…..go!"

He deserted the clothes. They tumbled down. He stood naked, stooping towards his father, with hands at his genitals.

"If you don't do it, I am going to mother at the market and tell her to buy me medicine!" Mauka ordered him to sit down. He washed all the enguu from his bloated wound and sent Nabangala to go and buy the white man's medicine.

"Today's children cannot live the life we have lived!" He said as he applied the antibiotic.

Chapter Seven

Old seasons died, new seasons were born but the boy refused to fizzle out his mind the agony he had undergone during initiation. The clanging of bells, the smears of bull dung, Mauka's deadly slaps and the thread by thread removal of the bandage festered on his heart. His mind burrowed in the blazing furnace of experience, the capital he had invested in the transition enterprise.

With time, Kisiang'ani compared it with the outcome. Society had taken him for a ride. He had gone at loss and could not see the future of the rite. Kisiang'ani who had counted on circumcision to appease Mauka to relinquish a coin towards his education felt cheated. His father's nonchalance surprised him. His extravagance nauseated him. Kisiang'ani spurned Mauka's decision to sacrifice a rotund bull for his circumcision and naught for his education.

Moreover, Mauka's insistence on former rules made the boy see the rite as a triumphant excellence of failure. His heart blazed with a strong internal agitation. His father was 'that right man' and them 'those always wrong culprits.' He was 'that always decorous father' and them 'those foolish ingrates.' How obnoxious! He was the Wanangali of their home and a haunting spirit of their existence.

Kisiang'ani saw him as the worst of men who seemed not to care a jot about anything. His was a crooked path to loss. The boy summarized his father as a man of no affections, a man with no purpose (save for dissipation) and a man of no ability.

He remained a darling of former rules and dressed a sour visage. The air in the home was so very miserable. It was defiant and despairing. His hopes plunged down the cliff. Kisiang'ani erected in his heart high mountains of hate against Mauka, his kinsmen and everything around him.

For his plight, he held Kimila- the customs of his people- culprit. Here was a culture in which brutes were crowned heroes, a culture in which vices were virtues and virtues vices; such a culture was worthless. Their home remained that poor and miserable slum. It was always below the pass mark of human habitation; today a replica of yesterday and tomorrow. Kisiang'ani went back to weeding erobo in Chebyuk to pay his fees.

By June 1958, Kisiang'ani realized that their farm was still fallow. Their neighbours had ploughed their farms as early as February and grown maize, beans and potatoes. Their crops blossomed as the Mauka's gawked ugly with weeds.

Mauka had made a step farther in his gross extravagance. He had acquired a new wife, Machuma. Consequently, he was seldom at home.

His absence had detrimental effects on the economy of home. It barred any attempt to farm as his blessing was missing. Butilu or Kisiang'ani could not release his oxen on the farm. It is this stringent rule that made the young man doubt the purposes of initiation.

Mauka made yet another mistake that embittered the young man. He had sold half of the farm to a Muyobo and migrated with his new wife to Kitali. A widow with six children, Machuma was a quick witted female. She was out for her main chance and before Butilu realized, Mauka was gone. With tremendous charm, she convinced Mauka to sell the land and move to the white settlements in Kitali, a region acclaimed as a sea of riches due to the presence of the white man there. Many sons of Mwambu stayed on the settlement as casual labourers.

Mauka had abandoned squatter life twenty years before and trekked all the way to Mount Masaba to grab a piece of land. But with Machuma's romantic influence, he had reverted to Kitali as a petty land owner.

With the entry of polygamy in the home, there was a shift from worse to worse than anarchy. The home became a boiling pot of combats. Mauka's hate for Butilu and her children rose to the summit and he was so incommodious whenever he reappeared from hibernation.

Life was so terrible. Here they were; children who were accustomed to obey under coercion, children who were bound by custom to watch their father assault their mother for asking him to give an account of the monies got from the sold pieces of land. Here was a son who was to applaud with automaton obedience a father who never cared what went down his gullets. Kisiang'ani's endurance was running out fast.

He could not understand whether customs were a moral license to marginalize some people. Perhaps they were guillotines set by men to kill women and children. Why would Mauka deny him the rights that custom stipulated? Why would he not be permitted to release oxen now that he was a man?

If Buchacha had visited their bushy home then Mauka would have been in for it. Obviously, he would not have tolerated his father's weakness. These were days of dissipation and Kisiang'ani had never seen his father sober. It made him doubt his great ancestry. The revelling made everything in the home and their reputation a squalid tale of poverty and misery. In all Cheleba, their home was besmirched as a place where sojourners neglected the hoe and suffered as casualties of hunger. Consequently, it was a place with children of ancient faces, subdued voices and pleading tones. Whenever a hen went missing, fingers of calumny could be pointed at their home where a hen was an unaffordable impossibility..

He had been sent home for fees again. It was nine in the morning. The sun was shrouded in a thick cloud. Tributaries of anger that flooded his heart violated all principles of reason and he blamed his father.

"Fights each night…, no food…, my fees… isn't paid…" Kisiang'ani complained as he flounced into the home. He was not as timid as Mauka thought. "I'll break his skull." He muttered. He knitted his brows. The vengeance within him rolled and escalated. The resultant fits of fury sought outlet to abate the rising strain. His father's oxen in the yard provided the outlet that averted all temptations of strife and vandalism.

Kisiang'ani had grown muscular. He got ashamed to idle with them and start complaining about poverty. He rose up and surveyed the bushy farm. It was green with weeds; their oxen chewing the cud in the shed. With the guiding hand of exasperation and instruction of defiance, he swaggered onto the cattle shed and untied the oxen.

He would not lack fees just because a reveller was boozing somewhere in Kitali. After all he was circumcised and in custom, he had a right to carry out such responsibilities. Furthermore, the state of their home never called for norms and customs. It needed action to be redeemed. An action that would immolate poverty and revert the home back to Buchacha's luxuriance. Customs that defended Mauka's damp ways to him remained hollow.

Kisiang'ani could not understand why the Wamalwas, with two hands like them, lived in abundance as they languished in misery. Those women who were eagle-eyed had already discovered the liaison between Kisiang'ani and Sitawa. They had condemned it and counted it among short comings of sending children to the iron sheets. It was degrading for Sitawa to marry in such a poor family. It haunted Kisiang'ani as he yoked the oxen ready for action.

Kisiang'ani lay on the ox-plough and Wafula whirled the strap to drive the beasts. They ploughed down the weeds on the farm. The morning mist slithered down the valley. Wafula singing a poignant tune. The lashing of the strap offered a suitable beat. Nabangala stole out of the kitchen to watch the remarkable risk in which they had plunged themselves. Butilu saw an impending peril.

They ploughed half way. Passers-by commended them. Wamalwa who had gone to Chebyuk to gather honey was extremely elated.

"A sweet fruit is known from a tender age, my son," he asserted, "keep it up, you'll change this family."

He shook Kisiang'ani's hand and left. Inspirited by these comments, the two brothers worked harder. As Kisiang'ani hoisted the ox-plough to evade a stump, a tall figure in a dark blanket stormed in. He saw his contorted face and spear tautly gripped in his right.

"Who told…you…to release…my…oxen…onto the farm?" He roared. His voice was thick with fury.

"I…ve…been…sent…for…fees….and…"

Kisiang'ani stammered, hands off the ox-plough.

"Your mother's b-!" He thundered obscenities.

The boy was lost for words. Mauka sprang forward. Wafula threw away the strap and disappeared into the scything weeds.

"I'm circumcised anyway!" The young man blurted.

"Tell your mother's g-!" Mauka snarled and advanced.

The assailant stopped, paced hither and thither and lunged ahead. His heart was stuffed with the fury of the buffalo. Kisiang'ani did not move. He was yielding to an irresistible desire to defy his father's authority and be free. He would not let this capital hand at oppression go untouched. He had lacerated his spirit, wounded his soul and embittered his existence.

Kisiang'ani forgot that the grotesque figure he saw before him was his father. He saw the ogre, Wanangali. Who had swallowed the whole family except him. He had to save it from its greed.

"I'll kill you!" Mauka growled and flung a stray hoe that lay by. It scudded in the air, bounced across lumps of soil and caught the big toe of his right leg. It chiseled a sizable chunk of meat and blood jetted out. It re-lived his past: Mauka's slaps, the knotting of blood vessels and the crude application of enguu to-

….torture…, him…and…yes…to…torture…him…

"It…is…you…who…should…pay…my…fees!"

He screamed and sprang up. Mauka raised his spear ready to attack. Kisiang'ani charged at him. A tumult rose in the home. Butilu ran at the scene. Kisiang'ani did not see the spear. He could not see Butilu, he did not see the on-lookers; he saw the immolation of tyranny.

He saw the enemy jerk his hand. He crashed on the ground and rolled ten yards forward. The women screamed as the spear missed the target and smashed an oxen's eye.

Kisiang'ani confronted his opponent. Custom wept, decorum cried and morality whimpered. He secured his neck and rained a great many punches from eyes, nose, mouth, teeth and stomach. With a head butt, he crushed his temple. The old man collapsed. Kisiang'ani braced for another offensive; a baton crushed the back of his head.

"Leave your father!" It was Butilu cursing.

Kisiang'ani turned and raised his hand to strike her. Wafula and Nabangala restrained him.

"I'll grind both of you into dust!" He glaring at them, but Nabangala entreated him to calm.

Men and women, young men and children trudged into the compound confounded at the outrage. Mauka lay prostrate where he had fallen.

"You fool! Why dare touch your father?" Snarled Livuva.

"The world is coming to an end!" Observed Matumbai.

Kisiang'ani's heart froze into a rock. He cared about nothing now. Did society care about him? Did elders practice the morals they hollered? He staggered his way out. The crowd gathered and was turning restive under Livuva's command.

"Who has ever cared about me!" Kisiang'ani screamed. His desperate voice hit the cliffs in the south and the echoes reverberated with a moving din. The crowd retreated upon seeing the despair that shrouded his soul. It is at this juncture that Wamalwa arrived and called for restraint. Kisiang'ani's move had impressed him, he had said, but his appeal to violence was absurd. He had insisted that, 'tit for tat" would only yield double loss.

"The boy should be summoned before elders," he had suggested.

The crowd assented to his piece of advice.

Wamalwa had left the scene deeply aggrieved by Mauka's misconduct. As much as the boy had committed an abomination, he had been provoked beyond his ability to withstand. His people gave a circumcised son freedom to enjoy all the privileges of adulthood. He could run the home in the absence of his father. Some even inherited their young step-mothers if the fathers grew old and senile. Why would Mauka fight the very custom he so loved?

Kisiang'ani had graduated from childhood. Mauka had to change his attitude towards him. But, the crowd did not think so. They cursed and lamented. Kisiang'ani picked his way along the scanty hedge. He stole his way out of their sight. He squatted near the well and saw his father spitting.

"Pooh! May the same happen to you!"

"Whatever you do to your father, shall happen to you also!" Matumbai added.

His eyes glittered with tears as he tottered up the muddy path to a place he did not know. All the human breath behind rolled against him.

But there was something in him that refused to regret. He refused to lop into self-pity. He had stood against organization of disorganization in the body of his society. Simon Kisiang'ani or Judas Kisiang'ani would retreat? Noah Kisiang'ani would die fighting.

They shook their heads. They condemned his blatant defiance. It was the first in the annals of Cheleba.

"Your father is your father," they said, "and a son has no right whatsoever to lay his hand on him."

Kisiang'ani tottered towards Kipsigon. He was not going there but his melancholic soul drove him somewhere. He desired to be alone, to talk to the cool breeze, the silent teak, the impending darkness and the still voice of death. These were his only companions, faithful and available enough to hearken to his tale of woes. Who in Cheleba would believe that his action was a consequence of Mauka's vexation? Who would believe he was a kind boy whose fine instincts had been bruised and reputation wounded. His ambition was no exception. There was no doubt that his rebellion had erased all hopes of Mauka's contribution towards his education. His people said that a milkman stroked a cow to maximize the yield. But foolish Kisiang'ani had battered the cow instead.

As the young man loitered in the cold night, Nabangala reached out for him. Beaten and worn out, she looked, but on her eyes he saw light beyond the tunnel.

"We've got to dress the wounds," she said approaching.

"Leave me alone, sister," said he with a subdued tone, "let me die!"

"No Noah," she called by his Christian name, "you have a bright future ahead. A man is the elephants thigh."

"Thanks, sister," he mumbled. She led him back home.

"You see where we can't see," Nabangala asserted "that's why you suffer more."

Kisiang'ani was busy, engrossed in his troubles.

The sun sank in Masolo and darkness spilled over the land. As they limped into the home, a rolling cloud of mist sauntered into the home. The ill-fated farm yearned for a steward who would minister to it. She desired a strong man to attend to her. She was a fertile mistress whose husband rejected, a discarded virgin whose bridegroom despised but debauchees revered. She craved for a time when she would be stroked by the hoe of life to end the shame of childlessness.

Kisiang'ani's toe and head throbbed with pain. Nabangala seated him near the kitchen and nursed his wound. She applied in it a pinch of salt and he retreated in the privacy of his cottage. He reflected about his life. What were his prospects? Who would pay his fees? He peeped through the hinges and glanced at the path that led to Cheleba primary. It narrowed as it approached Cheleba at the apex.

Chapter Eight

With superlative attempts of a discoverer, it was impossible to erase the ordeal from his mind. It had got him in a repulsive stench with his mother and Cheleba as a whole. The inner struggles he bore, the battles of self-censure, the feelings of rejection; how he longed to hurl them in the bliss of forgiveness.

He slunk back to monomania. Day by day, he experienced terrible feelings of isolation. He lived in constant evasion of his father. Who knew what he plotted against him? Kisiang'ani shunned every soul and wandered about like one banished from earth. He talked to the walls of his cottage and the voice of his thoughts. If ever he breathed a syllable to a soul then it was neither Wafula, nor Butilu. He either mumbled to Nabangala or remained a dehydrated husk: aloof, sulky and surly.

Those rare syllables were far from happy. They were bombs of boorish utterances, which would be halted by a fog of apathy that hung on him with a painful intensity. At the apex of his sorrows, Nabangala would reach out to right the wrongs of his heart by embraces that he objected with a gentle push. She would gaze at him in commiseration but he insisted on going somewhere beyond the rugged terrain, far away from Masaba to obtain a solace for his soul and solicit funds for his next cycle of education.

As she gave him a melancholy embrace, she hugged the wish to die and Kisiang'ani left for his destination vowing never to forget her. In rejection and acrimony, she had been a friend indeed.

He crossed the Okoro spring through a bush on the left of the main route to avoid Mauka who was marching in and staggered along the miry sloppy path to his unknown destination. He plunged into the thickest recesses of luxuriant green forests and wandered with the grey heat of the afternoon to his aunt's. He tottered in the orange haze of dusk along circuitous routes into the prosperous land.

The way ahead grew dark as the sun set behind him. Kisiang'ani felt a great deal better. His mind was suspended on the placid dais of freedom. He muttered in most emphatic terms that his decision to leave Cheleba was not futile. Beyond the mist was a blue haze. There lay a treasure that Mauka would not offer him.

He refused to cry. If he had come this far without Mauka's hand then worry was uncalled for. But, the way of life of Cheleba was instrumental to his bitterness. It was a culture that gave elder men a license to oppress, abuse, squander and walk away free. "I'll break their necks!" He muttered and flounced on. Having manfully laboured to meet the cost of his primary education, he bore a high opinion of himself.

He had weeded erobo and leased farms to grow onions, potatoes and maize, which he had sold to meet the cost of his education. All these engagements were the balm of his depressions.

After the fourth class, he had transferred to Chwele along with Sitawa. In spite of a few cases of absenteeism, Kisiang'ani performed exceptionally well. It was this that drew the attention of Stephen Grant, the British head teacher. His heart went out for bright pupils who toiled to remain in school. Grant never liked to see a brain missing school.

More than thrice, he had expressed a hearty desire to have audience with Mauka over Kisiang'ani's financial position in the school. But that year, Mauka had spent twelve moons in Kitali. Butilu had come to represent him. It had aggravated Mr Grant. He had declared her the first woman to conceive children without a man. Obviously, Butilu had returned home embarrassed.

If Kisiang'ani could recall better, Grant always complained about the failure of African men to master their passion. Perhaps in Europe men were so self-controlled given that there was no polygamy.

His prejudice notwithstanding, Grant had expressed a lot of concern.

"Is Mauka your father?" He had asked.

"Yes sah."

"And why does he hate you?"

He had declined to answer. That is how he had done his last two years in primary school. He had completed on hire purchase whose term installments were settled by Mr. Grants benevolence.

The white man had shown love, the love which his own father could not. Did someone expect him to send the white man packing? Where was he heading? He was on the way to his aunt, who lived as a squatter on the white man's farm in Kitali. The white man fed his aunt.

In his pocket was an admission letter from the newly launched Friends School Kimusingi. The school had been started amid tribal fracas. Trouble had began when the white missionary assumed that Luhya was one dialect assembled Maragoli, Idakho, Tajoni, sons of Mwambu and others and taught them religion in Maragoli language. The sons

Mwambu got confounded. Where a Maragoli said ing'ombe-a cattle; a son of Mwambu expected 'ekhafu.'

With time, this media of instruction in schools irked the sons of Mwambu. Their children fared badly in religion and education and they began protesting against it. They confronted the missionary and told him that they descended from the eldest son in the Luhya family with a distinct dialect and culture. It was therefore intimidation to be grafted on a young sibling in Kaimosi.

The missionary was stunned at the realization and gave them a Friends School in Kimilili. Here he was, honoured by fate to be counted among the first students of this great school.

Meanwhile, the young man exulted in the attributes of his people. Sometimes he doubted whether they were indeed Luhya. Perhaps they were just Ugandans. The courage and skepticism that overflowed their natures distinguished them from other Luhya. Complacency and sycophancy were not chapters in their unwritten constitution. Diligence was their trade mark and courtesy their attire.

Something shuffled ahead of him. It startled him to the present. He was manfully determined to arrive in Kitali on foot. How he wished that his melancholic waves subsided. The winding path narrowed and came to a close. Darkness spilled upon him. Alert as he would, Kisiang'ani could not perceive any vestige of human habitation.

The thought of coming face to face with a maumau fighter or home guard deepened his anxiety. He pondered over the recent capture of Dedan Kimathi and froze. A twig snapped. A giant bough swayed, east-west; it crashed onto the ground. His heart pounded. Fear melted him. He braced himself for flight.

Kisiang'ani cast a timid glance northwards. What a dreadful sight! A dark, mobile hillock hurtled at him. All trees were giving way. The fiend raised the tusk, whirled it a few yards ahead as if to sniff him and rolled on. The earth trembled as he moved. Frogs hushed when he grunted, fire flies smothered when he sniffed and ants waned with a single thump of his foot. Indeed he was in every way an irate king

Kisiang'ani scuttled through the bush and ploughed his way through the papyrus, he skipped over the jutting thorns and reached the road. The beast tracked him. Big branches saluted and grass lay prostrate to give way for the irascible sovereign thing. The young man reached a massive gully and halted, the beast in hot pursuit. In a single jerk, he hurled himself across it and landed in the middle of the road. A lorry swerved and missed a tree by an inch.

"Your mother's t...!" The men on board cursed. The ugly creature reached them. It hoisted its mouth up the lorry.

"Jump in!" the driver shouted at Kisiang'ani on the opposite side of the beast.

The boy leapt into the driver's cabin and sat on a man's lap. The lorry sped away from the fiend.

"Where are going?" Asked the driver.

"Kitali," he replied.

"From where?

"Cheleba,"

"On foot!"

"Eeh."

"Never try again."

"And you're called?"

"Kisiang'ani."

"Thank Wele for your life. The beast would have tramped you into nothing."

The old man said as Kisiang'ani alighted in town. He looked beaten. He sulked over the experience. Did he have a future? Was he destined to live? He trudged to Ford Farm with a drooping neck.

Chapter Nine

So strange was the way they named it. They called it Foti instead of Ford. What a daring adventure he had launched. It was a ripe fruit of his long cherished desire to know and he was determined enough to move beyond the cave of Cheleba.

Kisiang'ani exulted in the knowledge that he was a voluntary exile from Cheleba, driven out by its medieval distractions of violence, ignorance, and curses.

The black African workers resided on one side of the farm in tiny huts isolated by narrow alleys. They were grass thatched, mud walled and overloaded. His aunt cooked from one side of the shanty and slept on the other with her husband and children. The full extent of the hut was repulsive and offensive by reason of an asphyxiating cloud of smoke that meandered with a serpent gait in every nook.

How foolish he had been to join the camp of those who judged by appearance. He had supposed there was no one where there were people. He had supposed there was no life where it was. If there was love in the world, if there was affection on earth; it was here. In spite of their low material condition: the poverty of attire and scarcity of money, they loved fondly and devotedly.

Among them was warmth so unrivaled; so unusual. Their instincts were fine. Like elated chicks in the wings of their mothers, the children sat with merry countenances and attentive ears savouring their mother's narratives. Some chanted songs of merry, out in the yard. Others swapped witty riddles and others shared small talk of any happenings of the day with charm.

Nangila: Namunaii?- Riddle, riddle?

Children: Kwiche. - Let it come.

Endi nende kumukunda kulinebichikhi bibili bibofu
nende bibindi bikali bititi.

I have a piece of land that has two big stumps and many
other small ones.

Mulongo: Papa Lumati, mother and all of us.

Nangila: No.

Wangila: Wele Khakaba, Mwambu and Sela.
          Wele Khakaba, Mwambu and Sela.

Nangila: Tawe
          No.

Mukwana: Omukhulundu, omukhaya wewe nende
libukana
          The pastor, his wife and the church.

Nangila: Tawe,
          No

Kisiang'ani: Enyanga, kumwesi nende ching'enyesi.
          The sun, the moon and the stars.

Nangila: Orio yaya
          That's true, brother.

There followed a round of applause for Kisiang'ani.

Mukwana: Namunaii- Riddle, riddle?

Children: Kwiche- let it come?

Mukwana: Wanakhatandi sabonekha ta; atimila mukhayu,
akhukhosia lupao nofwa
          Wanakhatandi is invisible, he moves in a small
hut, he points a piece of wood at you and you die.

Nangila: Babalimu bakona mumapati
        Teachers who sleep in iron sheet roofed houses.
Mukwana: Tawe
        No.
Mulongo: Bang'osi na bafumu babapa bantu bikumba
        Seers and witchdoctors who bewitch people.
Mukwana: Tawe
        No
Kisiang'ani: The white man, moves in a car and kills you using a gun.
Mukwana: Orio omwana wa khocha. That is true uncle's son.
        All were awed by Kisiang'ani's wit.
Kisiangani: Namunaii- Riddle riddle?
Children: Kwiche- Let it come.
Kisiangiani: Khuyukhuyu paaaa!
Mukwana: The sound of a train.
Kisiang'ani: No.
Nangila: The fruit of the fig tree.

The audience laughed sarcastically at her. Repa wondered what kind answer was that.

Kisiang'ani: No.
Repa: The night runner who runs scaring people at night.
Kisiang'ani: Yes, aunt is right!
Chidren: Mother is right! Mother is right!
Kisiang'ani: Bikele bine alinda bikele bine ba bikele bibili.
Four legged watching four legged for two legged.

Repa: Hey! What a riddle!

Mukwana: If mother is unable, what about us?

Children: Mother is unable! Mother is unable! Mother is unable!

"Kisiang'ani!" a hoarse voice called from outside.

"Papa," Kisiang'ani replied.

"A circumcised man squatting by the heath stones with a woman and children?"

It stung him.

Kisiang'ani rose strolled towards Lumati. He was a man of bland voice and friendly air. He was a tall man, small headed but with spirits the size of his height. Everything in his world was bright and gaudy. More than ever, he hated anger outbursts. Depressions, bitterness, and animus did not form a paragraph of him. He sizzled with bonhomie; his eyes twinkled with a hearty expression of good humour.

Lumati was a peculiar friend of the Mauka's. The bottle and snuff were the prop of his existence. However, he was in good graces with his wife and children. A fact, Kisiang'ani ascertained this evening was that his wealth was scanty. The rest of him remained foreign.

The young man became nervous. He was not sure whether Lumati knew anything about the scandal. But he consoled himself with Lumati's love for education. He vowed to exploit this to cleanse the awful stench on his name.

Tonight, he appeared so very energetic with consistence in chivalry though without sufficient evidence to give him the trait. At the sight of Kisiang'ani he laid his staff, stood up and proffered his hand for greeting.

"How're you, son?"

"I'm alive."

"Muno, muno; muno, muno," they greeted, shaking hands.

"You took your exams?" The old man asked.

"Yes, father."

"What did you get?"

"Twenty seven points."

"Shake my hand again." He held out his hand.

"You're a man!" Lumati said. He sat back and adjusted his blanket.

"So to which secondary school are you going?"

"Friends Kimusingi."

"Our school which was begun in Kimilili recently."

"Yes, papa."

"Shake my hand again."

"But, I have no fees, papa. That's why I have come." Kisiang'ani broached his subject.

"Bas, you're a real man!" Lumati said ignoring the boy's request, "when you do that son, you strengthen the elderly like us. You are the banana sucker that props the falling mother at a withering age and takes over after she's dead and gone."

The old man stood, sneezed and blew his nose. He wiped the stray bits of mucus with the back of his palm and slumped back on his three legged stool.

"When Repa told me that dung about you beating my brother in-law, I did not give it much ear." The man said, his eyes twinkling with a roguish expression of humor. He cast timid glances at Kisiang'ani whose heart palpitated as the sharp nail plunged in the scar of his heart to re-live the chronic wound. He braced himself for the worst blow to hurl him back to those haunting memories. He felt crushed. Perhaps he had judged the man quickly.

Fortunately, the hammer turned the other side to claw the nail from his bleeding wound.

"My brother in-law should stop smoking marijuana and take his children to school," Lumati said and broke into a mechanical laughter.

"You're lying!" Repa shrilled from the smoky hut.

"A, ha! Ha! Ha! Ha!" The man laughed to draw away the nephew's attention.

"Didn't you blame our son, very much?" She added.

"Any way," Lumati whispered in the young man's ear, "I only tell you one thing, your father is your father. Do not touch him. Even if he shits on you, just run away."

Kisiang'ani nodded with utmost sincerity. The cordial manner through which the chastisement was carried out touched his heart and he desired to become a member of this family. Here was a man who had abandoned the thorny ways of his people and embraced the roses. He was monogamous and the young man loved it. To crown it all, Lumati had awakened to the benefits of education and out of his five sons, one was a teacher like Situma. Sifuna, for that was the son's name, taught in Karatina.

"You've done well," Lumati said after a pause, "although I have nothing to give you as you can see." He gestured his hand around. Honestly, everything denoted poverty. Kisiang'ani began to see the darker side of the white man.

"The white man has taken everything from us; our chicken, cattle, goats and sheep. He sends his boys to collect taxes and you don't ask anything. Last moon Mukhwana, that slim boy, was sick. You know the African science?"

"Yes, papa, did you call me?" interrupted the cheerful boy.

"Bones?" asked Kisiang'ani.

"Yes, bones. No, son I was just telling Kisiang'ani something about you. The doctor removed bottles from his stomach. We spent all we had on him. That's why we have no milk in this house, a ha!" He blew his nose again.

Mukwana was already at his feet. "The riddle! The riddle! He did not tell us the answer pa-a-a-a!"

"Papa, what help can you offer?" Kisiang'ani entreated with dismal look. The child seemed to divert his melancholic feeling.

"Alright, sit here, your brother will tell you the answer," Lumati pampered Mukhwana.

"Now..now... the riddle!" He cried.

"I think Wesonga should take you to Sifuna at Karatina. I'm sure he will assist you," the old man said in emphatic terms.

"Pa-a...pa-a! the riddle!"

Kisiang'ani's heart limped with delight. His face beamed. He turned to the boy and with a cheerful face said:

"A dog looking after a cow for a man."

Mukhwana was overjoyed. So was Kisiang'ani. No more did he look back to the crushing scandals of his past. No more did he behold the shameful briars of Mauka. Before his mind's eye were blossoming flowers, falling ripe oranges and a highway of a brilliant silver making a wavy headway into his hazy destiny.

Chapter Ten

The new images on the dailies never missed his political eye. Kisiang'ani gazed at the briskly rising blacks with admiration. Jaramogi, Mboya and Ngala. All in one, they called for the immediate release of their hero. Kisiang'ani looked at it anxiously. How innocent were 'these monks' to apply to a hellish field perfect standards absolutely at variant to it.

Had he been Odinga, he would have formed the government. Such opportunities, the young man held, were rare and only the naïve slunk back to shout 'Uhuru na somebody.'

His second year at Karatina had become hell. His shoes were sandals, his shoe brush a discarded tooth brush and towel, a tattered vest. The hopes he had nursed in Sifuna's generous hand shattered in the gutter of improvidence. Out of two hundred, he had paid forty shillings only.

Kisiang'ani slunk back to wander in darkness, a darkness of bitter meditations. He avoided every soul, loitered about alone and remained distant and bookish. He would stagger around the school, friendless enough, mumbling no whisper to a boy or a girl. His laughter was a minute quiver and if he tried to appear before people then he certainly never did in church or recreation room.

There Kisiang'ani had been all the time, just there; the same dry piece of wood, the same miserable emblem of poverty. They had scorned him, those well bred girls from Nyeri. They sneered at the poverty of his outfit. Of course you could not tell the colour of his patched up shorts. They mocked the bloated toes of his feet and any other insults their snobbery would find.

No doubt Kisiang'ani was a child of many sorrows. In spite of his misery, he neither refrained from hard work nor endorsed intimidation. He was Buchacha's descendant. He savoured words at night; consequently his academic performance was exceptional. He remained impervious to unreasonable criticism and whenever they stirred him, he became very violent.

The boy ate by divine grace, dressed by divine grace and learnt divine grace. The brook, however, dried when Mr.Gachanja, the head teacher, insisted that each student at Form Two had to pay registration fees for Junior Secondary Exam. His survival was brought to a halt.

Kisiang'ani borrowed five shillings from Sela, Sifuna's house help, and boarded the train home. The shots that scorned him would not miss the lonely grotesque they had always seen under the Mugumo tree brooding. They had known him as scantily as the late Dedan Kimathi. Although they underrated him, Kisiang'ani exulted in the fact that he had maintained his tenacity; he had not fallen prey to the deception of those girls.

Kisiang'ani sat on his settee and thought sentimentally about his life. His face depicted the deepest agitation as if the creator had announced his last day. The unpleasant thought that pretty girls would never spare a moment for a poor boy like him drained his self-esteem. Nonetheless, he dispelled it with the exhortation that he had remained a young man of pure morals and clear foresight.

"Home is home." He thought. Doubts set in. He wished Mauka changed his mind to assist him. He had been too young to understand. Indeed a father was a father. He was already missing him. He tried to imagine the number of wrinkles two years had added to his hardened face. He thought of going down on his knees to tender an apology. No, to repent before his father and rid this burden of guilt. But, missing was a guide to assist him unload the haunting burdens of his past.

Then would Kisiang'ani have stretched his arms and surrendered to that guide and deliverer of human troubles. But where was such a guide? Why did He watch him toil? Why would He give him a cruel father? Why would this creator permit his father to pee on children? Why would He bring him on earth via a poor and miserable family? The young man had a barrage of questions for his creator.

They always set in whenever he thought about home. They embittered him; they stole his peace. He, however, knew well that he did not hate home but Mauka's presence in it remained a calabash of pepper in a lump of honey.

"Those girls mock me. Aaah!" He changed the subject of meditation, "They imitate my… walking…and call…me 'unexposed,'" He reflected. It was sour to remember. But he silenced them with academic prowess. In history, he had scored everything more than five times. At one time, Mr. Gachanja had replaced his label from 'Walking disaster' to 'Mark harvester' after he scored 100% in two subjects. In short, Kisiang'ani was no doubt a mentally gifted boy.

The train rumbled down the great rift as darkness stuffed it. He turned hither and yonder. A sweet fragrance caught his perception. Kisiang'ani desired to enjoy human warmth if but for a minute. He yearned to part with bad thoughts that often shut the door of hope. He cast a quick glance on his left and wow! A beautiful plump girl shared his settee. She was about twenty two years of age with an alluring brown complexion and permanent grin. Oh, she looked familiar to Kisiang'ani.

"Hi," the girl greeted.

"Yah, I'm fine," Kisiang'ani replied in a whisper.

Her voice tickled his heart and more charming she became. It was sweet and familiar. Her eyes seemed to beam in the darkness and sent a romantic luster that he had never before witnessed. Kisiang'ani sizzled with extreme sweetness of desire.

"You look familiar," the girl said. Kisiang'ani got amazed. Noticing his shock, she proffered her hand for a shake, smiling. The boy felt at home. He shook the soft hand with pleasure. He took a passionate stock of her. Her features were tender and sweet.

"You girls refuse to talk to me at school," Kisiang'ani complained.

"That's you, a ha!" She cooed, "When you meet people you're always absentminded."

"Troubles, my friend," he said.

"What troubles? Have fun in life Kisi..." The girl abridged his name with a sensual touch. She sat up and gazed at his face. She was astonished; there was a lot of sorrow in it. She flung her hands sloppily and they landed on his. Blood rushed up his veins.

The boy was not himself. Doubts assailed him. Was it realistic for a queen of her stature to love a miserable boy like him? He was absolutely unsuitable for her. He doubted with palpitations of the heart. She was a slut taking advantage of his poverty to infect him with a disease.

No, perhaps he was too rash. He changed his mind. The mere thought of holding this pretty girl in his bosom was an attainment few boys had accomplished. An unattainable fantasy would soon be a reality. He yearned for a swan to shed off haunting memories that threatened to shorten his lifespan.

Furthermore, the young man beheld a god-sent opportunity to test his manhood as the elders had advised.

"How do you feel when you touch my hand?" The girl whispered in his ear.

"Super...oh!" He cooed. Kisiang'ani heaved with uncontrollable passion.

He had never met a maiden so graceful and daring as well as charming. It was time he knew her name before he bent his principles just at an acute angle. Kisiang'ani desired any moralist to sympathize with him because in a great measure he had been deprived the roses of life and presented with thorns. Gradually his bright side of life was unfolding and loud calls for virtue could not deter him.

He did not want to be childless as the elders had warned. Even the long time he had taken to respond to her feelings, he bet, let her confuse him for an impotent man.

"What's your name?" He asked moving closer. Solid darkness filled the train.

"Wambui."

"From?"

"Kitali."

"Which class are…."

"Alas! You don't know me Kisi? Grade two with you."

"No, no, no, no."

"I sit behind you my dear…oh my dear, you don't see?"

The last sentence drove Kisiang'ani mad. But something struck his mind.

"Do you think I'm as poor as you are? Look at your toes, they've bulged with hoards of jiggers. And your rotting teeth carry a life time of plaque…, I'll never admire you!" Kisiang'ani raises his hand and slaps her. She screams. He raises his foot and smacks her down. Three boys appear to end the fight.

"What are you pondering about?" Wambui startled him to the present.

"Our..."

"We fight to become friends, my dear."

Her voice was soothing. Kisiang'ani felt comforted.

"In fact you ought to marry me after school," Wambui added, wild with pleasure.

It surprised the young man. How could a girl propose to a man? She had said it with airs of a person who knew the ins and outs of love. Oh, no. She was far from purity.

But the temptation to crush her in his bosom was so great. It would drown his sorrows. Had she not told him to have fun? How else would he find it? Who else would carry him on wings from the dreary world to the Kingdom of pleasure? Only Wambui would do it.

"Why do you shy off? Aren't you a man? Speak," Wambui whispered and lay her head on his chest. Kisiang'ani hung his soul at the acme of passion. His heart throbbed violently. He panted fast. He surveyed around. Many were asleep; he could only hear the rickety motion of the train. He conceived a strong admiration amid sharp voices of doubt. A maiden proposed through gestures. Whores proposed to men directly. Many assertions flitted through his mind.

She passed her hand along his lips. It reminded him of the thing called kiss. He had seen white people do it on a street in the city. He passed his arm around her small back and kissed her. The girl reciprocated. He did it again. She returned a violent jerk and the affluence of her fragrance ignited a fountain of passion in his heart. An expansive pool flooded. There were chaotic motions of the battlements of passion: arms caressed, lips sucked, tongues rolled, saliva fused; heads jerked back and forth and hearts drummed into each other. Tribe and class wept miles away.

The battle subsided. They stared in each other's eyes, tired and tipsy.

"I love you," she cooed.

"I love you," he replied and fell into her bosom.

Kisiang'ani regretted his previous lack of confidence. He was not a nonentity as he had imagined. He was an honourable man. His sensual desire re-asserted its rights. They kissed themselves lame. He fumbled with her skirt. She sighed. She murmured into his ear, "Let's go to the toilets."

Quitting his seat, he staggered along the corridors, her arm in his, towards the lavatories...

*****

Kisiang'ani reached home at noon. Their home was overgrown with weeds. As annoying as ever, Mauka had sold five acres of land and spread word in Cheleba that he was on his way to Kitali. News had run through Mount Masaba that Hon. Mubeyi, the torch bearer of the sons of Mwambu, had stumbled on empty land in Kitali. He therefore wanted all the sons of Mwambu to leave Mount Masaba and join him there.

Like many other children of Mwambu, Mauka beheld an offer he could not pass. He made up his mind to sell all his land on Mount Masaba and migrate with his family to Kitali. With his modicum knowledge, however, Kisiang'ani found the rumour a falsity. It was a fib, the major weapon in the battle of politics. His father's innocence would bring them to ruin.

In his study of history, Kisiang'ani had discovered, to his surprise, deceit as the first ingredient on the recipe of political success. He cherished this argument and supported it with examples across the globe. Politics, he could say, flourished by sheer humbug. He pointed out the cunning that characterized the two world wars. They depicted corruption, contrary to the nature of civilized nations.

Kisiang'ani questioned American policy of neutrality. It was a trick to arm Germany against the then super powers for her own good. The fall of Europe only paved way for her rise. Then he thought about the Lustiana. How German submarines triumphed over British warships to sink Lustiana, an American ship, only Britain could explain. Didn't allies control sea routes? Kisiang'ani was not a fool to believe such crap of history.

It is along this line of thinking that the young man dismissed Hon. Mubeyi's promise of manna. He saw the man as a cunning hunter busy setting a snare to catch prey for his tummy. Therefore he would persuade his father never to sell the land.

He had to do it with tact so as to stroke the cow this time round to obtain milk from it. As the sun went to Masolo, Mauka showed up in high spirits.

"E, he, he! Welcome home son," he said.

"Thanks, papa!" Kisiang'ani replied.

"How is school?"

"It's good."

"People want you to become the chief of Cheleba. Eat books, son. Return and lead your people."

"I've got no fees father. I can't even register for exams," the boy asserted.

"Has Sifuna not done it?" He asked with confidence.

"He paid forty out of two hundred shillings."

"I'm selling this land to migrate to Kitali so...I'm..."

"What's in Kitali, papa?"

"Mubeyi, our first born son who arrived from the white man's land a few seasons ago, is now our eye. He sees the way and we all follow. He is the fire that burns all scything weeds ahead of us. He will be our king when the white man leaves. He will grip the cow by the horns for us to milk it."

He paused to smoke his pipe. Kisiang'ani surveyed the old man. He looked gaunt. He was tipsy as was his custom.

"E he he, he!" He chortled, "That's why I'm selling the land to move and live near him. I'll use part of that cash to pay your fees."

Kisiang'ani fixed his gaze at him. He wanted to take advantage of his situation to dispose more land. Warm thoughts left him. He spoke,

"Leave the land out of this."

"Let me get married for him to learn," said Nabangala.

"Tell your mother's b-!" Mauka insulted Nabangala.

"That's uncouth!" Blurted Kisiang'ani.

"This is my home and you can't tell me what to say!" Mauka growled and struck his staff onto the ground.

"All right you shan't sell land any longer!" Kisiang'ani declared without emotion.

"Tell your promiscuous mother that I'll sell my land!" He shouted.

Kisiang'ani remained unusually calm. Mauka rose and disappeared into the infernal darkness. 'See how history repeats itself!' The young man thought. He had not wished to instigate violence but it had repeated to re-live past wounds. He had irritated the cow before touching the udder; uncertainty was all that remained.

How foolish he had been to think that the gratification he had had the previous night was a premonition of the impending success. On the contrary, it forecast failure. Nonetheless, it was a balm of his heart throughout the distressing night. That initial whimper that caught his hearing after plunging his sword in the groin, the dripping of blood that succeeded to seal their hearts; the violent wave motions that culminated into a spirited combat ushered them into bliss. They stuck on each other, lips sucking and the throat groaning. It had challenged his mind set; not all who proposed were promiscuous.

Stretched out in his blanket, the young man discovered that he was handsome enough to attract someone's daughter. His heart limped with joy. His self-value skipped a stave higher with the thought of Wambui's promise to marry him.

But where would he take such a beauty? All in all, the desire to have a woman by him to share his burden remained supreme. Bush telegraph had it that Wafula's wedding would be held one moon from then. He had to do something to avoid being overtaken by a young brother. He resolved to marry after his exam.

The following day, he woke up with a bright sun above Mount Masaba. The birds sang, the grasshoppers twanged into oblivion and the butterflies fluttered gaily in their short lifespan. He walked into Nabangala's hut and was greeted by a brown envelope on her stool. Blankness and boredom reigned in the hut. The letter was addressed to him in her queer hand writing.

Dear Noah,
It is not my want but I is went
Take money and go school. Eat
Books I'm went with Wanjala for your fwis
Read, we wili sheya fruit.

Kisiang'ani was shaken. He had treasured Nabangala's warm company. In those moments of rejection, she had remained the closest companion. She had hugged clouds of despondency out of his bosom on his way to Lumati's. He had loved her fondly. It was a love matched only to Wambui's but as destiny would have it, the beautiful soul had left to be with the ugly Wanjala.

He conceived a foetus of envy for Wanjala. God forbid, that Nabangala should marry this idiot who could not pronounce the first two letters of the alphabet. He had taken advantage of the poverty in the home. The rumbling famine, prevalent jiggers, poor diet and Mauka's violence had pushed her into the vulgar business of self-sell. With his coming, she had got embarrassed to do it in his presence and taken French leave.

He had rejoiced to find her lovely, plump and tall. But her exaggerated size of hips and bosom had awakened his suspicion. Though he had waved it aside as petty, it dawned on him that he would have made it the punch line of all their conversations. Then would he have righted the wrongs in her sister's heart. Nabangala had died for him to live. She had become poor for him to flourish.

Kisiang'ani took the money with beads of tears on his eyes. He brought the wad close to his mouth and spat saying,

"May Wele reward you, daughter of Buchacha. May he give you sons; twins and triplets." The sum total was four hundred shillings.

As Butilu was still uprooting arrow roots at the well, she saw the sulky figure of her firstborn son tip toeing up the miry path like a bank thief. His hands made gestures like a father computing a year's family budget.

'I won't waste all this bride wealth at school!' He thought. He knew without an iota of pretence that with prevailing economic difficulties, he would not make it to advanced levels of education. Kisiang'ani could not ignore his age. In two years time, he would be thirty. He would be thirty without a good hut, a bed and a spouse. That would be shameful. He resolved to set aside two hundred shillings for Agricultural projects to prepare for his marriage.

PART TWO

Marriage and the Rise

Chapter Eleven

The morning breeze brushed them as they steered their hoes around the stems of crops. Kisiang'ani's three lines led the pack, Wafula's line followed closer, Butilu's followed suit then came Esther's and Nang'oni's.

"That's a true son," Wamalwa who was passing on his way to gather honey in the forest commended. He was walking along with Matumbai.

"He tightens his grip on the hoe even after swallowing the white man's pill at the iron sheets," he told Matumbai.

"But our son should control his anger," replied Matumbai, "our people say a stubborn elephant never preserves its task."

"But he will lift the banner of that family," maintained Wamalwa.

Whether they called him Kisiang'ani fanatic or Kisiang'ani holic, Wamalwa would neither defend himself nor apologize. Truly, he loved the young man. Wherever he went from Kikai to Rikai, he flattered him. He exhorted young people to follow his footsteps. The white man's attempt to turn him into the proverbial Wanakhatandi was utter fiasco.

"Wanakhatandi read so much until he refused to eat esaka (bitter vegetables)," he would say, "but our son not only eats esaka but grips the hoe."

Indeed Wamalwa's testimony was accurate. Kisiang'ani's new management had brought a handful of changes. He had ploughed down gawking weeds (using Mauka's oxen) and in their place shone dancing leaves of maize, beans, bananas and sugar cane.

How fertile their farm was. Kisiang'ani got fascinated by the treasure they had lain on for decades without knowing. You stabbed a set of sugarcane on it and it shot up after two days.

Kisiang'ani had put up a rectangular hut with a grass thatch, yet another wonder in Cheleba. Rumour darted on the political pew. Two national parties had been formed to lead black Kenyans to independence. They argued over the nature of government best suited to the country. The squabbles dispirited the young man. In fact, one of the sons of Mwambu strongly backed the opposition.

Their hoes thudded at irregular beats to get the daily bread. Why would he focus all his energies on politics? Wamalwa had once told him, "The stomach carries the head." Politics was the head and he could not venture into it on a hungry stomach. Even those who praised Jomo and Tom watched for their main chance.

He stopped weeding to stretch his back and before him appeared Sitawa's image: overwhelming confidence, sweet smile and care free attitude. She smiled into his eyes and blood tinged up his body. He gazed at her overflowing hips and ravishing face. He was overcome by the desire to have her. He untucked his T-shirt to cover the fly. His heart pounded with extreme passion. He breathed a sigh---

His face misted into the alluring beauty of Wambui. There she was, the mighty guardian of his heart, whose recollection embittered his existence. Few believed it but Kisiang'ani never counted himself among them. Only a beast would have withstood that magnitude of loss. The girls and boys in the school could not accept it and worse was Kisiang'ani.

The wicked robber of human kind had broken into Wambui's soul and stolen her spirit away. His darling had painfully departed to the world of permanent repose, the world of eternal peace that she had missed in this world of strife. In spite of encouraging him to make fun, she could not make fun of what she had found at home.

The white man had arrested Mwangi wa Thiong'o on trumped charges of harbouring a maumau and hanged him. The news were a pill of aloes to her spirit. She could not imagine life without a father. She had rejected entreaties, plunged into a trance and went for the bottle of dichlorophenoindopheno. The siblings had rushed at the scene; they had come very late.

Two men had sauntered in the school a few days before the final Exam and confounded the community about her sudden death. The school converged to observe a moment of silence in honour of the deceased; Kisiang'ani whimpered and scampered away from the assembly.

"Follow him," Mr Gachanja directed some students.

Kisiang'ani had scuttled hither and thither shouting fragments about Wambui. The boys tried to grip him but he threw them down and sped towards the hillock on the western end of the field. He then sprung up and let his body crash with a thud. His feet kicked, his bosom twitched and tears flooded his new shirt. The boys saw absolute sincerity in all his actions.

He mourned his sister and they also joined him to weep. They learned from him and there ensued a mighty screech of despair and melancholy in the school. Mr Gachanja wondered what manner of girl Wambui had been. Girls die. So do boys. But, such a magnitude of grief that involved foreign tribes never arose.

Only the students could tell better. Wambui's love had had no bounds. She always cherished the society of every human being. Most of her friends came from other tribes. Like any human being, she had weaknesses. Wambui was quick-tempered but she forgave immediately after the quarrel.

She had taught them an enduring lesson: True love traversed tribes, races and classes- the three major shadows of reality. Her ghost had haunted him in dreams. It made him resolve never again to unlock closed doors until marriage.

At present, he was planning to call on his fiancée as part of preparation for marriage. In spite of his formal education, the young man was well informed about the customs of marriage among his people.

In many cases, the young man accosted his father to express his desire to marry a certain girl. The father then thought about the girl's family. If there was any close blood relationship, the young man's request would be rejected. If the father established no hindrances, he would then proceed to have audience with the girl's father.

The girl had to be aware before hand. The boy would have wooed her before telling his father, otherwise nothing would start. Kisiang'ani had finished this stage. Wooing was not easy during Buchacha's times. The maidens were not as easy going as Wambui. They were strict, gross and hostile. Those who belittled a boy could challenge him into a fight. A man had to be brutal and muscular. In the case when he throttled such a woman, she would take him up as a suitor.

It was very risky for the young man to go straight to the girl's father and express his desire to marry his daughter. It would earn him a historic beating. His father would go with a bundle of snuff in banana sheath and say,

"I have a handle at home but it has no hoe, please, give me a hoe. I wish to fix it."

The girl's father would tacitly understand and reply,

"Give me the key to unlock the door to parliament."

Parliament never meant offices with people making laws. It was dialogue with the girl's mother and the key, the bundle of snuff. If she loved the young man and the family background, she would simply ask, "What has he brought?"

The girls father would then present the bundle of snuff and word would be sent to the young man to prepare for dowry payment and wedding. This was the formal way as far as Kisiang'ani was concerned.

But Kisiang'ani dismissed it as a preserve of the rich families among the sons of Mwambu. The poor families of Mauka's calibre singled out the informal way. It was despised but most popular in Kisiang'ani's times. It was a means through which the assertive sons of Cheleba punished their irresponsible fathers using custom.

Meanwhile, many rumors made their rounds in Cheleba about Kisiang'ani and Sitawa. Some claimed that, Kisiang'ani was impotent as a consequence of his disobedience to his parents. Others said that, Sitawa's path to the womb had been clogged by the white man's science. They could not be persuaded that a normal boy and girl could be unmarried at twenty nine.

In spite of the slander, she knew what she had sought since those days when she had run away from her father's cattle. It was abstract but it had set her mentally and economically free. But, that did not mean that she had wavered in her firm devotion to Kisiang'ani. She loved only him and desired him day and night.

Although she sometimes burned with passion, she had never done this thing that instinct instructed her so well. She believed Kisiang'ani's letter that he had preserved himself for her. Standing behind the kitchen, Sitawa's heart pounded with a certain craving for something she had denied herself twenty nine years now. An expansive void escalated in her soul. It was a vacuum no one in the home could fill. A wave of loneliness swept over her. She hated herself. Was she too ugly to get married? Was she too old to attract him? Why did his eyes rove more at Rita whenever he visited the home?

Two of her young sisters had married off two years before and it was shameful for her to continue loitering in Wamalwa's compound. His father had already shown obvious signs that she was unwanted in that home. He kept flattering Kisiang'ani to draw his attention. Her mother, Simbi had told her the previous day that the kitchen was too small for the two of them.

Mamai's pigeons flew by and perched on her feet. Realizing the presence of a human being, they glided to their nest. They began singing and mating. They were merry love songs. An inexplicable yearn for Kisiang'ani engulfed her. She desired to surrender herself as a willing pilgrim on his back to be carried to those unknown pleasurable kingdoms.

His giant stature stuck before her: broad face, dark complexion, expansive chest and bull shoulders. He was a prominent man. His fame all around Cheleba charmed her. He was a pillar of diligence, a monument of exposure and a pyramid of courage. He was to her the embodiment of the ideal husband. How many in Cheleba had stepped in the city? Even Sitawa herself had not. He had dined with the sons and daughters of Mumbi and it made her to be proud of him. He would have married one of them but he had resolved never to fall in love with even one. It was a great privilege just to be called by his name.

"Linet Sitawa Kisiang'ani," she muttered with delight. But his recent liking for Rita worried her. She was a woman like herself. Her mother usually said that a small thorn killed an elephant. A woman was a woman as long as she had the looks and feminine wit. Men would adore her regardless of her social standing.

She knew the power women wielded over men. Kings sometimes ruled in women's names. She therefore set forth to get him before a coup. Darkness spilled over the home. Simbi began singing a song to Rita in the kitchen,

Simbi: Pilingali yauma	*The wedding is lively*
Pilingali yauma	*the wedding is lively*
Rita: Uwu yauma, huu	*Oh, it's lively*
Simbi: Yaumila mwitukhu	*it's lively in the mansion*
Yaumila mwitukhu	*it's lively in the mansion*
Rita: Uwu yauma, huu	*Oh it's lively*
Simbi: Nendumukhana	*If I were a girl,*
Nendumukhana	*If I were a girl.*
Rita: Uhu yauma ,huu	*Oh it's lively.*
Simbi: Senje burende	*I will not get married,*
Senje burende	*I will not get married,*
Rita: uwu yauma huu	*Oh, it's lively.*
Simbi: Bapila chirungu	*They beat with staffs ,*
Bapila chirungu	*They beat with staffs.*

Sitawa no longer feared. She thanked her mother for warning her about marriage life but he would rather have Kisiang'ani beat her than tolerate her mockery. A shuffle of feet startled her from her reflections. She lifted her eyes and saw a dark figure that transformed in a moment into Kisiang'ani. She rushed towards him.

"How are you?"

"I'm alive." He replied.

"Looking for…"

"You sweetie." He cooed.

"You lie."

"Why, Linet?"

"Kisi you think I don't know?"

"What...do…you…mean…"

"You love Rita, don't you?"

"No please, I just find her attractive, period!"

"More attractive than me? Is….am...I..."

"You're more beautiful. I've missed you big time, darling!"

He fondled her palm. Solid darkness poured in and geckos sang romantic tunes. He pulled her closer. Her features were tender and body, soft and warm. He touched her breasts and she recoiled from him.

"Don't do anything," she whispered.

"All right, but you should spent the night with me today."

"I shall not!" She said with a bold firmness.

They strolled away from the Wamalwa's. Kisiang'ani was gradually getting drunk. He was between intoxication partial and intoxication complete. They staggered round a bend and started climbing a steep hill to Cheleba primary school. Kisiang'ani's breath was short. He craved to know what lay beyond the knees of this beautiful girl.

The girl evinced unusual attachment to conversation. She shared the experiences she had gone through; her struggles to pay fees at Lugulu High School and the average performance in class. When she came to rumours of barrenness that

Cheleba had fomented about her, he got an opportunity to woo her. He extended his arm across her small back and caressed her. She did not resist. Stars shone over them.

"You're the dearest darling of my soul." Kisiang'ani whispered.

"You lie," she replied.

"You're the backbone of my life, the strut of my breath."

"You lie, dear. That's Rita," she persisted.

"You are very beautiful," he flattered her.

"Thank you." She said losing her stiffness.

"We must spend the night together," he suggested.

"I can't do that. You haven't told my father," she argued.

"Even if I die now and descend into the grave, even if Mauka struck me dead and..."

"You'll not die now! Darling, don't say that!" Sitawa said, his neck in her two hands.

"Even if Butilu expels me from the home, I shall never leave you. I shall hold pure and strong the indelible memory of your love, your warmth and rejoice in the fact that my name, my suffering and my tears were fondly stored in your warm heart." He broke down and wept. Wambui stepped in his vision.

"Don't cry," Sitawa pleaded.

Why do you shy off? Aren't you a man? Make fun Kisi... the voice persisted.

"I love you Wa...m...Sitawa," Kisiang'ani erred.

"Who is this Wasitawa?" She became furious.

"That's just a tongue slip," he said in a composed manner.

"I won't marry in a dishonorable way," she asserted.

"I won't marry formally," he declared.

"Why?"

"I've got no father to make formal arrangements," he revealed.

A period of silence succeeded with Sitawa on his shoulder. She thought about Kisiang'ani's situation. Her father Wamalwa had never concealed anything from her. He always spoke in favour of Kisiang'ani. She was well informed about Mauka's laziness, extravagance and irresponsibility. She reached a decision that her darling needed her.

Furthermore, the geckos had stopped singing and crickets would soon retire to bed. It was approaching ten. Her parents would not be happy to see her walk back late in the night.

"Then we must reach your house," Sitawa said with an air of moral firmness. She was tired of dirty rumours, Simbi's silent insults and Wamalwa's talk about him. How long would she suck her knuckles? They reeled along meandering paths, the girl repulsing his attempts to kiss her with pushes. Was this her culture? Why would he deny her the right to breath? Why would they use mouths when there were tools meant for the purpose.

A cold breeze blew across their bodies. Dogs and bitches intoned romantic tunes. Kisiang'ani stepped in his hut with moon rise. Streaks of light penetrated through a chink. The hut beamed with the ray of light and celebrated for her blessed deliverance from loneliness. She was an over-worked expectant mother cherishing the arrival of the house help. The floor was overloaded with buckling chunks of cow dung.

They stepped in the bedroom and the maiden refused bedding. Was it substandard? A six inch mattress separated from the floor by three cow hides. On the right hand side of the bedding were three hearthstones.

The girl pulled out one hide from the floor and lay it on top of the mattress. He kissed her, he kissed her again. She could not understand. The battle began and raged. The gate to bliss was narrow and he fumbled desperately to open it. She was strong and pure. He gathered his strength and banged but the combat tilted against him. He despised himself. He recalled Matumbai's advice. He lifted her onto one of the hearthstones. He grabbed her with all his strength and hurled his last blow.

She hissed and complained of pain. The gate flew open, the curtain ruptured and blood oozed to seal the covenant of their marriage. The blood trickled and percolated into the hide to form a permanent mark. This stain would forever be an eligible sign of Sitawa's honour and purity in the society.

Chapter Twelve

Trees have ears and darkness has eyes. Crickets and fireflies keep their diary. That is the only way Kisiang'ani could explain the mysterious circumstances that had befallen his territory on the third day. How else could he explain how news had reached Wamalwa to ascertain his daughter's presence at the Mauka's? Had he not plotted her flight at night? Had Sitawa not remained indoors for three days?

But when he rose on the third day to usher in Nambuya, Sitawa's paternal aunt, he thawed with astonishment. In a pretentious trance, she pranced into the sitting room and pushed her way like a mad woman into the bedroom. Kisiang'ani was somewhat indignant. He wanted to storm the room and tell her off but Butilu motioned him to keep his cool. They were just the proceedings of marriage rites.

"E, he, he! Look at this hide!" She said in feigned surprise. The hide was in her hand. She threw a curious and cautious glance at it. In a lifeless grunt, she staggered through the main door with eyes on the bloody stain. She tumbled down the steep slope into Okoro springs and climbed the steep into Cheleba primary at the summit. She reeled away in a tipsy state.

She exulted in Sitawa. She had not embarrassed her father; he could strut there and demand anything he wanted. Wamalwa would be respected as a father who tended virgins. Now Nambuya dismissed all the rumours she had heard about her licentiousness. The 'iron sheets' had not spoilt her.

As an aunt, she had observed her. Whenever she returned from Lugulu, she picked the hoe and went weeding on the farm. She was not like other girls who painted their nails and sat basking on the sun. She envied her brother Wamalwa for having such a daughter. Nambuya wished the couple well.

Meanwhile the change of status had come with tremendous transformation in Kisiang'ani. He had shifted from the depth of sorrow to the summit of cheeriness. He that had never mastered the art of making friends now attempted to interact and chat with every heart. But some shunned his greetings with averted heads. The outrage he had committed years ago had besmirched his name.

Nonetheless, his equanimity was at once restored; he dressed his face with a lively appearance. She was a woman after his heart. His happiness was bound up in hers and her affections wrapped up in his. When she went out he became love sick; she was the rose of his eye and song of his soul. In short, Sitawa was the prop of his masculinity, the engine of his strength and spice of his dreary life.

Kisiang'ani thanked Wele for her. In their going out and coming in, they would stroll arm in arm in the bushy labyrinths of Cheleba. She would sway her hips ahead of him while stealing backward glances with romantic smiles. He would reach out for her hand extremely elated and 'drunk'. His mouth would bubble with honey, his passion quite bewildered with twangs of mating grasshoppers, moving chirps of birds and courting serenades of cicadas.

He would wink to her sweet smile; he would pat her huge bosom and wince with desire. He would smile, laugh, wink again and kiss her. She accepted it now with expression of face that implied that she was mighty in love. They would thaw into one of the bushes of Cheleba.

Oh, how happy they were. How distant problems were from them. Look where she would, no handsome man would be better than her darling. Marriage was not as Simbi had sang. On the contrary, it was a bed hibiscus.

Kisiang'ani permitted his passion to get the better of his life. In conversations, he digressed more often to the personal beauty of his wife and the worth with which he held her. Although in secret contrast with Wambui she fell back by a step or two, her brown complexion and sweet voice sent a man mad.

Leaving the past behind him, he consoled himself with Sitawa was a lady that made a man rejoice. Her smile would make the bond of love flourish. But if that daughter of Mumbi were alive, then he would have married the two simultaneously.

The voice of blame rose against him. Here was a man who went with his wife to fetch water, to grind maize and plait hair at Cheleba. Kisiang'ani was accused of assisting his wife in cooking hence disregarding the essence of circumcision.

Unlike the men of Cheleba who looked at spouses as domestics, Kisiang'ani saw his wife as a sharer of joys, sorrows, riches, dreams and all the rigours of life. She became Nabangala's substitute. Most religions saw a wife as a queen of the house or a helper rather than a slave. The younger man chose to swap this for the beliefs of Cheleba.

He loved her. He would not leave her to wander alone; he gave her company. He disliked the idea of men deserting their wives in Cheleba to carouse in towns far away. Why would a married man live alone? Kisiang'ani could not believe. He therefore resolved to pamper his wife Sitawa in a way that was shocking to the elderly.

The elders condemned the vice. They had never in their lives seen a husband accompany his wife to the bathroom. It aggrieved Kisiang'ani that society interfered with his privacy. Little did he know that there was nothing private in marriage among his people.

That is why a week after his marriage, Butilu had scolded him for not only marrying casually but also an old woman. The suitable wife for him was six years younger. Kisiang'ani had told her that she wasted her sugar prying into affairs that by no means concerned her. Butilu got surprised. A wife did not belong to the individual. She belonged to society.

"Your tastes aren't mine, so is your experience..." he had burst out.

"It's also good," replied Butilu with scorn, "he that rejects advice lies on the path of death."

"Are you cursing me, mother?" he asked.

"I'm warning you, an older woman will give you hard time."

Kisiang'ani remained adamant. He had never thought of marrying a teenage girl. First, she could not share his big dreams. Second, she could easily confuse marriage for sex. Third, she was still a baby to be pampered yet he needed a mother to baby him. Butilu corrected his third reason: all women were babies who needed men to baby them. He was wrong to seek Butilu in Sitawa.

Even curses would not change Kisiang'ani's mind. He had vouched never to do what the youth of Cheleba did. They abandoned mature girls in favour of teenagers. Many argued that younger girls were more obedient to authority. To put it in realistic terms, teenagers were more passive and would applaud everything with automaton obedience. Hence was their dislike for older girls and hate if they were learned.

A learned girl was not only belligerent but also defiant to coercion. How would a man of Cheleba rule his house without an iron hand. He growled and thundered. Women and children scuttled and sprinted to the rhythm of his voice. A woman who argued with the husband was intolerable. It was repugnant to the norms.

He recalled men like Buchacha who did not tolerate a divergent view from a son or a wife. His savage heart was impervious to discussion and violence was the meal of each day in the home. A wife, it was said, had to be beaten to be a wife. How embarrassing it would be for an inherited widow to complain that her new husband was the first ever to beat her. It could as well be said that she never had a husband.

In short, Cheleba concluded that Kisiang'ani was not Buchacha's blood. He was a weakling who feared his wife. He sat in the kitchen like a woman and pleaded with her to permit him go out. Situma's attempt to explain to them that the young man was as brave as Buchacha hit a wall.

He taught them that in science there was something called water cycle. Rain water flowed after rainfall into rivers, oceans, vapour, and clouds and then fell again. It would be absurd for one to say that clouds were not water because they hung in the sky. They scorned at Situma's artificial wisdom. They wished she cited a proverb from the language of Mwambu.

Buchacha obeyed all the rites of the sons of Mwambu including Khutumia kamaika, which Kisiang'ani despised. A bridegroom had to fabricate a situation, work himself into a hollow rage and thrash the bride within the first month.

"Where is that comb...hey? ...why...are...you...dilly-dallying...esh? ...are you growing horns? ...wham ...you must behave!" It was something like that to fulfill the demands of custom.

Kisiang'ani had defied Maratani's calls to perform the rite on the basis that a woman was a person. He reasoned, she perceived pain; physical and mental. That was a sufficient reason to bar him from unnecessarily assaulting her. The elders had stormed out of the gathering never to make him a chief. What manner of chief would he be? The kind of leader who tramped on the very traditions that gave them identity was not worthy. Maratani vowed never to appear in his home unless he died, to walk the arena. In case his marriage flunked, he was to blame.

Unlike other newly married men who ate from their mother's kitchen a number of months after marriage, he had begun cooking his food long before marriage; yet another taboo he broke. A circumcised man was not supposed to touch a cooking stick like a woman. *Had he not fixed those stones-* he mused at himself- *his manhood would have let him down.*

His wife did not belong to the society. She was one of the concrete realizations of his diligence. Had he not schemed to get her, he would have raised the dowry single-handedly, to liberate himself from the bother of society. He held the opinion that his life, wife and education was his personal property. What was society to do with it. The toil he had undergone in attempt to attain a status on the hierarchy of society impelled him to renounce many aspects of his culture. In his opinion, his troubles emanated from the thorns of the culture of his people.

*****

Fresh news flew around. Jomo had been released from prison and many in Elgon Masaba cherished his oratory and militancy. To Kisiang'ani, the excitement was sycophancy.

Whereas the young man saw the militancy as a precursor to dictatorship, to Mauka it was a sign of strong leadership. He doubted the kind of education Kisiang'ani had received.

Kisiang'ani yearned to live in a society where citizens were free to question proposals made by leaders. Where society insisted on total submission to elders regardless of their character, mediocrity prevailed. He feared for degeneration of the nation to anarchical times of Buchacha.

These were not times when a father sentenced his child to death. He had doubts about Gichuru. How could a man so able and handsome step down for another... a prisoner. Was he a circumcised man? Didn't sons of Mumbi circumcise?

In spite of the short rains, the air was misty. The sun had risen above Mount Masaba but the morning mist was a great obstruction to fulfill its traditional role. Sitawa's belly was inflated by the germinating seed of life. Far down the valley were Mauka's cattle chewing the cud while peering in the misty depression in Masolo.

Resting at the humid front of his heart, Kisiang'ani pondered over his aspiration in life. It had cost him his relationship with his father and denied him the pleasures of youth. He yearned to stand before children and contribute towards their growth and success.

"One plus one...?" He muttered. His heart throbbed pleasurably.

It faded and gave way to anxiety after the afterthought that he might fail to obtain the object of his pursuit. As matters stood, there seemed to be rising hopes for Sitawa who was totally immersed in 'scratching' the slopes of Mount Masaba'.

A female pigeon flew in his direction, soared above his head and perched on Sitawa. She jerked her arm violently and scared it away. Kisiang'ani roused his face and surveyed the rising escarpment beyond the Okoro springs in the south and there he caught the horrid sight. They were sturdy young men with hides and skins around their waists. In their right were spears. They strutted into the home.

They picked their way through the miry sloppy paths, labyrinths of waterlogged passages and scything weeds. They shuffled around a bend before they swaggered into the Okoro well. As they marched into the home, Kisiang'ani identified the ring leader as Mamai. He got excited; his scheme had worked.

They were valiant emissaries of the Wamalwa's to penalize Mauka for his irresponsibility. With great precipitation, they triumphed over the sharp incline that ascended into the Mauka's- a formidable army. They headed for the cattle shed. Fifteen of them remained outside as guards as twenty others entered to untie cattle. No man in the Mauka's dared to oppose. Any violence meted out on the culprit was justifiable.

Immortal astonishment descended on Wafula. It roused in him extreme anxiety. He had married ahead of Kisiang'ani and his dowry had to be paid first. He regretted his decision to have married among ignorant people. Had they mastered custom, he would have been rescued like his brother. He was about to shout but looking at their ferocious airs, he froze. The men fearlessly led all the twenty-two heads of cattle away. Forthwith, Kisiang'ani anticipated life-long contention with Wafula.

Chapter Thirteen

It was a capital example of how brains encountered brains. Those who wallowed in foolishness had no chance to prosper on Wele's earth. The hyena would never get provision among the son's of Mwambu. This is why Wafula had no other way but sink in the downward spiral of misery. But those who mastered ingenuity emerged heroes like hare.

Was hare ever punished? Didn't he swindle? Wasn't cheating just cheating? Perhaps hare's was virtuous cheating and his, a decorous humbug. Kisiang'ani had aped him and blossomed. Mamai had returned in company of twenty armed young men and who silently released ten emaciated head of cattle, the remnant of what they had taken. Mauka could not say a word; custom had been obeyed.

He had been duped by his witty son. But one thing his son had to know was that he had to fend for himself. There was nothing droll for him. He had to become what he wanted to become in spite of his decision to marry. In Kisiang'ani's view, he was not half way his ladder. With the recent declaration of self-government, hope flew in the air.

Kisiang'ani hungered for his long awaited object. He desired a well-to-do life. He yearned for repose from a hand to mouth existence. He wanted to grasp a piece of chalk like Situma, teach children the way to success; the proceeds of which he would buy a farm and settle near Masolo. This subject always presented itself to him in flowery colours whenever he gave it mind. Nonetheless, the wedge that his trick had planted between him and Wafula dulled the colours.

Kisiang'ani ignored the seething jealousy and focused on the important. He lived for something and he had to attain it.

He needed economic muscles to climb the ladder but the scanty harvest he had obtained the previous year disheartened him. The onion yields had been meagre. The leaves had flourished but bulbs as emaciated as match sticks. He had to do something to evade future losses.

Events in the home seemed to spell trouble for him. Friction sizzled between his wife and that of Wafula. Sitawa was very diligent to match with Nangila, Wafula's wife. She dug almost every part of the home leaving Nangila a very small portion. Sitawa woke up at cock crow and retired at sundown. She had to do it because Mauka's head of cattle had been paid as dowry. But it dimmed Wafula's economy and soon Mauka would be compelled to subdivide the land. How thorny it would be! It sent jitters down his spine.

Wafula was never himself. It strained their relationship. Kisiang'ani could not broach the subject of land subdivision; he understood Mauka's reaction pertaining such matters. Furthermore, he had not an intention of settling in Cheleba. Meanwhile, Wafula accosted the Kinsmen to assist solve the problem. He incessantly complained about Kisiang'ani's scheme to take all the land even after the family spending everything on his education.

Kisiang'ani was a Wanangali whose mission was to swallow everything in the home. Of all the relatives who promised to help, he could count on Livuva, who had a secret despise for Kisiang'ani. He vowed to apply all his wit to ensure the villain left the home. How thankless some children were, they had said. The Mauka's had denied themselves basic needs to sustain Kisiang'ani in school. How could he come back to take all the land again?

Kisiang'ani withdrew his attention from domestic affairs and thought about politics. Jomo was behind the steering wheel driving the baby nation. The thought that Kenya had attained self government remained the balm of his heart. It meant golden opportunities for the black man to rise from slavery and poverty.

He heard grand names around him: Tom, Odinga, Ronald, Daniel, Bildad, Ngei, Jomo, Muliro... It was young Tom who remained popular in Cheleba. His mastery of the language of the white man endeared him among many. They loved his nature: cheerful and overflowing confidence. As the nation braced to send the British governor packing, Kisiang'ani prepared to welcome his first son. He was apprehensive about the forthcoming experience.

The August of 1964 was a special month to Kisiang'ani. Fate commanded a bouncing baby boy into their lives. He was plumb. He had threatened Sitawa's life. He had rejoiced but got dispirited upon realizing that it was Mamai's replica. To crown his wonder working wit, he had named him Mukesi, which means 'the bright one'.

There were faces of merry in the home. Relatives beamed with delight as cradle songs ambled over the compound. Mwanambeli, the first born, had stepped in the home, a blessing from Wele. He was a son of valour, a son entitled to Buchacha's leopard skin. Mauka who had appeared in the home in one of his impromptu visits could not be left behind. He presented a cock to the mother via Butilu amid congratulatory syllables and added twenty shillings to go towards busaa. Wafula (who had sired miserable girls) was send to go and call Wamalwa, Matumbai, Wanyenya and other honourable elders to celebrate the birth of a first born son.

It was another sodom apple for Wafula to chew but custom had to be obeyed. Butilu was the happiest. She ululated and danced joyfully. She slaughtered a cock for the mother and took the house as her own. How he loved her daughter in-law. A son mattered a lot to her. She now knew the shortcomings of having daughters. Nabangala had returned with nothing but tears and three pot bellied tots for her to nurse again. As for dowry, she had yielded two goats; Mauka had grabbed them by force.

It had been a scuffle to reckon with. Wanjala, Nabangala's husband, had sworn by his manhood not to release any dowry because he had found 'her fences broken.' He had complained that the fence at the breast, at the lips, at the hips and groin, which were worth three cattle each had been destroyed. She was a good for nothing whore; consequently she was not worthy a cow.

All this prompted Butilu to see a daughter as a good for nothing foreigner who benefited outsiders. Perhaps this is why the sons of Mwambu compelled men to pay their dowry as a consolation to the family for the loss. Nevertheless, Butilu did not see any profit in it because during circumcision the maternal uncle who received bride wealth had to relinquish a bull to his nephew. It went without saying that if the sister begat many sons, the uncle parted with many bulls. It hence prompted every man to desire sons and sons only.

Moreover, Butilu ascertained the fact that, a son remained in his father's land and carried with him the family's identity from generation to generation. How would Nabangala carry her father's identity from 'diaspora'? Impossible. A son was better. He was even circumcised so that by shedding blood, he would be strongly bound to the blessings and ways of his people.

She thought about his name. It had to come from one of his great ancestors. They did it on the third day. Mauka insisted on the boy taking the name Buchacha, that legendary hero who lived in the pre-colonial times. Matumbai suggested the name Milisio, Buchacha's great grand father. The puzzle could not be solved. Three cocks were named after three of his great ancestors and hurled on the roof of Mauka's hut. They shrieked and tumbled in terror. The red cock, Buchacha, shrieked aloud, left the path taken by two others and perched on the leopard skin on the ground. There ensued a clap of applause as Mukesi received the name Cecil Mukesi Buchacha.

He was Mukesi Buchacha, an eminent man whose anger knew neither tribe nor religion. Great was Mauka's affection for his son for siring a Buchacha for him to behold. How he despised Wafula for begetting girls. He wished his son sought for a wife who produced 'male eggs'.

By December, the new black president was sworn in. A few sons of Mumbi were given their land. In Kisiang'ani's view, it was erroneous to say that Kenyans had received back their land. No one had lacked this in Cheleba. It was more than enough. Perhaps the hope for jobs was the greatest news at the time. If a republic meant hundreds of idle jobs then Kisiang'ani had a reason to rejoice. He was vigilant enough to grab every opportunity. He did not wait for fare. He did not look for a bicycle. He was extremely desperate. He lumbered along the bushy alleys of Cheleba onto the murram road in Chwele and trekked his way to Bangamek. He wanted to check at the District Education Office. He reached there and cast eyes on the notice boards:

RE: Recruitment of Teachers.

What else did he want? That was sufficient. His heart palpitated with joy. He buoyed up with hope. His fears were brought to an instant halt.

"Applicants are required... to those with passes in Kenya Senior Secondary Examinations (Division III& IV)" This shut him out but never say die, he fought on. Those with passes in Kenya Junior Secondary Examination will be considered later. He sighed. There was no need of despair.

In spite of his delay, Kisiang'ani exulted in his wife. Sitawa would join the profession ahead of him, yet another taboo broken. He did not care about Kimila. His darling would soon join Situma to the great dismay of many. How absurd it was for a woman to be employed and leave the husband at home. Such a woman would 'grow horns', lord it over her husband and desert him.

As a man ruled by progress and directed by foresight, Kisiang'ani beheld an exquisite opportunity to tread across the boundaries of poverty. He saw this as a carte blanche for alleviation from 'scratching' as the only mainstay. Like any other man pretty romantic about development, Kisiang'ani thought with a touch of sweetness.

The thought of his kinsman struck him. Although he had carried a vengeful attitude towards Sifuna since those days of anguish, the bubbling pans of jam on his mind dispelled his wrongs. His apathy had remained the best illustration of the evanescence of human assistance and ambivalence of human favour. Was Sifuna not his kinsman? Was he not an inspector at the District Education office.

He knew where Sifuna resided in town. Evil or holy, kinsman was a kinsman. It was quite impossible to suppress the urgent desire to see him. He would not mind joining him in laying one or two bricks to erect a shrine of fortune in his home. He set forth to say jambo to his kinsman. To call on such an office without greeting a relative was the worst antipathy intolerable among the sons of Mwambu.

A relative was cherished more and above the closest friend. Consequently, a wife was nothing to compare with a relative. Only fools like Kisiang'ani disclosed their hearts to wives.

"Eh, eh eh! Welcome cousin!" Greeted Sifuna with passion.

"How have you been?" Kisiang'ani found his voice.

"I've been alive, muno, muno, muno, muno yaya," said Sifuna at every hand shake.

"How has your work been?"

"It's good now that the mubeberu, as jomo says, has left."

"They won't harass you when you talk politics?"

"We're now free!" Sifuna screamed.

"I've seen some adverts cousin."

"You've passed through the offices?"

"Yeah!"

"In fact I've been thinking about you, cousin."

"Let me prepare a cup of tea for you before we talk."

Sifuna said and rushed into the kitchen.

He had grown taller and walked with a slight stoop. His streamlined face carried dull eyes of monkish quality but his lips were inscribed by a permanent smile that advertised his communicative nature. He was the kind that promised all and did nothing. Sifuna was a fountain of optimism; an outgoing man who beheld so great things that he never bothered about small things. He would rather buy a car and sleep in a gutter than bog himself with small huts at home. He had neither bought land for himself nor his mother, Repa. She was still a squatter. A visionary man Sifuna was.

"That man is an orator," Sifuna shouted from the kitchen.

"Who?"

"The president."

"That's true."

"And the vice president?"

"Good in English."

"That's how Luo are, good in English."

"Why?"

"Their syllabic structures are similar."

"I'm lost," Kisiang'ani shook his head, amazed.

"Cousin, I've a big interest in English. Luo words like kuon, ugali, have same syllabic structure with 'town'."

"Just go and teach in Ukere university, cousin."

They both laughed.

"But the way he defended Jomo against the mubeberu- white man- was stunning." Sifuna went on.

"Quite stunning cousin," replied Kisiang'ani.

"And that governor, pooh!" Said Sifuna, "that the mzee is a leader to darkness and doom."

"Maybe he wasn't wrong," Kisiang'ani mumbled.

"That man is an elite, cousin. He did not graduate from any useless African college."

"Cousin remember, he's a maumau."

"So?"

"He should be our Chief of General staff," asserted Kisiang'ani.

"Explain further."

"A militant man will use a lot of force."

They sat down for a cup of tea and discussed many topics. With the advent of freedom, topics of conversation were never wanting.

"My wife comes soon and a hen's life will come to a sticky end."

"I'm not hungry," Kisiang'ani lied.

"Of course you may not be but you can't visit a kinsman and return on an empty stomach unless he is hyena."

"Eh thooh, sure," affirmed Kisiang'ani.

"Now tell me caso, how did you carry on since you finished form two?"

"I took my exam..."

"I'm sorry you found me in a financial wilderness," he said looking at him askance.

"I understood," Replied the young man.

I understand you couldn't leave those daughters of sausage and spend a coin on me.

He said mentally.

"Shake my hand," Replied Sifuna, "that's true kinsmanship. You don't hold grudges against a kinsman." He looked relieved.

"True, no need," whispered, Kisiang'ani.

"So you finished at KJSE?"

"Yes, caso."

"I can't assist you now."

"I've someone with KSSE at my house."

"Who...?"

"My wife."

"Shake my hand cousin," he rose on his two to proffer his hand.

"Why are you people happy?" A shrill voice pierced the air of the house.

That was Nafula, Sifuna's wife. She was a slender, tall woman. To a great extent, she was a plain Jane. Her cheeks like limps were fat. Her instincts were rough. Nafula spurned above all things extensions. Many a time she literally chased relatives out of her house. Their room, she would shout, could not accommodate those crowds that streamed in from Cheleba and that she hungered for private moments with her loved one.

Such vagabonds in her view were a hateful intrusion into her much cherished privacy. She emitted an awful stench back to Cheleba. Her name became a curse among the relatives; in a little while, they recoiled from her. In spite of her thorns, she had brought forth six sons in Sifuna's bosom. It was a gift that had knitted the strongest bond of marriage between them. Even with decades of experience in urban life, Nafula still exhibited high degrees of ignorance. You would find her walking barefoot in town, she could shout at an acquaintance, a hundred metres away in a Central Business District. You could find her using a knife to cut tissue paper. Although Sifuna being a professional teacher had a hard time to prepare lesson plans to instruct his wife to adapt to the changing world.

How he always wished she was educated. She always enjoyed seeing his hand dance and reel along that white paper. She would convulse with sincere laughter. It remained a riddle how her husband's pen would dance along the paper drawing small things that he read and got a lot of money. Indeed it made her love him most.

Here he was with a boy whose ambition he had tried to suppress but was fortunate to get a learned girl.

"How are you, In-Law," greeted Nafula.

"I'm alive," replied the young man.

"Very good of you, caso! Very commendable," Sifuna
went on

"Which school?"

He asked, a lump blocking his throat.

"Lugulu."

"That's great!" The man shouted with a tinge of envy,
"Shake my hand again, caso," he stood on his two feet.

"Good," he said reclining on the settee.

There was silence.

"What did she get?" Sifuna asked as an afterthought.

"Division III."

"She is qualified cousin!" He screamed, "Shake my hand
again."

They shook hands with a incomparable rapidity; two
strong men of Buchacha invincibility. There was no thought
of defeatism, but, that of success. There was no look of
hatred but that of forgiveness. Evidently there was no face of
myopia. Indeed a kinsman was a kinsman. However rich one
was, he could not live without them. The presence of Sifuna
at this office would do him a great deal of good.

It was time he reconsidered his attitude towards the
customs of his people. He thought repeatedly. He doubted
whether all his suffering emanated from the thorns in the
customs of his people. Nonetheless, there was this devilish
thought which condemned Sifuna's offer as a terrible act of
corruption whose fruit was a snare.

"Isn't it nepotism?" the fiend asked.

"My wife has qualified," he defended himself.

Then let her apply without Sifuna's help, the fiend argued.

"No, this is generosity of African people," he replied
mentally, "it's corruption in the western sense!" He muttered.
He suppressed the fiend and rejoiced in his wife, Sitawa. He

wondered if Wambui would have merited that job. She had a pretty body with an empty head.

Kisiang'ani set forth for Cheleba the following day. He trekked all the way. The day was sunny and the thick clouds on Masaba were gradually misting away down the gigantic valleys. The orange orb of the sun stood poised in the sky to dispel all the crawling mist. He strutted on. His mind was crowded by the darling object of his pursuit. He dared dream, stride by stride of the splendid life in the profession of his desire. His attire was by no means sight friendly. But he wished the on-lookers ripped his soul open to behold the majestic splendour of his impending ambition.

He swaggered around the multitude of winding paths with a well constituted mind. He arrived home in the forenoon and found his dear wife still on the farm. She followed him behind to the hut and served him a dish of Ugali.

"How was the loitering?" She asked immediately before he had tasted the food.

"Now there you spoil my day," Kisiang'ani replied gently.

"Yes, you just went wandering."

"Who told you that?"

"I told myself because you did not tell me."

"I went to check at the education office."

"Why?"

"To find out when UTs will be recruited."

"Forget those things and let's work the farm," Sitawa advised, losing her temper.

"No, we shan't go on harrowing these slopes, dear."

"No, no, no, we can't leave each other and go to school…"

"Oh, no dear! Love is appreciable but we must think about a better future."

"Don't waste time there," Sitawa said, sobbing.

"No, beloved, we won't go on scooping these slopes. What's the difference between those who never stepped at school and us?" Kisiang'ani said more to himself.

"But there is nothing we can do now," she insisted, tearfully.

"There's dear, why should you discard your ambition?" Kisiang'ani asked.

"Those were childish dreams, let's now face realities," argued Sitawa.

"Yes, the reality is that tomorrow you accompany me to Bangamek to be recruited as UT," Kisiang'ani announced with the air of a winner. Sitawa brightened up and embraced him. How fortunate to be under tutelage of such an astute man.

He was a gentle man who just blushed at her emotional outbursts. She rested in his arms for some time; a cock's life met its sticky end.

Chapter Fourteen

od's punctual yardstick of time did not wait. Kisiang'ani with his wife became teachers and students. The school of life had ignited quite a lump, some of wit, on his mind and the axioms he had created were a lasting testimony of the same.

Your attitude determines your altitude was such one. "Your attitude determines the magnitude of your latitude and longitude," was yet another. Repeatedly, he exhorted his wife never to sacrifice his dreams on the altar of marriage. In his jokes, he insisted that 'a pawpaw' ambition made one grand but a 'guava' ambition made one miserable.

Kisiang'ani's prominence was on the lips of many a man and woman in Cheleba. His diligence had paid dividends. He had become a mighty proprietor of tens of cattle and hundreds of goats; the sole rival to the ailing Situma Barasa. There was a pompous display of affluence, the Mauka's had never seen this before.

He became a great hand at all sorts of farming, crop and animal into the bargain; they yielded thousands of eggs, tens of bags of maize and hundreds of hides and skins yearly. As poverty packed to leave, Butilu smiled gaily. How excited Wamalwa became. His expectations about Kisiang'ani were fulfilled.

Machuma sent her children to come and borrow. Kisiang'ani provided for them profusely. In his heart of hearts, he feared the arrows of jealousy that were mounting to defeat the ends of his diligence. But he remembered Buchacha's maxim, tears and fears never ought be familiar with manhood.

Kisiang'ani made yet another discovery. His monthly income was far less than the profits of his farm projects. What he had despised was more paying than what he had adored. He earned much more by tilling land than chalk and that is how he learned to become a master of all.

He was at school and home with a typical enterprising face. He anticipated buying a lorry soonest possible. Upon hinting Sitawa about it, he came face to face with capital "NO'.

"This is not the place," she declared. He promised to think over it.

He renovated his hut, constructed a new kitchen and put up a better hut for Butilu. Mauka tripped in frequently with stunning humility. His motive Kisiang'ani well understood.

Kisiang'ani trudged home today in a sad mood. The previous night, he had dreamt eating roast meat. It never augured well. Among his people, such dreams were not taken for granted. He flounced around a bend and felt strength deserting his knees. They trembled with mysterious uncertainty. He staggered into the compound and perceived profound stillness. Every gaze was fixed at Butilu's hut. Every ear, keen. Something had happened to his father, he concluded.

In a spur of a moment, Butilu sprang up and let her ageing body fall with a heavy thud. She emitted guttural shrieks and kicked her legs in the air. Tears streamed and the bosom heaved. She tapped her shrivelled thighs, patted her swinging breasts and darted confusedly. She rolled in scything weeds, refusing to be comforted. She objected entreaties to calm.

"They have finished him, they have finished him!" She wept.

"What is it, mama?" Kisiang'ani asked.

"Your father is gone! Your father is dead!" She said amid tears.

Kisiang'ani broke down. Mauka had not been ill. Something fishy might have happened.

"Where do I go…. Where do I go… Mauka... Mauka…. Mauka! Who poisoned you? Who is this jealous man?" She wept musically. She stamped her feet and plunged in a trance. Other women: Simbi, Machuma, Nang'oni, Nafula, and Nelima joined her and there was a roar of screams.

Crowds poured in to share the sorrow as custom demanded among the sons of Mwambu. Death was an evil and sorrow had to be shared by all whose ears got informed of its whereabouts. When Maratani arrived and failed to control himself, there ensued a thunderbolt of despair as men, women and children screamed. Kisiang'ani could not withhold his tears. He let them flow. Mauka's failures notwithstanding, he remained his father and he could not imagine that he would never see him again.

Furthermore, it was time to forgive the person for his soul to stroll peacefully across the river of life to the land of Buchacha, Milisio, Puraimu and other ancestors. They packed their goods the following day and left for Kitali. Mauka Milisio Buchacha was buried in a one acre piece of land to the surprise of many. It was during the walking of the Arena on the third day (for peaceful distribution of property) that Kisiang'ani discovered something: Mubeyi's promise of manna had been a falsity. The sons of Mwambu who had migrated from Mount Masaba in league with his promise had ended up as squatters.

Of the twenty acres he had sold, Mauka secured only an acre in Kitali after months of dissipation. Machuma had borne him five sons to his delight. In the arena, Maratani decreed that the five had a right to inherit half of the ten acres in Cheleba.

"And if you think you're a man, stand up and oppose it now!" He had growled in Kisiang'ani's direction.

Kisiang'ani was absorbed in his thoughts. He had warned his father against falling prey to Mubeyi's words. He had plunged the family in a crisis as Mubeyi enjoyed at the capital city. He was now a minister. He learnt that it was good to be principled in life. They had seen him as a rebel then. They had spurned him but what he had warned had come to pass.

How absurd humanity was. It rejected a sceptical man and condemned a critical mind yet these were the very natures that brought positive change. He got encouraged. Revolutionary men, he came to note, knew the truth; and truth was scanty in the world. Consequently, they were rejected.

He thought of Mandela, Mugo wa Kibiro, Aristotle, Socrates and Jesus of Nazareth. They possessed qualities so elevated for earth to comprehend. Subsequently, they got rejected.

That was March. Schools had closed and so he left for his in-service teacher training after the funeral. The following night, he was ushered into a dark world. It was a strange place. He heard the hoots of owls, wails of cranes and chirps of marlets. Never before had he come across such labyrinths. They were waterlogged passages winding around a cluster of huts. The hedges were ill-trimmed. The ground was rocky and vehicles rare. It was forlorn; lizards and grasshoppers complained of negligence. But the absence of rugged terrain made Kisiang'ani love the area.

He could also see that the place had no jiggers. A violent whirlwind then roved around. His belly tightened with fear. He braced himself to flee but it turned into Mauka.

"Don't run away, I'm your father," he said in a friendly tone. He took him by wrist and led him to the outskirts. They stood facing the Tororo plug in the distance.

"This is your land," he asserted, "although it's taboo to migrate south ward, your rebellion has brought you here." He paused as if to allow him understand and proceeded, "but in the darkness, see that which sees and not the blind."

Kisiang'ani rose up only to find himself at college. He neither told his wife nor Butilu this message that the ancestors had revealed.

In April, Repa appeared in Cheleba, a shabbily clad old woman with shrivelled features. She was a guest with an air of most rugged minded mortals. Her eyeballs danced with jealousy, the neck craned with extremity of desperation and the heart pulsated with revenge. The home was gay and warm as it always was. The woman entered with a gait that tacitly proclaimed she was on far less pleasant errand. She looked fragile and would pick a quarrel at the slightest provocation.

Kisiang'ani gave his aunt a warm welcome in spite of her presentment that hung over him. After lunching, she gave a haranguing sermon about the need for the couple to shun selfishness and assist their relatives. Kisiang'ani's composure was instantly in a state of horror-stricken astonishment. Sitawa almost fainted with shock. Repa proceeded saying that many a young man who had got jobs after Uhuru, had squandered everything and forgot the very relatives who had 'slept on water' to keep them in school.

"They eat pluu pandi (margarine) and chicken as their relatives eat enderema, (traditional vegetables)." She shouted casting a scornful look at the remnants of chicken on the plate. Kisiang'ani with his wife remained silent. Her scheme hit the wall.

"My children, do not forget us," she appealed to emotions, "I met you when you were very poor and miserable," she paused for Kisiang'ani to get the point.

"And I assisted you." she proceeded, "we took you to Karatina. Lumati took you to Sifuna and…." she sobbed, "and now you don't care about me?" She cast a bold glance at him. Her tone was rising. So was her temper. Kisiang'ani wished Mauka were alive to face his sister.

"And when Lumati passed away, you did not even appear…appe…ar….aaaa…" she cried glaring at him.

"Auntie, I was busy…"

"Too busy to bury a man who accepted you when your father had cursed you? Hey! Too busy to bury the man who educated you….u…you…beast!" She groaned.

The words tore through Kisiang'ani's heart like Wambaya's knife. The mention of the curse burrowed in his past wounds. Gloom flew over the room. Thick clouds of mist crawled in the giant depression far below the home. Generally, he was touched by his aunt's situation and explained that from the inmost recesses of his heart, he had never forgotten her. He added that the hundreds on his hands to feed and dress were the root of his negligence. He said as an afterthought that he thought Sifuna took care of her. The name, Sifuna, stung Repa.

"Bad manners!" she blurted, "don't mention Sifuna!" She clicked.

Silence resumed. Tension built up.

"Sifuna educated you so that you can assist me!" She screamed.

Butilu appeared at the door to see what was amiss.

"Now aunt what do you need from me?" Kisiang'ani asked.

"Two blankets, a mattress and three kilos of sugar."

"I'll buy," Kisiang'ani promised.

"And if you fail me…" Repa stammered.

"Who's cursing somebody here!" Interrupted Butilu.

"We took him to Karatina and now you eat everything alone!" Shouted Repa.

"I'll strangle you wicked woman!" Butilu screamed and charged at Repa's neck.

A commotion ensued. Repa lost a few rags of her dress before Kisiang'ani separated the two.

"You dog! Since my brother died you want to eat his wealth alone!" Repa said screaming.

"You hyena, why do you lust for my son's wealth, don't you have Sifuna?" Butilu replied.

"Let's wait! Should he fail the promise you'll know that I am his aunt!" She warned staggering towards the exit.

Kisiang'ani became jittery. Depressions knocked at the door of his heart. He cursed and regretted. He was fed up by the milling crowds of dependants, he was unhappy with Wafula's attitude; tired of everything in Cheleba. Relatives and relatives streamed into the compound, some too distant to make out the winding chain of relation. They all presented themselves for provision. Could a man not be left to enjoy the fruit of his labour?

Here was another one. A mother of a very important man, District Inspector of Schools, evading the root cause of her misery in her home to besiege him. A river flowed along the line of least resistance. Why would she curse him over something she had no right to? Which fees had Repa paid?

He wanted to rise up, follow her and bluntly tell her that Sifuna had paid forty out of two hundred shillings. He was ready to refund him.

But he recalled Sifuna's kindness during Sitawa's recruitment; he recoiled from lamenting. What assistance was it? He wondered. Had Sitawa not qualified? Why had he enslaved himself? He wished he had obeyed the fiend. They had qualified for the jobs. Their colleagues had gone with certificates and had been employed. They enjoyed the fruit of their labour without strings attached. Her arrogance stung him too. What right had she to talk to her thus. Oh, what manners; uncouth and ill-bred.

"I'll rebel and she'll do nothing,' Kisiang'ani muttered. He thought about the prophetic dream. He could now see the reason why Mauka had told him to migrate southward. He had to move. He could not sit around as a fraction of his father.

Kisiang'ani pitied young men who looked at their fathers' inheritance as their only source of wealth. Assuming the father had an acre of land with two sons, he would subdivide it into half an acre per son. Such a son would be a half his father yet a son was a whole number. He was a full tree, not a branch.

He did not sleep that night. He was busy counting his money while comparing it to the land values. Sweet sleep seized him at an hour when sleep is very seductive. When he stirred from it, the hut was boiling. The walls hooted and smoke seared his eyes; it choked his throat.

He stood up and in a single blow threw open the window. He picked Sitawa, drowsy as she was, and flung her through the window. Before she could know what was going on, the man handed the weeping baby to her. He saved a few more items before hauling himself out of the collapsing roof. A red hot charcoal landed on his right arm as he swung out. He sustained an sizable burn.

What an incidence. Inside was his radio, certificate and bedding blazing into flames. How fortunate he was to keep his identity card and passbook in the pajama suit. Wise he had been to keep his money in the bank. Butilu and Sitawa wept. Looking at them, he was seized by a temporary spell of pity. He paced up and down the compound in a state of agitation. Here was one of the most trying moments of his life. However, he consoled himself that the experience would enable him to discover his promised land.

"Did I not tell you?" Sitawa said between sobs.

"Didn't we warn him?" Butilu supported.

"What!" he barked.

"This is not the place to get rich," Butilu said crying.

"For how long should we be poor?" Kisiang'ani said, fuming.

"Jealousy, In-Law," Sindani, Matumbai's son advised.

"I saw Livuva fleeing to his hut immediately the scream pierced the air," said Wanyenya. His tone was conspiratory.

"He must be the man," whispered Sindani.

"He must pay for this!" Kisiang'ani thundered and lunged ahead.

"No, no, no, no, no!" Shouted Sindani.

"Restrain him! Restrain…my…son!" Cried Butilu.

"They're witches!" Asserted Wanyenya.

Wambilianga restrained him. He calmed and Sindani drew him aside.

"Leave these witches alone," he advised, "they're jealous of you. It's not good to prosper in the eyes of those who saw you poor. They wished you failure but Wele has seen you through. Come, let's go to Okoro, the land of Bamia."

"Can I get fertile land among Bamia?" Kisiang'ani doubted.

"There is a lot of it," he assured him.

They found a private place and chatted their way out. Sindani pinched a bit of snuff into his nose and proceeded to pour into him a synopsis of life in Okoro. They discussed land values, fertility and the security of the area in general.

The following day saw the transit of the Kisiang'anis to their land of destiny. Kisiang'ani swaggered from behind, Sitawa ahead with their fruit of companionship. They descended the steep slopes, slipping on the rotten leaves in bushes as they shuffled along the labyrinths with perfect keenness.

Before his eyes stood the day he surveyed his father's land, the day he had noticed the poverty of his mother's hut and resolved to dig erobo diligently to realize his aspirations. He had desired to buy a piece of land near Masolo, built an iron roofed house, and marry a teacher. There she was; there he was enroute to his place of purpose.

As they plodded along, his dear wife would skid. He would skip forward to grip her arm to save her health and that of the son.

At Cheptais, a market in the plains, they boarded a lorry that dropped them at Lwanda. They picked their way through the marshes and bushes to Okoro market. They met Sindani waiting for them. He directed them to the village. They passed through bushy alleys, clusters of absolutely untamed bushes and struggled through thick climbing plants. Sindani's wife, Choina, welcomed them in her kitchen where they put up as they prepared to settle.

Chapter Fifteen

Five thousand shillings was not a sum to stumble upon in a hamlet like Okoro. But, to the amazement of tipsy Okorians, Kisiang'ani could afford more than this. Within a few months of his arrival, he had erected a stone walled house, acquired twenty acres of land from Reja, Masengo, Pusi, Okaanya and Sindani himself. He had used both cash and cattle as a medium of exchange.

In spite of his progress, something was going wrong with his dear wife. A strange disposition seemed to have perched upon her. After completing her in-service at Eregi, she was no longer the submissive Sitawa he had known. There was not that sweet lady she had known. There was a grumpy and coarse woman in her place. Everything he said, she subjected to detailed scrutiny. She analyzed its ins and outs before dismissing it in his very eyes.

A good house for instance was not the dreary cave Kisiang'ani had built. In her opinion, building began by thorough consideration of those qualities that made a suitable site: Infrastructure, security, water and many others. Okoro in itself was inappropriate. Her husband would do better to consult her before doing anything.

He had bought a farm at so remote a place that their best friends could not visit. You tottered through bushes like a Muyobo on a raiding errand. Shoes became an unnecessary burden as you had to wade through river Okoro before you trekked tens of kilometres through potholes to school or hospital. Why would she suffer so much just to buy a pen? Sitawa foresaw great suffering for their children.

When it came to the house, her husband built a 'big hall' only partitioned in 'wire mesh' fashion. She appreciated the building material-stone- but there was no style. A small house with sophisticated architecture could do better than 'the hall'. At the outset, she reserved her comments like any other woman to secure her position in the marriage. Children were this security; they provided a living bond in an African family.

The creator proved so generous to them. Their offspring increased in quick succession, from one to four. Three of whom were sons. Butilu was excited but Kisiang'ani desired more daughters. But sons for Sitawa were a ground to assert herself. She spoke her mind and fracas ensued. Their marriage was attended by strife.

Waliaula, the padre of the Anglican church Okoro, reached out for them. Kisiang'ani saw the church as a means to dehorn his insolent wife and took it with stunning zeal. Waliaula insisted that legitimizing their marriage was paramount if they intended to serve the creator effectively.

On August the sixth 1976, Kisiang'ani with his wife, Sitawa, tied a knot in presence of hundreds of Okorians. It was yet another circumcision ceremony for him but it magnified his dignity. After evaluating his commitment to the vows, he was appointed the church secretary.

As a man of God, he had to welcome all and minister to their needs. They milled into his home from Okoro and Cheleba. Machuma's sons came to beg. Nabangala also appeared to ask for her share. Had she not sacrificed her future for him to succeed? Kisiang'ani would have done well had he prayed to his Maker for guidance. Unfortunately, he was too busy to pray.

He acted out of human feelings typical of Buchacha and all his antecedents. Furiously, he told Nabangala that her lust, not empathy, had driven her into marriage. She had embarrassed him, he had repeated and ordered her out of the compound. Nabangala had wept the whole day. How wicked human nature was! How fast her brother forgot that day!

That...day...after...he...had...fought...Mauka...and...I...was ...the...only....person...in...Che.....who...stood...by...him! Nabangala had wept, strapped her tenth baby on her back and trudged back home, leaving her vengeance in Wele's hands.

Kisiang'ani then stepped up his war against 'beggars'. He withdrew all his assistance from Machuma's sons and chased them whenever they came. He never argued with a step brother. He shouted and they ran.

"Loafers! Numskulls! Go back and work!" He could insult.

He only feared Simbi, his mother-in-law. As he complained about it to Sindani, the latter bluntly told him that it was both unchristian and anti-African to chase one's relatives. He gave him an example of Namunyu who lived in Sitabicha. This old man hated people so much that when he died, the villagers could not know because he had even chased his wife away. It was a hyena's visit to the hut, which drew people's attention to his rotting corpse.

"In-Law," had asserted Sindani, "when you see everybody complaining about you, don't ignore it. Your aunt made noise, now..."

"Keep away from my affairs!" Growled Kisiang'ani.

"And why did you tell me?" Asked Sindani.

"Don't say..."

"It's me who brought you here and our people say a man who despises advice is on the path of death."

"Witchcraft, that's what you all know."

"In-Law, beware Mauka's arrogance, you forget too quickly. Beware Buchacha's pride. If you have ears listen. The hyena thinks a river isn't rain or rain isn't a river."

Sindani had gone his way. Butilu arrived to assist him to send away pests that destroyed his wealth. She confronted Simbi with heart-breaking insults. A widow for two years now, Simbi's heart was too fresh to tolerate harangues. She packed her scanty belongings and trekked back to Mount Masaba. Sitawa's attempts to intervene and placate her were futile. She even refused her fare. The old lady got hurt beyond repair.

The Kisiang'ani's were at throes of change. The laughter that prevailed the home died. The warmth and freedom that sprung up every evening sunk into abyss and a new lord assumed the reins of power. Kisiang'ani stopped going to church; Sitawa followed suit. The strain in their relationship could not permit them to go there.

Perhaps they never knew what they were inviting. Had they been sensible, they would have ignored their quarrels and pursued the right path. Their human weaknesses blackmailed them and the club of fate struck.

His arch enemy intruded the home. She foamed with rage. She carried the aunt's authority without pretence or imposition. She knew the power she wielded over him and her appearance was as sudden as death. Her eyes were the angry eyes of a leopard and feet the agile paws of the lioness. Her mouth was the dreadful mouth of a crocodile and hips, the shrivelled hind of a hyena. As she stormed in the home, he braced for the worst.

"Welcome aunt," Sitawa said, when she entered.

"Welcome aunteeeeeee!" She mimicked.

"Ouch, why quarrel in the morning?"

"You've denied me what is rightly mine!" Repa screamed, her hands akimbo.

Kisiang'ani paced around the home, confounded by the turn of events. Butilu was not around to counter this terrifying situation.

"Auntie, do you have any queries?

"You think there's nothing wrong? A child lying to me!" She shouted with fierce voracity.

"Do you want free blankets?" He complained, "Sifuna did nothing to assist me!"

There followed an awkward pause. Shattered promises thronged upon her. Unrequited kindness taunted her soul. Her heart failed her; she could bear no longer. How vain the 'boy' was! She regretted having defended him against her brother's curse. How recklessly he had disregarded the kindness she had shown him. With insensitivity to her breaking heart, absolute indifference and contempt for all Lumati had done, he had taken to selfish gratification. He had amassed a lot for himself forgetting the masons of his foundation.

His words had awakened unpleasant recollections in her breast, womb and waist; recollections that could not permit her skirt to remain there. A temporary siege of lunacy seized her. She reeled around the home exulting in her customary authority. With the airs of a much injured paternal aunt, she stepped out of her prison of humility and unleashed her punishment. Her skirt flew away from the loins and the blouse from her bosom. She stood naked- an emaciated dark grotesque.

"You've become rich and spat on the breast that nourished you!" She screamed, patting her breast. She pranced forward and proceeded, "I toiled with Sifuna for ten moons in this womb." She screamed touching the womb and pubic hairs, "And now you refuse to give me just a blanket to cover my thighs! I'll show you the spot through which Sifuna came to earth!"

"You can't force me to give you things!" Roared Kisiang'ani, "Put on your clothes!"

"Uuuuuuuuuuuuwi!" She screamed, "Look at Wanangali! You're Wanangali!" She raved mad. The tumult rose in the home. Reja, Masengo and Pusi swaggered into the home. Sindani kept his distance.

"I'll show you!" She blurted, "the spot where Sifuna…" she stammered. She turned to display her private parts to Kisiang'ani and his young son. Her shrivelled thighs and flimsy breasts presented the ugliest drama in the theatre of Okoro. She turned to show him the wrinkled back. She then bent once, twice and thrice. Kisiang'ani saw the hips expand to reveal the inexplicable contents of her bottoms in each cycle of the act.

In the first transports of his emotion, he rushed back for the spear and attacked the woman. He wanted to kill her. There ensued a tragic display of hostilities. Repa ran round and round in a zigzag motion, gasping to the caning by the wooden handle of the spear. Kisiang'ani followed and battered her nude body. He cast away the spear and kicked her groin. He pulled her breasts. She screamed. He kicked her buttocks. She fell head first. He picked the spear to kill her. Reja caught it from behind. They wrestled. Masengo arrived and they pulled Kisiang'ani away.

"You will never prosper!" Repa shouted.

"Ugh, you, go!" Thundered Reja, "I'll swim in that thing!" He roared pointing at her vital spot. Blood streamed from her lips, back and pubic area.

Okorians shook their heads in astonishment. It was a savage performance. Reja and other Iteso neighbours had never seen a woman walking naked in the broad day light. In Okoro, a woman's genitals were her husband's secret possession and she had no right to uncover them in the public.

Repa's scandal spoilt the reputation of the son's of Mwambu all the way from Okoro, Lwanda, Moding and Cheptais. It spread across the villages by petty gossips and Kisiang'ani's dignity was terribly wounded.

"Is that how a woman looks?" Mukesi had asked as Repa walked away.

"Shut up, son!" Kisiang'ani ordered and entered the house.

PART THREE:

THE SLIDE

Chapter Sixteen

Open the window and let the climate come in had grown to become his cliché. It was said that in his opinion, air, weather and climate were the same thing. He was a master of all. Within two years of reign, he became a professor, engineer, a doctor, his majesty, her majesty, his highness and his Excellency, Ida Bakora Abba.

In his speeches on public holidays, he boasted to be the conqueror of the British empire and the cock that mated every pretty hen on site. He argued that he was anti-Christian, anti-Zionist, anti-communist, anti-non aligned, anti-capitalist and all the 'antis' in the world.

Masolo was a small dungeon in hell. In her soul, Katami had a lot of pity for it. A country in which poverty was the identity card of every citizen. Death was the national anthem; and fear was the staple food. Such a country was below the pass mark of sustenance and thereby unworthy of human habitation.

Katami was a girl of medium height, slender and brown of complexion. She had a pondering look of a seventy year old at sixteen. She was homeless after her home was ambushed by the 'Lion,' the president's terrorists. Katami had found the new president funny and scarry. She never had seen a face so cruelly contorted with firmness in autocracy, suppression and vigour of massacre. In sincerity of her young heart, Katami had not seen a country so queer. She never had heard of a nation so vicious with a president so savage.

Katami was surprised at such comedy at statehouse. He was fat with a monster look. He had an enormous round head with fat cheeks, bull's shoulder; clad in military regalia. His right hand stuck in the right pocket. It fondled his confidant who had empowered him to oust the predecessor from power.

He was irascible. He laughed merriest at the sight of falling men in front of firing squads at public squares. Katami had seen him laugh. It was a queer outburst, sudden and sarcastic. No son or daughter of Masolo joined his laughter. He could victimize you and charge you of treason at his volition.

Throughout Masolo, Bakora was known as a man with no ear for entreaties and heart for sympathy. He was a mahogany man and Katami had no doubt about that. His veins were full of pebbles and mercury. How else could a normal human being drink human blood. Rumour had it that he ate the flesh of his enemies.

These are the thoughts that wrinkled her lantern face. It was care worn. Her long flowing dress, however, proclaimed hope in her despair. It flowed tenderly over the distended waist and swept the path beyond the ankles.

She had tramped three days now. She counted herself lucky never to have encountered the police. The first day she had slept at her distant cousin's, and the other two in bushes, living on fruits and roots. In all this, fortune had been on her side. She believed it would be thus till the end.

She bore exhausted looks. Her feet were dusty and mind apprehensive. The timid nature that had come to be part of her character was a stunning evidence of the long years of oppression and suppression she had endured in Masolo. She had learned to obey without question. Men, for instance, had to be respected. You had to greet them on your knees.

Diligence was yet another ingredient on the recipe of womanhood. She had learnt that five in the morning, never ought to find a woman in a blanket but near the kitchen washing dishes, poking the fire and milking the cow. Katami grew up with hate for laziness at home and school.

Looking at her subdued airs at the moment, one would imagine that she had had no laudable ambition to cherish. Katami had aspired to excel at school and join Mengo University. But the strife that had ambushed Masolo with the ascent of Bakora to power smashed and discarded her longings.

The People's Republic of Masolo had plunged into perpetual anarchy after Bakora's successful coup. With the aid of the Yankees, he had overthrown Dr. Mukisu who had socialist leanings. The foreigners were extremely elated with his success. Katami could not understand all the words about 'cold' and 'hot' wars at that time. Had she stepped in secondary one, she would have explained.

But the Yankees, as her uncle explained, were happy to have this man in statehouse, a man worthy of every honorary. He was the general manager of the universe, the president of all religions and king of every street. Masolo was Bakora and Bakora was Masolo. After a few month's rule, the beautiful country became a dark hell of civil strife, cannibalism, rape, amputations, and other gross atrocities. Fear became the cement that held the regime.

Bakora controlled everything save for his passions. A pretty maiden never escaped his manhood. His six wives were a standing monument of his immortal passion for Negritude and the two wives that shared his bed each night a rubber stamp of his manhood. Whenever he made a remark, his ministers cheered; whenever he cast an eye on the hips of a minister's wife, they cheered louder.

He was nowhere and everywhere. He would appear in your church anytime to assess the 'treasonability' of your sermon. He would appear on your street anytime to evaluate the sanitation of his subjects. He could make laws instantly and criminals punished.

There were instances, Katami could not forget. Bakora had suddenly appeared in Binala, her village. The local administrator had made an impromptu party to appease him. After the party, he had stood up and said,

"Thank you very much Filikisi."

Everyone laughed at the pronunciation of the name Felix, the regional administrator. It annoyed him.

"Why tu you yusii white's names! We ara Africans!" He thundered.

Silence crawled over the crowd. He got pleased.

"Thank you all gentle men! A ha ha ha!" He burst out. No one spoke.

"Men fasiti in Africa! Not, women, we tell America, no, no, no!" Applause ambled over the town.

"When you come Paka in Mengo, hey, Filikisi, I'll revenge!" He declared. The crowd cheered.

Felix got jittery. Why would Bakora want to kill him? Katami likewise understood revenge as a bad word for the occasion. Bakora sensed the anxiety in the crowd and cleared the doubts,

"I mean I shall revenge the good party, what's wrong with you, fool!" He roared at Felix.

"Thank you, Sir!" Shouted Felix with automaton nods. He breathed a sigh, he was safe.

"Yes," proceeded Bakora, "I've just divorced my two wives because none of them attended this party, e he he he he!" He convulsed with laughter. Nobody joined him.

"Why are you quiet!" He snarled, "are you planning to overthrow meeeeeeee?" He screamed. There was no response.

"I now declare that sweet lady ...yeah...ha ha...near Filikisi my only wife!" The crowd cheered. He was still incensed by the previous silence.

"And Filikisi," he proceeded. Felix was already on his two.

"Binala people must be clean. They shouldn't dirtify our name aproad!" He purred and knitted his brows. Katami had sensed danger.

"These people in sandals!" He had thundered, "you, come here!" He beckoned at Katami's uncle, Mafwabi. Tension built up. He whipped a pistol from his pocket and pointing it at him roared,

"Eat it!"

Mafwabi faltered. Katami and the rest of the crowd heaved with emotion. She retreated and left.

Bakora surveyed the crowd and motioned The lion to be on guard. The munching had no sooner ceased than the meeting ground was shaken with such terror that children, women and men quivered. The Lion shifted swiftly from end to end arresting those in sandals. Screams rend the air. Gun shots. Gun shots. Katami recalled the incident with dread.

Forthwith, Bakora had dispatched the Lion to loot, plunder and rape in Binala because of their dislike for the law that prohibited wearing of sandals. Felix was arrested and charged of incitement, which was tantamount to treason in his majesty's opinion. And Binala had lain without a face of mercy, without a countenance of certainty; without an iota of peace. In their place were the boom of the murderer, a cloud of misery and the stampede of flight to exile.

Katami was not a bullet to remain in Binala. She enrolled on the list of fugitives and fled to Jomo's haven of peace.

A melancholy cloud shrouded her heart as she staggered along the bushy labyrinths, lonely and apprehensive. She trudged along the circuitous routes with hands folded at her breast, her chin upon them to a home beyond her knowledge. Her gait was that of an assassin banished from his motherland by Kabaka and condemned by Katonda to an uncertain lifespan.

How she was desirous of parting with her past rigours. She wanted to forget about this man in vain. Sadder episodes flitted through her mind. She thought about Bakora's jokes. Were they really jokes? She recalled one conference in which the minister for finance had appealed to the donor community to save Masolo from an economic crisis. Mr Walela had explained that the country needed foreign exchange to be saved from the crisis.

Bakora, like a great many disciples of Negritude at his time, was ambushed by solid shame. What Foreign Exchange was nagging Masolo? He reflected. Was he Mukisu's disciple? Could it be money? Coins? notes? Did Masolo lack mints to make that? Why would Walela stand up to embarrass the People's Republic of Masolo? He did not wait for him to devastate the shining beauty of Africa to a white audience. He had stood up to interrupt,

"Mr Walela, where is Mr Foreign Exchange so that we kill him!" The conference had broken into laughter.

"A, ha ha ha ha ha ah ha ha!" He joined them to appreciate his piece of witticism.

"His Excellency," Walela resumed, "foreign exchange is not a person, I meant the country needs foreign currency to..."

"Is that money?" Bakora roared. His voice was full of disgust.

The Yankees laughed. The chief justice could not school his laughter.

"It's foreign exchange..."

"Slave!" He blurted, "Go and make money. Mint it; don't shame Masolo over such small things."

Walela had apologized. Henceforth, Katami had seen so many notes in Binala. She had even seen a ten million shilling note.

She waded through river Lwakhakha into the new country; her bitter thoughts abated. But doubts set in. Would she live longer than today? Had she a future? What was the use of living? What if she drowned herself in that river? She stood and stared at the lapping waters. The bright morning sun that shone over Okoro drew her attention away. For a moment, she enjoyed the serenity and calm of the new country.

She trekked ahead in the morning breeze hundreds of yards to the North of Okoro River. She now planned how she would approach her employer, 'a greeting, then request for the job.' She trudged into an 'affluent' compound and her eyes fell on a neat talkative woman in her prime of life. She was busy washing utensils at the kitchen. She raised her head to see the approaching dilapidated figure.

Chapter Seventeen

"**H**ow are you, mother?" She greeted.

"We're alive, child," Sitawa replied.

"I've come from Masolo and I'd like to talk to you," she said.

"This early?"

"Yes, mum."

"Mukesi, Mukesi!" She called.

"Mum!"

"Fold one chair and bring it out for your sister!"

"Yes, mum," the boy affirmed.

"You must be very tired now," Sitawa sympathized.

"Yes mother."

The boy hoisted a chair onto his head and brought it where the young visitor was.

"Your name is …?"

"Phanice Katami."

"Where do you come from?"

"Binala, in Masolo."

"Masika we! Masika, hurry the tea up, your sister is dying of hunger!" Sitawa shouted.

Katami took a good stock of the compound. There was a giant stone walled 'mansion' enclosed in a trimmed hedge of cypress. The ground was Kikuyu grass. Along the wall leant a dark blue bicycle waiting to transport the owner to his place of work.

A tall man of dark complexion emerged from the house. Her blood warmed. Her pulse intensified. In his purple Kaunda suit, she could see he was bow legged. On his face, she saw a perfect gentleman. He had a refined speech that he punctuated in the phrase, 'Ehe thooh.'

She had no sooner cast sight on the man than she unleashed her best courtesies to earn his favour. She greeted him on her knees, her dress kissing the morning dew and face broadening with the most charming smile.

"How are you, child?" He greeted.

"I'm alive, papa."

"Ehee thooh."

There was a pause in which his airs seemed to relive past memories. She was lovely; he had prized her.

"Where are you coming from?" He asked trying to conceal his feelings from his wife.

"There're wars."

"Where?"

"Masolo."

"Ehee thooh, so you come from Masolo?"

"Yes, papa," she said, eyes dancing with passion.

"I wonder what's happening in Masolo."

"We ran away from The Lion."

"Bakora's thieves?"

"So you know it?"

"It's on radio daily," he replied, "so where will you people go?"

"Give me any job papa: washing dishes, bathing children..."

"All right, you're welcome home. Feel free first, we shall talk." Kisiang'ani said mounting his bicycle.

Something had stricken his soul. The brown face and amorous smile had reminded him of the girl he had loved once. He had always wanted to forget her, to forget that plump waist he had touched in a mobile lodging.

'Wambui, darling of my soul, why did you die to desert me in this cruel world,' he had muttered in the succeeding days. Katami was Wambui born again. In spite of her destitution, he concluded that the girl was beautiful and he could reclaim her into Wambui.

Obviously, Katami was absorbed in the Okorian job market as a house help to give Sitawa a breathing space. It was acutely back breaking for her to tackle the multiple roles and at the same time warm the bed. She embraced the new arrangement in spite of the girl's budding age.

Katami proved exceptionally diligent on whatever she lay hands. She was up by five to begin the many household chores. She would milk the cows, iron the clothes, make all the beds and set the breakfast table. Kisiang'ani conceived extreme fondness for her.

Whenever he returned from school, he could gaze at her with a painful passion. She was Wambui. Her expanding bosom and hips made a Wambui with the rise and setting of the sun. Her courtesy was unrivaled too. The spirit of servant-hood was permanently engraved on her. She was far better than Wambui. These coupled with her sweetness of voice tempted him to break the nuptial vows.

He would soon let religion go. He thought about it daily. Five months now, he had not stepped in the church and he no longer cared about it. Why would someone deny him the pleasures of life? The way she shook his hand on her knees! Which woman in his country could show him such respect? He paid her generously away from Sitawa's jealous eye. Expensive dresses that Sitawa could not afford were spotted on her slender body.

Katami grew rounder and prettier. The Creator had placed her in the hands of a man who possessed inimitable kindness to pave the way for the progress of her life, sustenance of her breath and propel her to towering levels of prosperity. What other power did a girl have in a male dominated world that was further wounded by insecurity? Beauty was the only option.

Violence belonged to ogres like Ida. Education was a preserve of those whom the creator had blessed to flourish in a haven of peace like the children of Mwambu. However, the woman of Masolo had no other door.

Kisiang'ani grew edgy over his marriage. His liaison with Sitawa had been a thing of children and he had been foolish to marry her. A woman who obeyed a man in Katami's manner was a wife a man needed. He despised 'the arrogant vermin' he had planted in his bedroom. She was vermin silhouetted in a white man's education and job. He had been duped, deceived by the ugly mask of schooling and the fleeting etiquette thereof.

He had been stupid to stop at appearance. He would have scrutinized the heart. He regretted he had done it out of his immature heedlessness. The theories of his peers in Cheleba struck his mind with horrid clarity. Younger unmarried girls were the most suitable partners. Whenever Katami knelt before him for a greeting, Kisiang'ani's heart sang.

Meanwhile the situation in Masolo degenerated. Walela, the minister for finance was assassinated at a public firing squad; he had declined to mint more money. The chief justice's corpse was found terribly mutilated. Masolians suspected The Lion's involvement; he had laughed at the president in a conference abroad.

Before Masolo forgot the sad news, Abba emerged with tidings. His accomplished magicians had stumbled on an effective cure for all physical disability. The lame, the blind and the lunatic had to assemble in Mengo, the capital. A few doubted the intention but when they heard him swear by the holy name of the prophet, they obeyed.

"Your ugly legs will be stretched, your tirty aye palls washed and doll ears repaired!" He shouted and convulsed with wicked laughter. Giant lorries and buses appeared. The cases were haphazardly hoisted into the lorries and sped to lake Masolo in the dark of the night. Giant cranes then appeared and with the help of The lion, the poor fellows were deposited in the waters of Lake Masolo.

How tragic it was for those who had no arms. How dangerous for the those without sight. How happy Bakora was!

"Ha ha ha ha ha ha ha ha!" He cackled, "eliminate the parasites"

"These lames, blinds, cripples and dumb dogs and ear-lesses are useless things that tirtify our country. They beg around! They asiemu us and spoil our climate in Mengo. If I get a beggar, I cut his head straight and... yes straight and give it to my dog for super, ha ha ha ha!"

He directed The Lion to shoot all swimming 'lames and ear lesses.' However, the valiant cripples like Namba Sita, who now stayed at the Sindani's, dived their way out. He had taken the sixth position in the contest for life. Following this, many physically handicapped, women, men and children; fled Masolo into Jomo's land.

Kisiang'ani thanked Bakora for giving him 'Wambui.' He loved the daughters of Masolo; they were the best in East Africa. Upon return from school, Katami brought him a basin, full of warm water to bathe; Sitawa sulking under a mango tree.

Trudging home, he wore a scowl. The fine feelings that had germinated in the infancy of their marriage had vanished in exchange for anger. He worked himself to bursting; so vexed he was with dispiriting reflections on the subject of marriage.

A dark cat crossed ahead. His heart limped. He made a few strides forward and came face to face with Choina, Sindani's wife. "Pooh," he spat with disgust. A man with a male first born was not supposed to meet a female first thing in the morning. A man with a female first born was not supposed to meet a male first thing in the morning. They never augured well.

His thoughts about Sitawa were morbid. He hated her now. He had to let her go. He only counted one obstruction: Religion. It was a foreign religion anyway. His ancestors did not practice it. Who was he to practice it? It curtailed his freedom to enjoy the luxuriant fruits of his labour.

Had he wanted to marry her anyway? It was Rita he had desired. These schooled girls were not the best. He was in a social dungeon and would free himself soon. Whenever he attempted to reprove his wife, she would cry and whimper. She always wept at the slightest reproach. He had not known she was such a baby. His heart sunk whenever she started crying expecting him to pamper her. And how he had concealed it in the initial days.

Kisiang'ani who had imagined that formal education relieved women of their sentimental nature felt cheated. The bitter truth crashed his soul. He was wearied of her outbursts, he was wearied of her harangues; he desired a subservient woman.

There was yet another lesson to learn from the bitter instruction of experience. Those beatings that Mauka was accustomed to unleashing on his mother were never in vain.

"But I blamed papa and defended mama…oh…, how foolish I was!" He muttered in the strongest melancholy tone. He conceived sizable pity for his late father, Mauka.

He wished his father were alive to guide him through this marital dilemma. He knew what his father would have told him to do. Had he not married Machuma? Did action not speak louder than words? Katami would be his Machuma.

A stray thought criticized his choice on ground of status. 'A woman is a woman,' he muttered, 'she fits any social class depending on her looks. Buchacha married even Bayobos,' he nodded.

'If Sitawa bound me to the church to oppress me, I'll rebel!' He resolved as he flounced into the home. The orange orb of the sun had stood on the Tororo plug ready to set in Masolo. The weaver birds on the eucalyptus at the heart of the home stood silently peering into the distance.

Sitawa sat near the kitchen breastfeeding the baby, Wamalwa. Katami emerged from the house, went on her knees and proffered her hand to the master. Sitawa glanced at the comedy, frowned and sneered.

"What did you have for lunch?" Kisiang'ani asked and whistled a gentle tune.

"You ask as if you have provided something else," Sitawa barked with a hoarse voice.

"I simply wanted to know what you had for lunch."

"Cassava, of course!" The mistress snarled. Tears brimmed her eyes. An awkward silence succeeded with mounting tension. Sitawa rose and flounced to the kitchen. She drew out a plateful of boiled cassava, cast it onto a dirty stool and pushed it near the master.

"Linet, I'm not a dog," The master said. His tone was bitter.

There was another pause. He contemplated.

"If you wish our marriage to continue, respect me and mature!" He added with venom.

"What wrong have I done...oh...oh...oh!" Sitawa whimpered as was her custom. Kisiang'ani rose and picked his way towards the Sindanis.

Chapter Eighteen

The punctual servant of Wele had already stood at the apex of Mount Masaba on the east when the wizened old woman emerged at the Kisiang'anis like a blue fly intruding the dining room at meal time.

"Welcome, ma'am," Sitawa said with a gentle tone, "you have arrived unusually early."

"Thank you child," she replied, "I arrived yesterday in Okoro."

"Mum, where did you sleep, then?"

"Sindani's home."

"You prefer Sindani to your son?"

"There was something to discuss."

"To discuss indeed," Sitawa mocked.

"Your anger always looks for troubles," Butilu asserted.

"Trouble indeed," she said, suspicious.

Butilu ignored the irritable mistress and spoke as if to herself.

"Sometimes I wonder what spirit forced you out of home and threw you among bamia e, he, he-eh!"

"It is far more peaceful than Cheleba," Sitawa replied without joy.

The discourse vexed the old lady and she heaved with distaste for Sitawa. Her arguments gave a few more reasons for her disposal. A woman who argued like a man and asked questions as though she were the head of the home, a woman who crumpled her husband in her armpit and wandered everywhere with him; such a woman had no place among the sons of Mwambu. Butilu vowed to utilize every means her hands could lay on to oust Sitawa.

Wherever did one hear that a wife criticized her husband? Such a woman was yet to be born. The attempt she had made to scrunch her son between her thighs was inconceivable. She was a witch. A woman had to remain in the kitchen and let her husband free in the family tree.

Butilu thought bitterly. She was inside the sitting room; Kisiang'ani had gone out for short call as Sitawa prepared breakfast. She surveyed at the room; it was furnished with a purple carpet, tens of chairs, five tables, two sets of sofa and other pretty articles that charmed her fancy.

'My son is doing well,' she thought, 'but this woman is the problem. She brings her mother and other poor beggars to pull him back!' She muttered.

"Welcome mother," Kisiang'ani said sitting in a sofa.

"Thank you mama, muno, muno, muno, muno," they shook hands again.

They then sat down to swap countless tales. She talked about heavy downpours in Cheleba. She then recounted the sad story of Wambasi's son who had been surrounded by Bayobos and chopped into piles of meat. With an edgy air, she declared that the continued existence of the sons of Mwambu on Mount Masaba was uncertain. She turned to Matumbai's son in a happy tone.

"Wambaya cut him very first and all the things fell on the ground, e, he! maiwe!"

"Oh, God! What happened, then?" Kisiang'ani asked.

"He was taken to hospital; his things were inside salty water."

"Then?"

"The things died in water, pooh, maiwe."

"A, ha?"

"A lot of blood oozed out."

"Did he die?"

"He slept. He left us."

"I should take my son to hospital, and be circumcised."

"Whose, grandson? Buchacha's? You bury me first!" She swore.

Kisiang'ani hoisted two folding chairs and led his mother outside. It was the best place to converse on specific subjects. He turned into a boy and sentimentally complained about his wife.

"Please, mum. I find it very hard to live with Sitawa."

"Continue."

"She doesn't respect me, she doesn't care about me, she throws food at me."

"Son, understand women. They change at certain times of the month."

"Mum, that I know but Sitawa is just rude."

"E, he."

"Katami washes my towels, my underclothes and she grows my bananas," he said in a sad tone.

"Oh son, your bananas?"

"That's why she should be my second wife," he broached the subject

"Oh, but many wives bring problems. You saw how we suffered, son."

"But it made me to work very hard."

"Wasn't it suffering?"

"No, mum."

"Did I not warn you about old girls?"

"You make me to think mother."

"Yes, our people say that the pot that cooks bitter herbs never loses its bitterness. Always take advice. If you reject it, you lie on the path of death."

"I hear you mother," he said nodding.

"A wife should be at home, to warm you, warm food and grow bananas."

"Surely, isn't that what the name woman means in our language?" He made a discovery.

"Omukhasi," Butilu uttered and pondered.

"Khukhasia means boil or warm," He explained.

"A wife should therefore warm the husband and warm his food," asserted Butilu.

"Yes, she should not teach out there," he added.

"Of course now that she has trained, she should do something to avoid being a goal keeper," Butilu argued.

"It's all right."

"Son, don't send her away but it's good to have a woman who'll remain at home, cook your food and grow your bananas," Butilu asserted. Her tone was conspiratory.

She returned to Cheleba the same day; she had accomplished her mission. With the innocence of the new born, she thought her son would do everything within the boundaries of reason. It happens not so with a man who hates a woman he had loved. The volley of hatred rolls and destroys even life. In a few days, the seed of discord germinated and flourished in the Kisiang'ani's.

Kisiang'ani chose a new direction of life, a life contrary to the nature of his conscience but in league to the whims of his soul. Incessantly, he lusted for the marriage of his animal instincts. He craved for a wife who would pamper him in his mistakes; kneel before him, shake his hand and kiss him when he arrived from school. He wanted a tender hearted woman who would not bark at him but comfort him.

He wished Sitawa knew the needs of his life. Destiny had deprived him three needs since his entry on earth; these were: love, love and love. They were the cry of his heart, the desire of his mind and medals of his pursuit. Affection had remained a foreigner to him. His late father had tyrannized him to the level of cursing him, his aunt Repa had followed his footsteps and now his marriage, the supposed solace, turned out to fan his agony. It reduced his hopes into a heap of rubble.

He now abhorred his home. He did not want to rest his eye on it. It was a spring of torment and a sea of sorrow. Who was Sitawa but a dead woman? She was a corpse in bed. She had infected him with coital Marasmus. Many a time she had resisted his advances; she felt pain. Savages had chopped off her engine hence the incompetence in the sport of life. Had he tasted her before marriage, he would have made sound judgment. But only Katami gave him a reason to live in an otherwise empty tomb.

The sons of Mwambu did not circumcise girls. Nevertheless, there were those cheeky ones who were tricked by Bayobo friends into it; Sitawa must have fallen prey to this. He flounced his way to the Sindani's, a man who had suddenly emerged as his most intimate friends.

'A woman who throws food at me will no longer be my wife,' he muttered as he skulked, 'a wife who leaves the house help to make my bed! Katami is mine as life lasts. I must act now. I'll defy religion and obey my mother!" He resolved. His mother's line came to him, *it's good to marry a woman who'll remain at home to cook your food and grow your bananas.* He swore to obey the advice to the letter. Even the Christian religion taught total obedience to parents. He recalled her mother's song in childhood:

Papa ne mayi   *Father and mother*
papa ne mayi   *Father and mother*
Papa ne mayi   *Father and mother*
Niyetala yefwe   *Are our lamp.*

Nabalomanga nokhaulila *If they advice, we don't listen*
Nabalomanga nokhaulila *If they advice, we don't listen*
Nabalomanga nokhaulila *If they advice, we don't listen*
Nikwo kubelekeu   *Then we are ill mannered.*

The song was a balm to his soul. For the first time he was the daddy and mummy's son. He swaggered into the Sindani's and the host stood up to receive him,

"Welcome, Omumaina (My age mate)."

"Thank you Omumaina, bakoki muno muno muno muno!" They shook hands happily.

Sindani resumed his task of weaving after the greeting.

******

"That is a fair attempt," Sindani said.

"Why do you say that?" Kisiang'ani asked.

"You're coming back to the right way."

"I've always been on the right way."

"No, I've never seen Omumaina, smeared with mud at dawn, ruled by a wife, except you!"

"I've never been ruled by a woman."

"Lies, In-Law! That woman rules over you, why can't you marry another one, then?"

"One wife is enough for me."

"Just say your Christian friends are on your neck."

"No!" Kisiang'ani blurted.

"Yeah, they have put you in jail and you can't enjoy anything anymore!"

"I enjoy!"

"What? If you don't even taste busaa? In-Law, you got circumcised well but religion spoiled you!"

"I taste busaa."

"From where? Fanta is your busaa," he pulled phlegm and spat, "you should be free In-Law, free indeed."

"I am free, In-Law," defended Kisiang'ani.

"Omumaina, why should you eat cow peas daily?" He whispered.

"I don't want to make a mistake my father made," he teased.

"You speak shit In-Law," he pulled phlegm and spat again.

"I've no wealth to keep another wife."

"You're a teacher!" Sindani reminded him, "mwalimu should not eat cow peas, daily."

"No, I've no problem with that," he argued.

"Yes, there's a problem In-Law."

"Never."

"Then go away and don't visit me again!" Sindani thundered and dashed into the house like the old man who forgot a pipe in Nandakaywa's intestines.

He emerged with a semi calabash full of busaa.

"You said you take this, hey?" He asked.

"I....em…" Kisiang'ani stammered.

"Bakoki, you either wet the throat with me or go and never return!" He growled.

Kisiang'ani was at loss. To sit with Sindani, drink beer with him and converse about bamaina and marrying many wives was inconsistent to the religion he professed. He was a church secretary in Okoro. But where would he obtain the courage to woo Katami and rebel against the priest? The pot of beer was the only source.

He accepted the offer and gulped the drink down his throat. Sindani ordered for more and he cleared it again.

"You're now a true Omumaina, who marched naked at five in the morning," Sindani flattered him.

He nodded silently.

"After this, be a man. Vary your diet. I have this myself," he showed him three fingers.

Darkness had smothered Okoro and the villagers, as often did, went to sleep. Men, he bet, were in their wives' bosoms to multiply the human species. If there was a commandment Okorians obeyed then it was, "Go ye and fill the earth." The chirping birds cheered on. The crickets applauded too. The yelps of mating dogs conquered all.

Hunched in her blanket, Sitawa kissed her knuckles alone. It had never been thus. By now she would be in smarting bliss. Although unpleasant, his being with her made life bearable. Loneliness would kill her with worries.

The dog barked. It startled her sweet thoughts. A whistle succeeded to soothe it to silence. Sitawa suspected the arrival of her husband and braced herself for the best. Ten minutes went; she did not see him. A little noise caught her ear from a distance. They were laments and sighs.

"No, no, I don't want," a female voice whispered.

"Ah, you're old enough," a male voice insisted.

"No, no, you're my father."

"Relax, you'll enjoy."

"No, mother will hear," she resisted.

"Forget that, you're so sweet, dear," he cooed.

He persisted step by step. Her resistance waned as his forearm moved from her bosom downwards. Katami surrendered herself to this man; so caring, gentle and kind. He was a father who possessed the guts to provide for her to liberate her from misery. She let go her antagonism and clung on his wings to be shifted to those distant realms of pleasure.

The slayer of loneliness struck and they swung together. They flew across the valley of solitude, over the marshy gullies of boredom to galaxy, descending to Orion and back to earth stuck on her Messiah. She curled like a serpent as she pushed him away. He fell on his daughter Rachel. She complained. Embarrassed, he pulled up his trousers and stole away. The meat had tasted better than cowpeas.

The ball changed hands. Mukesi, Masika, Rachel and Wekhanya tumbled on it. Their father never missed lunch of late. Sitawa did not come for lunch and so they were free to have all experiments in the laboratory of passion. And they were tipsy; they reeled in lechery. Kisiang'ani exulted in her; she was the Esther who had come timely to save him from the arrogant Vashti. Sometimes he pulled her before their presence to kiss her and take her to bed.

Mukesi was disturbed. He saw Katami call him, "Let's hope up and about." And he followed her through the maize farm, down the banana crop to the coffee farm.

"You can't get me," the girl called as they descended downhill to the heart of the coffee farm. A grass tripped her. She fell and lay supine under a banana sucker. He perched on her and together they sang. That was two years ago.

Now he was dejected to see his father show those advances at her. It was a mixture of depression and jealousy. Anxiety set in too. Why would his father step where he had stepped? With time, the ball rolled into Sitawa's bosom. She would not idle to watch the ruin of her house.

On one of those mornings, she marched to the kitchen, found her cooking and pounced on her. With the agility of the lioness, she ripped her clothes, smacked her down and bit her.

"Oh, mama, why…beat….me….?" Katami pleaded.

"Man…hunter!….fake!" screamed Sitawa.

Blood trickled down Katami's face. Mukesi who was untying cattle in the shed darted to the scene to try and separate them.

"Leave her…please…mum," he entreated.

His attempts were an exercise in futility. Katami's face was a piteous sight. It was blended with red spots; chunks of meat had been severed from it.

"Papa, come…come," Mukesi called his father to intervene. Kisiang'ani showed up in under pants; Sitawa extricated herself from the enemy and fled.

"Shit! You are feaces!" Kisiang'ani growled.

Audible silence was the response.

"Because you've taken the law in your hands, I declare her my wife!" He thundered.

He wiped his dear wife, gave her first aid and led her into his bedroom. He was fed up with a lioness in his home and was prepared to defy Waliaula and be happy.

He picked his straw and flounced to the Sindani's. It was a misty morning and the air was gloomy. The weaver birds did not chirp; neither did the marlets. Anger smothered him. He reached Sindani's home and unfolded to his friend a synopsis of his problem.

"Such a woman should be given a thorough beating!" Sindani roared.

"I fear for my marriage," Kisiang'ani said.

"Are you a man? Did you skip her over cooking stones?"

"Oh, no!" He said in a regretful tone.

"That's your problem, In-Law," he shouted, "You pampered her throughout."

"Now she'll bring Waliaula and I don't know how it'll be," he complained.

"In-Law, why do you worry? That's a small matter."

"Big issue."

"No, buy liquor and arrange some ceremony to welcome the new bride. Once they see beer, they'll run away."

"Thank you, In-Law."

"Welcome, In-Law a, ha, ha," he chortled, "that's why it's good to love your people."

"I'm arranging it right away," replied Kisiang'ani.

"You can't die alone, In-Law."

Kisiang'ani reached home and ordered for fifteen litres of busaa from Masengo. Katami quickly arranged a party with all the courtesy in her power. She swept the compound, fetched water and prepared the venue for the festive moment. When the sun was overhead, Sindani, Reja, Masengo, Pusi and Wabomba staggered into the home and sat under the Mango tree.

They sat surrounding a big pot of busaa. Upon arrival, they jerked their straws, plunged them in the pot and began sucking and shaking. Kisiang'ani was troubled in his heart. He tried to suppress his conscience in vain. He tried to imagine how he would react before padre Waliaula in that tipsy state and failed.

Sincerely, he could not imagine the turn of events. How he had loved her in those infant days of their marriage. She had been dear to him. They had had lovely moments: the laying at the roadsides, the kisses that had left them weak, and the promiscuous use of words- *I love you, my dear, my sweet darling-* which had separated him from his relatives. He recalled his nuptial vows all the way to *ONLY DEATH SHALL TEAR US APART.*

It irked his soul to know that he was a liar. How many of those lavish vows had he kept? Where was his promise to stand by her in all troubles? No, the church had forced him to say, "YES I DO," he muttered. Kisiang'ani resolved not to keep a lioness in his home. She was dead too.

"Circumcised women are fake!" Kisiang'ani blurted like a man rising from sleep.

"These Bayobos are wrong!" Shouted Wabomba, "Who told them to circumcise girls!"

"To encourage men to marry many wives as girls were many," Sindani asserted.

"No!" Shouted Reja, "To stop them sniffing!"

"Yeah," affirmed Wabomba, "circumcised women don't catch the flame easily…"

"E, he hewa!" They chuckled simultaneously.

"So whenever they went hunting for months, their women could wait for them," Wabomba added.

"Is that why mine was a virgin when I married her?" Kisiang'ani revealed.

"Is she cut?" asked Wabomba.

"Is she a Muyobo?" enquired Sindani.

"Their clan are Bayobos who were assimilated by our people. In fact, the midwife had to 'cut' the knotted scar." Replied Kisiang'ani reflectively.

"True, Bakolati, true…, marry another woman," asserted Wabomba.

A male voice greeted them. They raised their faces to behold Waliaula and Sitawa. Kisiang'ani's heart limped. It stirred. He had been caught pants down.

"Noah," Waliaula called his Christian name, "is this what a church secretary should do?"

The words stung him. He did not reply, but he rose, swaggered to where Sitawa was and grabbed her neck. Waliaula tried to save her; it was too late. He struck her nose. She collapsed. A blow landed on her forehead. She screamed. She tried to cling on the sleeves of his shirt but he kicked her. She flew and fell at Waliaula's feet. With the resilience of a soccer striker, he followed to kick her again but Reja grabbed him from behind.

"Don't beat a woman like that!" Reja thundered.

"Give me a machete! I'll kill them both!" Kisiang'ani purred in Sindani's direction. A tumult rose on the compound. Waliaula had begun retreating. Neighbours paced into the home to witness what had befallen their church secretary.

They shook their heads, embarrassed. They took Sitawa to the hospital. Waliaula stopped and with a bewildered face spoke a few words at Kisiang'ani, "Remember your vows at the podium before a multitude of witnesses. God is not a fool, what you sow you reap. I am not to blame." He shook of the mud on his shoes and trudged away.

Chapter Nineteen

isiang'ani now settled down for polygamy. Forthwith, his reputation was tarnished. He however maintained that he was positively enroute to success. Whether she put every romantic machine into life or all the chapters of law in force, Katami would remain his dearest wife and Sitawa, the object of his bitterness. His hatred for Sitawa was inextinguishable and he was desirous of seeing her dead and gone.

He was determined to extend his antennae to reach out for every artifice that cunning could device to secure Katami's position in the home. In his monologues in the bushy alleys of Okoro, Kisiang'ani argued that he was impelled by diverse circumstances, foremost of which was custom, and then came Sitawa's pride and disrespect.

Nonetheless, he fought waves of guilt: a man of great potential he indeed was, and would not have tolerated intimidation from a mere wife. He wished that each grain of piety in him died a shameful death to be liberated from oppression.

In his privacy, Kisiang'ani regretted his defiance. He had been rash, a voice kept reminding him. At such moments, a melancholy air would hung on him and tears would glimmer on his eyes. The iota of light in him would sear him with blame but he would console himself that his action was an illustration of the instability of human love and uncertainty of masculine passion.

But how again on earth would he stand out and shine in Okoro? How else would he stand as a high authority in counseling in Okoro? His mind would sink down to the bitter past, shift to the recent skirmish and arouse anger in him. The man who had began his house on a well constituted mind deteriorated and degenerated into the realms of the weird. He acknowledged that his delicate mind had frozen into a rock and the heart a granite; impervious to correction.

Sindani said it. So did Reja, Khaemba and Pusi. The delivery of his defiance had hurt them; he had done it to extremes.

He deserted Sitawa to live in the most abject solitude. He compelled her into the belief that her former house maid was her co-wife. A tense draught blew across the home. Kisiang'ani was the janitor to protect the queen from assault.

At Okoro Anglican Church, Padre Waliaula grossly condemned Kisiang'ani's scandal. He warned the flock against polygamy,

"It's a primitive act of pagans," he asserted.

"To hell...hell...with the lot of them," Kisiang'ani cursed when the assertion reached him.

'I'm...fed up...with...a...wingless...life...intoning of hymns...you half understand every Sunday and throwing a few coins in an offertory bag; a boring primitive routine- heck!' He had muttered.

His hatred for religion was confounding. He lamented, "Continual talk about the very things-testimonies-yes: 'I was baptized in 1928 and hence forth I haven't seen any good thing in the world. I left the sweet things of the world- so you know there're sweet-smart girls with lovely waists...some exult in education and others in money but me I exult in The Lord...my wealth is no longer on earth but in heaven, so is my car, my education and friends...heck!'" Kisiang'ani mimicked and cursed. *Didn't Jesus tell his disciples they were his friends? Which Bible did Waliaula study?* He would shake his head as he skulked through the alleys of Okoro towards home.

He did not miss his lunch at home; Katami was there. The tenderness of her bosom remained a mighty consolation in the ensuing spells of depression. A change that remained palpable was the violence of depression; it was the blessing he had mined from the ordeal. His feet were dusty this afternoon. The overhead sun had vaporized moisture from his body; he strutted ahead with big strides inconsistent to the quality of his gait. He was determined to use less than thirteen minutes to reach home to touch the tenderness of her body to deliver him from the strain of his crumbling soul. And he wallowed in the past as he swaggered home.

His aunt Repa struck his mind. What she had done in his son's presence tormented him. Kisiang'ani could not make out how a thinking person could put down her underwear and perform savage gymnastics in the broad daylight. He became skeptical about the norms of his people.

"Is this what Kimila brainwashes people to do?" He asked himself. "Bloody fools, I'll depart from them!" He swore. He now hated tradition and vouched to create his own culture, not Western, not African; a unique culture somewhere.

Perhaps you would accuse him of straying from actual meaning of culture. Kisiang'ani defined culture as a way of life of an individual. There he was: a displaced being, a nameless creature; a blind man in identity crisis, rejected by kin and kith alike. An abomination he was in the church and an outrage to the norms of his people. Kisiang'ani became a ball of mercury in the world.

But he had one bosom friend. Sindani remained warm and reliable. His hand would guide him till death. And the light of his countenance died down; dreadful waves of commiseration swept over him. A drop of tears stole down his eyes in utter regret of his father's death. He desired Mauka's guidance in the rugged gullies of life.

"Papa…papa!" He muttered amid missiles of sorrow. He wept at his rejection, he wept at the fingers of blame against him and wept at his tattered family.

"Forgive…me…daddy….forgive…daddy…, I was only a foolish boy." He pleaded.

All of a sudden, the air around him was filled with Mauka's presence. He could see his leopard skin on that circumcision day. His unkempt hair was there too. The snuff in his left and the spear on his right came so conspicuously to his sight. He said,

"Kisiang'ani, you're my first born, named after Kisiang'ani Kurima, my father. Don't shame me. Stand as a man without a flicker of an eyelid. See, all these eyes are watching you to see how you'll face this test. Life is fire, you must endure the tests of life." He had led him to the surgeon.

His burden got lifted. The purpose of his initiation dawned on him. His people wanted to prepare him for the tribulations of life. He had overcome the harrowing ordeal. What was the decision to fall in love with Katami to compare with that experience? Was there anything to really make him bitter?

"Nothing," he muttered as he skulked into the compound. What he saw hurt him. Katami was playing hide and seek with Mukesi and other children.

"Katami! Where are you, Katami?" Mukesi was shouting.

"Nonsense!" Kisiang'ani roared with a rising rage.

'What a painful sight.' There was something on his eyes that awakened a dreadful sense of fear. His grimace was plainly discernible from a distance.

"What's wrong, papa?" Mukesi asked in a friendly manner.

"You puppy!" He insulted, the first time, "From today, she's your mother!"

Mukesi got scared. His father had never called him that. Something was amiss.

"Why should we call her mother?" The innocent Masika asked.

"Lie down all of you!" Kisiang'ani thundered, "Your ugly stomachs on the ground!"

He plucked cypress branches and closed in on them. His face expressed utmost disgust. He unleashed tens of strokes upon them.

"See you in the bedroom," he ordered Katami as he whacked the children.

"Papa! Oh papa! Forgive us!" They entreated him.

"She is your…?"

"Mother!"

"She's your…?"

"Mother!"

"She is your...?"

"Mother!"

So went the questions and strokes. The strokes of the cane moved from the shoulders, back, buttocks, shins, calves and stomach. He ignored their twitches and groans of despair. With the squeals of children, the home sizzled with apprehension. Mukesi tried to stand up and, *'Wham!'* Kisiang'ani smacked him. He smacked him again.

"Uuuuuwi!" The boy screamed, his nose torn and blood streaming down his shirt.

His father was no longer his father. The boy came to realize. His life hung on the precipice.

Mukesi sprang up and ran. Kisiang'ani pursued him and through the coffee farm they ran. Masika took off too. The toddling Wekhanya called for the end of violence.

"Don't kill them papa!" He pleaded.

"From today you'll know that I'm Kisiang'ani, son of Mauka!" He roared on his return from the vain attack.

"If your mother teaches you to disobey me, you'll all leave this home," he declared. His booming bass shook the home. He swaggered into the house and flung the door shut.

"Sleep properly!" He ordered his new wife. She turned and faced him.

Chapter Twenty

Kisiang'ani sat in Sindani's hut in the evening enjoying the warm friendship. There was Sindani, there was Khaemba, there was Wekhombe and there was Reja with straws dipped in their pot of existence. In the hut were howls, grunts and chortles of tipsy men who could not face the rigours of life in a sober state of mind.

The most conspicuous figure in the hut was Reja. He was a boorish tall man who had never in his life learnt the essence of decency. His trousers were so patched up that people could not tell its original colour. His hair, ever in sturdy shreds, gave one the picture of the porcupine.

If there was a philosophy he cherished in life then it was dissipation. It was a didactic he recited daily; marriage did not matter to him. Today he was happy after selling an acre of his land. He was rich. He kept wrapping tobacco leaves in five shilling notes and smoking them.

Kisiang'ani watched him smoke fifty shillings but was more absorbed in his life than Reja's. Bitter meditations bombarded him. They were thoughts of agony he dared not breath in words. The painful realities of life closed in on him and he stood the best chance of catching hypertension. He shook his siphon and sucked the liquor with an alacrity that declared the drink a perfect solution to his problem.

Sindani came in with Gramophone, inserted the disc and turned it on. The singer sang the famine of 1980:

A lazy wife, should return to their home,
The '80 famine, was severe,
To those with lazy wives,

A good wife should grow cassava
And harvest debes and debes.
A lazy wife should return to their home.

"Like your wife, e he wa!" Squeaked Reja at Kisiang'ani.

"Shut up, uncircumcised man!" Shouted Khaemba.

"Don't call me that?"

"What? Why should you comment on marital things when you know nothing about marriage?" Asked Khaemba.

"E, he hewa! To hell with marriage and circumcision!" Reja cursed.

"You're a waste of space!" Wekhombe insulted.

"Food is food whether you grow it, borrow it or buy it, e he hewa!" Chortled Reja.

"In-Law, these are the ogres that eat our wives. Be alert!" Sindani said facing Kisiang'ani.

The latter was disinterested in the topic.

"And eating is eating, he he wa!" Proceeded Reja in his characteristic way, "whether you use dirty mouth or clean mouth, the food will end up in the stomach!"

"That's why you fold your foreskins with a rubber band and cheat our daughters that you're circumcised!" Shouted Wekhombe.

"We must circumcise this fellow!" Roared the tipsy Sindani. He licked his fore finger, tapped the dust on the ground and licked it again.

Kisiang'ani listened to the conversation. The topic had digressed from what interested him more. He needed the answer to the lazy woman. Okaanya who had not spoken a syllable pulled phlegm, spat and then roared, "A lazy wife should not be sent away! Wait….I finish…," he stopped Sindani from interrupting, "give her a thorough beating!"

The sun set over Okoro and solid darkness assumed the reins. With a new marriage friction, topics of meditation were never wanting. Kisiang'ani thought about the day's skirmish with his children. Rambling experiences struck him, they enslaved his mind.

Sitawa's brawl with Katami, his revenge for Katami, his rebellion against the church, Katami's games with Mukesi and the punishment he had given them. Her painful whimper after plunging his baton of life was a balm for his mind. However, it made him doubt his competence in the art. No, he wanted to punish her, he defended himself.

All of a sudden, a mysterious fear descended on him. His hair stood erect and heart throbbed turbulently. Someone was tickling his soul. He was numb with fear. Someone was urging him to grab the man on his right. He gathered himself to ignore the voice but it was too strong to ignore. In a trance, Kisiang'ani jerked his forearm and grabbed Wekhombe, imploring, pleading and entreating.

"Give me that thing! Give me…!"

Wekhombe tried to resist but Kisiang'ani overpowered him. He was relieving him his attire when the man found his tongue.

"Calm, I am a diviner."

"Go on!"

"I've a charm around my waist. I'm amazed at your discernment."

"Bring it here," Kisiang'ani said with a tremulous voice.

"No, I can't. You shouldn't touch it now. You have the gift of divination; there are rituals to be performed to initiate you in it. All your problems…"

"Who initiates!" Kisiang'ani growled with a booming bass.

"I can do it."

"Welcome, home."

"Remember the service isn't for free," asserted Wekhombe.

"At what price?"

"Two brown bulls, two lambs and three goats."

"I'll try," Kisiang'ani agreed as he took a proper look at him: voluble, slim in tattered woolen coat. It was too dark to see his trousers.

He bid him farewell and staggered about his way home like a rebel accursed by Wele. He tottered through pot holes and bushes in the infernal darkness. He skulked through the labyrinths, rising rage mounting in his savage chest. He skulked ahead, an enthusiastic admirer of anarchy and vandalism in Okoro. His left stride lauded fury and the right, violence. He contemplated a separation and a divorce respectively. He doubted, they were far more painful.

Okaanya's line flashed on his mind: A lazy woman should be given a thorough beating.

It was the better option. He soon discovered that he had lost his bearing and taken the wrong route, home. The new challenges never gave him a chance even to think about his physical path.

He retreated and picked the right one. Solid darkness hampered his movement. Twice he tripped over stones as he approached Okoro River. It hummed a poignant tune. It was fat tonight; the recent rain season had abated her hunger. Slowly, he waded through the cold waters that reached his navel. As he approached the other end, a cold rope spiraled up his right leg from the ankle to the shin. He jerked it but it wriggled swiftly up his thighs.

Kisiang'ani stirred up, dived in the water and swarm as he threw violent kicks in air. The aggressor let go his foot. He reached the muddy bank of the river and something rattled. He shivered in the cold, his teeth chattered and clothes dripped. He stopped and peered at the source of the rattles. A hissing sound reached him. His senses got alerted. He made one stride forward and saw a cylindrical pole jerking the head backward and forward. He tried to proceed but its neck bulged as it braved itself for combat.

Kisiang'ani would not waste his time with a serpent. He had killed more than a hundred. He tightened his grip on the bamboo that stored his siphon. He kept a keen eye on the enemy. The latter rose to spike and he flung the bamboo with a diabolical gusto.

At a rising momentum, it picked the viper, lifted it diagonally and deposited it yonder with a thud.

"A man is a man," Kisiang'ani flattered himself. He trudged uphill to his home.

His attire was soaked in muddy water. A savage voice ordered him to remove it and walk nude. He removed his clothes, save for underwear, and plunged in a trance. He gripped his clothes on the hip and tottered in the dark. His head spun round and round in a transport of frenzy. Darkness grew thicker in the lonely wet bushes around the river. The silence of frogs made the place a grave yard. He had to do something to dispel the fear and anxiety. He began to sing a song and melancholy feelings overpowered him. Tears streamed down his eyes as the song reminded him of his father:

Papa ulila	*Father listen*
Papa ulila malilo	*Father listen to my cry*

Papa ulila   *Father listen*
Papa ulila malilo   *Father listen to my cry.*

Mauka ulila   *Mauka listen*
Mauka ulila malilo   *Mauka listen to my cry*
Mauka ulila   *Mauka listen to*
                                     Mauka listen to my cry
Mauka ulila malilo

Nese ndichaye   *Where shall I go*
Nese ndichaye kang'ali   *Surely, where shall I go?*
Nese ndichaye   *Where shall I go*
Nese ndichaye kang'ali   *Surely, where shall I go?*

The song lifted the burden on his soul. He named all his ancestors by substituting Mauka with tens of them as if they were a solution to his problems. A mystic strength descended on him and he braced himself to destroy all his enemies. He had the energy to kill padre Waliaula, smite Sitawa, Repa, "ugh Repa!" He swore over the name and skulked on.

Meanwhile, Sitawa was busy arranging rags on the floor as bedding for the children. It was her daily routine. Each evening, she threw rags on the floor, one after the other for the boys to sleep on. Her husband did not care about them. He left very early and returned late. If he returned early, he appeared only in Katami's room.

After supper, the children asked for entertainment.

"Mama, tell us the one about Nandakaywa," Mukesi requested.

"No, tell us that about Simbi," Wekhanya asked.

"Long long time ago," she began.

Hare lived well with other animals. The Leopard, Antelope, Goat, Sheep and others. After a while, there was drought in the Land. Animals not only went without water but also food. The Goat walked, walked and walked without hope of finding either leaves or grass. Many animals died hence denying Leopard the privilege of finding prey. Antelope watched helplessly as her fawns succumbed to hunger and thirst. In contrast, Hare always had enough to eat and save for tomorrow.

One day, Goat paid Hare a visit and asked him where he got the food. Hare was muffling lots of meat while leaking his fingers. He chewed and swallowed noisily.

"Do you really...really want to know where I get my food?" He asked.

"Yes, my friend, Hare, I wish to know this place."

"Up the hillock, come tomorrow and I will show you."

"It is alright," Goat accepted the invitation. The following morning, they set off for the journey. They went uphill and down valleys, crossed rivers and streams until they came to the Mumbo hill.

At the foot of hill, Hare gave his final instruction:

"Remain here and wait as I climb to the peak. When you hear the sound, *Bwa...bwa...bwa....bwa...bwa*, step aside. That is not the food, alright?"

"Yes..yes...yes!"

Affirmed Goat with automaton obedience.

"When you hear the sound, *ndiiiiiiiiiiiiiiiiiiiiiiiiiiiiii*, open your eyes, your mouth and place your head in the way! There the food comes! Alright?"

"Yes...yes...sir! Yes!" Affirmed Goat.

"Ha ha ha! Goat will be killed, he will be killed!" interrupted Wekhanya.

"No...no...Goat is just obedient, we should be obedient!" Retorted Masika.

"That's not obedience, it is foolishness," Said Mukesi.

Goat waited patiently.

"*Bwa...bwa...bwa...bwa,*" came the sound. He stepped aside. A huge stone rolled by.

"*Ndiiiiiiiiiiiiiiiiiiiiiiiiiii,*" came the shrill.

The children chimed, "he opened his eyes, he opened his mouth and placed his head in the way!"

"E he he!" Sitawa screamed with laughter. The stone hit his head, broke the skull and spilled his brain.

Hare descended the hillock, packed Goat in the sisal sack hoisted it on the back and made away.

He flayed Goat, cut him into pieces and smoked him for future use.

Antelope came to visit him after a week. Hare's mouth was surfeited with meat.

"My friend Hare, where do you get all this food?"

I am lucky to find some more food, he hewa! He laughed more to himself.

"At Mumbo hillock. We go uphill and we will find food," Hare replied.

"Is hay there?" Antelope asked.

"In plenty."

"Mummy, somebody is singing," Mukesi warned.

"Who?"

"Daddy's voice," the boy said and rushed to the door.

A pause of apprehension ensued.

"It's papa and he's very dark!" Mukesi screamed. He was standing at the door.

The hoarse voice approached the house. Sitawa shut the front door. Silently, they listened to their heartbeats. Mukesi was so worried. Sitawa lay her hand on him and said, "be strong, life is a battle." He felt comforted.

The voice came singing. It was a desperate tone:

Nalila Kisiang'ani Nalila *I weep Kisiang'ani I weep*
Nalila Kisiang'ani nalila *I weep Kisiang'ani I weep*

It was the mention of Kisiang'ani that convinced Sitawa that the performer was indeed her husband.

"Open the door you fools!" Kisiang'ani growled. An ear-piercing bang followed. The door gave way and blew off the oil lamp in Sitawa's hands. Mukesi darted closer to his mother. He saw a dark phantom seize the pregnant lady by the neck and strike her face. She collapsed on the furniture and screamed but the blows muffled her voice.

The spook followed her on the floor flailing its fists and kicking her haphazardly. The children screamed and it attacked them. The fists traversed from Mukesi, Masika to Rachel. Sitawa rose to defend them and the spook kicked her womb. She collapsed and rolled with a yell that got swallowed in the hullabaloo. Reja appeared at the scene and flashed his torch at the nude father.

"Is this why you got married? To beat women and children…e hewa hewa!" He scorned and challenged him to a bitter combat. They wrestled. Reja flung him onto the ground.

Mukesi rushed to call Choina, Sindani's wife; Sitawa had not risen from the ground. Three women arrived to check Sitawa but Kisiang'ani picked an axe and chased them away. Reja and Sindani combined forces and overpowered him. They tied him on the mango tree. The women examined

Sitawa's femoral system. It had been injured and blood oozed. There was no hope…there was no hope…

"I must kill this wicked woman!...I…must…kill her." Kisiang'ani shouted as the women carried Sitawa away.

PART FOUR:

THE FALL

Chapter Twenty One

He trudged around a corner on the bushy path and picked the main route home. Down his heart was a bliss having skipped over another hurdle in his life. He was a mixture of contradictory emotions. He looked confident and resigned. He walked with a brisk and frail stride. His exam had been easy and difficult.

The dreary in school notwithstanding, Mr Mareva, or Mr Nowhere as they called him, made a big difference. As much as the principal complained about his shabbiness, and scruffy beard, Mukesi admired his attitude towards life. He had once caught him reading a novel in his English lesson and he had said, "It will take you, nowhere." The class had roared with laughter at his characteristic use of the word. He had then started, then added:

"*Youngman, I read five hundred novels, they took me nowhere. I wrote six of them, nobody published, they took me nowhere. I sang songs, I took my students up to the nationals, they gave me awards, they took me nowhere!*" The class sat ready, waiting for the chorus:

"*And I married four wives and sired twenty children, they took me---?*"

"*Nowhere!*"

"*When I was a young man like you, I was a school captain in Mang'u; it took me…*"

"*Nowhere!*"

"*I was handsome, spoke good English; I was proud and sensitive, it took me…?*"

"*Nowhere!*"

"*I was born in a rich family and I despised my poor teachers…!*"

"*It took me…*"

"NOWHERE!" The class had thundered.

This scene always set him thinking. Why would Mr Mareva assume such an attitude towards life. Perhaps Mukesi's idealism would lead him nowhere. He grinned. Mukesi anticipated a super performance in only half of the subjects. The other half would go burst. A few years before, the boy had made futile attempts to convince his head teacher to relieve him the burden of taking Mathematics. Mukesi had desired to let go 'the big brother' along with his step brothers in the laboratories.

Mr. Nabumali, the principal, became extremely indignant. Infuriated, he ordered the Boarding master to rush the boy to the sanatorium for diagnosis. He speculated psychosis and other mental anomalies. Having tested negative, he candidly admonished the boy and maintained that his query was a preserve of the lunatic. Mathematics and sciences were the core of the curriculum and each Kenyan pupil had to attempt if he were to proceed to any tertiary institution.

Mukesi liked the arts and humanities. He specifically cherished literature but Mr Nabumali denied the department the necessary tools to nurture his talents. The library was half empty. He saw numerous science text books with five novels only. Whereas Mathematics had two teachers per stream, English had a teacher for every four streams. The result was poor instruction in the languages with scant coverage in areas like poetry and prose fiction.

Those ten subjects that Ministry of Education had put on the curriculum baffled him. Did it ever wish him leisure time? You had to be 'a book worm' to pass. Consequently, he had had no time to read any of the five novels in the library.

In his seldom venture in discussions, Mukesi told his peers that the social sciences had more impact on students than the physical and natural sciences. A thorough study of *Things Fall Apart* for instance, enabled learners to unearth shortcomings of masculinity through the prime mover.

His peers respected his line of thought because he never failed literature. Mukesi turned out to posses some unique features. For instance, he never did things because people did them. Passive loyalty to custom per se was variant to his nature. Subsequently he grew to loathe the paternalism typical of his people.

The way elders, his father no exception, imposed their opinions on individuals was distasteful to him.

In his private studies, the young man had discovered that the Western world progressed owing to the freedoms and liberties individuals were accorded. In relation to this, Mukesi often desired an international dais to convince African societies to relinquish paternalism and recognize the individual.

You are because I am became his dictum. He held that the Creator made the individual; from him proceeded society. It was hence absurd for the latter to dictate everything at the former. Who fathered the other? If the views of the two clashed over something obligatory, the offspring ought to submit. Mukesi saw it as unethical for the sons of Mwambu to impose the circumcision rite on everybody.

"Just say you're not circumcised," Wesonga, one of his classmates had blurted.

"Now, friend, why are you circumcised?" Mukesi had asked him.

"It's our culture, that's…"

"See that's thickness, you did it because others do it!" He had left him alone.

Mukesi was a tall boy of slender built. He was dark of complexion and seemed to avoid human society. He was a loner at home and school. He locked himself in rooms and read voluminous books. In his proximity, you would not miss: *Pickwick papers, Readings in Philosophy, A tale of Two cities, Native Son, Old Goriot* and *Crime and Punishment*.

His failure in exams, however, proved him not brilliant. He was quite religious but seldom stepped in church. Generally, he yearned for the western way of thinking; freedom of association, expression and choice even among children. The rich environment in which children were raised appealed to him. He detested the savage conditions in which he had been raised.

Worst of all was the informal bureaucracy among his people. Male chauvinists appointed themselves in high offices to batter their wives and children. They were cowards of cowards. If indeed a man was brave, why wouldn't he fight strong men only?

Mukesi sauntered ahead. Darkness flowed over Okoro and fireflies darted hither and thither. An owl hooted in a distance. A hyena cried. A melancholy cloud perched on his brow. How he wished never ever to see his father tyrannize his mother. He was fed up with the incessant anarchy and vandalism. He was a man, even without circumcision and he would not condone intimidation from any illiterate person based on 'backward traditions'. As an adult, in his own right, he would make his own judgments without the guidance of society. A baby grew into a toddler. For how long would people think for him in the mask of desire to see him through? If he would not be entrusted with making the simplest decision like circumcision, when would his reason mature? For reason, as he had read, grew by making choices.

Mukesi was sick of coercion, sick of paternalism and sick of autocracy; the trio that ruled many African communities. They erased genius hence underdevelopment on the continent.

Children were puppets to obey all the customs. 'What is, is what ought to be,' he thought. He shook his head. 'A murderer of creativity,' he muttered. 'And you obey what you are taught from the past, you obey whose author you know not because the customs are the property of the collective mind. They're transmitted for their own sake..., any critical..., look at them is confronted with hostility..., such are the rude children...'

Mukesi shifted his suitcase from his right to his left and trudged on. The grotesque image of his father stood in his presence. He hurtled through the dark room, a naked ghost kicking at anything. He pranced over the children. They screamed. Sitawa came in their rescue, he kicked her womb. She yelled and keeled over. Mukesi darted towards her.

Blood..., blood was all over her. He ran off to call the Choina; it was too late. The bouncing baby girl had gone....., gone.

"Oh dear sister, were you destined to live so shortly?" Mukesi asked in a melancholy tone of voice. He was under great agony and anguish.

'She would have become a great woman in the world, who knows!' He muttered. Mukesi became superstitious. He now attributed the absence of daughters in the family to the ordeal.

The strength of the buffalo descended on him and he now thirsted for rebellion. The perpetual anarchy that had stormed the home after Katami's rise in status fanned his depression. How he craved a cessation of violence. He braced to purge the turmoil out of the home.

"Fire is the only cure for fire," he muttered as he reached the gate.

"Mukesi! Mukesi!" Masika cried with joy. He dashed to call other people.

"Welcome son," Sitawa said with little animation.

Mukesi sat in front of his mother's kitchen and surveyed the compound. The beautiful hut he had left was not the smoky thing he saw. The pretty house he had left was not the cow shed he saw. The smart Kisiang'ani he had known was not the unhinged grotesque he saw this evening. There he was in a cattle boma, a boozing house for a home.

"What happened to my hut?" Mukesi asked, sharply.

Sitawa became all jitters.

"Papa burnt it down," Masika ejaculated.

Sitawa's attempts to silence him failed.

"Why?" Mukesi asked.

"You wrote to him that you'll go to the wood."

"So?"

"So he said you're uncircumcised and don't deserve a simba (man's hut)."

"And the doors on the main house?"

"Dad cut them down," Masika proceeded.

"Why?"

"He said that mum should build her own house to compete with young mother."

"Who's asking here as if this is his home?" A growl rose from Katami's house.

"Did you burn down my hut?" Mukesi asked to provoke his father.

"Do you know whom you're asking that?" Kisiang'ani asked in a rising rage.

"Just touch me! Won't like it!" blurted Mukesi.

Kisiang'ani picked his sword, sprang out and attacked his adversary.

Mukesi hurtled in the dark, tripped over unknown obstacles and took the archway from home. He ran. Sitawa and Katami yelled. They implored. They placated. The boy swerved northward and Kisiang'ani crashed in the compost pit. His ankle sustained an injury and it hampered his progress. He changed his mind and returned limping and panting in gulps of fury.

"Go and never return," he roared.

"You're training an army to fight me," he shouted at Sitawa.

The tumult drew knots of people into the home. There was Khaemba; there was Okaanya.

"What's wrong here," Okaanya asked, tipsy.

"This musinde thinks he can fight me because he has finished form four."

"Circumcise him!" He shouted and struck his staff on the ground, "make arrangements, circumcise the boy and all rebellion will end!" He returned home.

*****

It was a great day for Kisiang'ani. A time to prepare the home for a great occasion. It was a time for kinsmen to visit his family, familiarize with his children, rejoice with a pot of liquor and chunks of meat as they witness the circumcision of a son who was entitled to the leopard's skin. The episode that had befallen him the previous day was no longer in his heart.

Although given to short tempers, Kisiang'ani did not hold grudges over conflicts with his children. He accepted that conflict was an undeniable fact in human existence. He therefore woke up to start roofing Mukesi's hut, the hut he had set ablaze. He never needed to argue with a child.

'Inflict pain on the kid and bad manners will depart,' he muttered. In any case, bickering with a musinde, the uncircumcised, was akin to an abomination among his people.

There was this presidential candidate from the lake who showed up in Okoro to ask for votes. Okaanya had told him point blank to remove his trousers and be circumcised before he could contend with a circumcised man. More insults had followed, then stones. The son of Ramogi had fled. Whether a son rejoiced or wept, circumcision was the only measure of manhood among the sons of Mwambu. It had to be done in league with all the customs of the people. It was a precursor to marriage and other adult privileges like leadership. Education was respected but circumcision revered.

Kisiang'ani marched out of the compound in a tattered pair of trousers. His red underwear protruded through two holes at the buttocks. His hair was unkempt and the shirt emitted a stench of sweat and chang'aa. The weaverbirds on the eucalyptus were absorbed in an early morning song to welcome the heavenly day. He ploughed his way through the dew and tottered to the Wanjala's.

Wanjala was a local carpenter in Okoro. He was indebted to many Okorians; he never finished his assignments on time. Yet he never could resist the rustle of a note.

Twice it had landed him in prison where he refined his skills in carpentry. Whether his crimes were conscious or unconscious, he returned from the prison with new skills to propel his business to heights of insolvency. Even this task of roofing the son's hut had been given two months before. Kisiang'ani had hoped that Wanjala would finish it before his son's return. But, the man had kept on postponing till it had come to this. Fortunately, he had found him and they rushed home.

Wekhanya and Masika darted to the scene to see Wanjala work. He gauged the size of the wall, the pieces of timber; picked the hand saw and cut. He picked the hammer and drove the nail into his pieces of timber. He joined two central trusses with the roof pole between them. He hoisted them and the pole pointed to the sky.

"What's that for?" Masika asked.

"It's custom," Wekhanya replied.

"No, it stands for a man," Wanjala explained.

"How?" Masika wondered.

"As long as it's there, a circumcised man is in the home."

"Is that why it's sharp?" Masika said, amazed.

All of them flew into pearls of laughter.

"Yes boys, and that's why only circumcised men need simba," Wanjala asserted.

"Tell them, Wanjala," Kisiang'ani barked approaching.

"Yes, how are the plans?" Wanjala asked.

"Ten bags of maize, for making busaa, three bags of yeast, one bull, two goats and so on…"

"Ei, ei, ei! How did you manage all that with all the fees at Chesire High?" Wanjala got surprised.

"Sacrifice, brother. The boy had to go without fees for some time".

"You mean…"

"He had to stay home the whole of second term."

"Circumcision is very important anyway," Wanjala proclaimed.

"Otherwise you'll never be given honourable burial."

"Your corpse will be circumcised first," Wanjala completed.

"But I have a foolish son, Wanjala."

"Ei?"

"He mocks my kindness. He says he must go to the wood!" Referring to the hospital.

"O lolo maye! I haven't got you well, am I dreaming? Tell me well," Wanjala said, confounded.

"I swear! My son wrote to me. The letter is here."

"A good son knows that circumcision is for his own good!" Asserted Wanjala.

"Eeeeeh!"

"Like my cousin who lives in Sitabicha, the boy lost his father two years ago."

"Huh?"

"Two weeks ago, he came to me and said, 'cousin my initiation has come. I want to be a man. I've sweated; I have two goats, two bags of maize but lack yeast and other few things, would you please chip in?'"

"That's a son who's serious with life, a son who's educated," Kisiang'ani asserted.

"Or we can do this, brother," he spoke to Kisiang'ani, "hold him."

"What do you mean?"

"Seize him and circumcise him," Wanjala clarified.

"You can't do that, Wanjala," blurted Mukesi who was eaves drooping, "I'll dismantle your dental formula."

"We can do it!" Kisiang'ani screamed the place down.

"Never!" The boy bleated.

"Yes!"

"No!"

The boy emerged out of the lantana hedge he had been hiding and stared at his father. There ensued an awkward silence in which tension intensified. Children watched the scene with jitters.

"Who has bewitched you?" Kisiang'ani found his voice.

"Society."

"How?"

"Forcing people."

"All of us have passed through it, son," Kisiang'ani softened his stance.

"I can't do it just because you did it."

"So?"

"Go and tell all the relatives that I've refused to get circumcised."

"Impossible!"

Kisiang'ani growled. The assertion incensed him.

"Or I go to the wood!"

"To the wood?"

Wanjala and Kisiang'ani asked simultaneously. The words confounded them.

"I've finished form four. I can't skip around with bells like a grasshopper," Mukesi declared and both of them laughed. Kisiang'ani shelved his anger for awhile. He then shook his head. He did not blame his son; he had taken after him. In fact, he wanted to permit him to go to hospital but he feared his relatives and friends. The boy had to submit for them to start the first stage: *khuchukhila*.

Chapter Twenty Two

ukesi either wanted to become a Christian or sort out his issues cleverly like Hare. Yes..., Hare. He remembered his mother's story before she was first assaulted by their father. She had completed the story later after recovery:

"Antelope like Goat followed Hare to the Mumbo hillock. When they reached the foot, Hare said, "Remain here and wait. When you here, *Bwa...bwa...bwa....bwa...bwa*, step aside. When you hear the sound, *ndiiiiiiiiiiiiiiiiiiiiii!!* Open your eyes, open your mouth wide and put your head in the way to receive the food."

"Yes, I will do," Antelope said with absolute obedience.

Hare reached the summit of the hill and pushed a huge rock downhill. It came *Bwa...bwa...bwa....bwa...bwa*. Antelope stepped aside. Hare picked a sling, loaded it, and cast the stone. It moved *ndiiiiiiiiiiiiiiiiiiiiii*. Antelope opened his eyes, opened her eyes wide and put his head in the way. The stone hit and broke the skull, spilling Antelop's brain. He collapsed and died. Within no time, Hare was packing her in his sisal sack. He had got the meat of the next ten days. On reaching home, he flayed her, smoked her and stored the meat on his firewood rack.

Two days later, Leopard had marched in. He was shocked to find Hare wolfing chunks of roast meat.

"My friend, Hare, where do you find all this food yet all animals are dead and besides there is no water..."

"Follow me to Mumbo hills and I will show you the food?" Hare interrupted rudely.

"Are you sure?"

"Pretty sure."

They set off the following day to the hills. On reaching the foot of the hills, Hare gave his usual advice: When you hear *Bwa...bwa...bwa....bwa...bwa*, step aside.

When you hear *ndiiiiiiiiiiiiiiiiiiiiii*, open your eyes, open your mouth and put your head in the way. Leopard nodded and waited. Hare climbed uphill and pushed a huge rock. It came rolling, *Bwa...bwa...bwa....bwa...bwa*.

Leopard stepped aside. He braced for something worse. All of a sudden, he saw a stone come his way. He dodged and then lay prostrate, feigning death. With eyes half closed, he saw Hare come in excited mood and shove him into a sisal sack.

"Fools...fools...I will eat all of them!" Hare said to himself.

No sooner had he hoisted him to his back than Leopard clawed his ears. Hare abandoned his sack, sprang up and fled. Leopard disentangled himself from the sack and pursued him but his efforts were fruitless. Since then Hare and Leopard are enemies. When Leopard finds him he kills and eats him. Mukesi wondered whether he should use wits like Hare to tackle his father or Leopard's method of confrontation.

The day had ended without success. Their attempts to make the young man appreciate the benefits of circumcision had hit the wall. Kisiang'ani had resolved to bring him before five elders the following day to try and reason together. Sitting under the mango tree, Kisiang'ani pondered over his own experiences. He too had had his queries with the rite as a young man.

It had rained the previous day and dirty pools of water idled at the centre of the home. Dark clouds that hung in the sky braced for a fall. Kisiang'ani could not associate the clean rain water with the dirty pools in his compound. Only Mr. Gachanja of Karatina would have reminded him that the clean waters he saw pouring from the sky originated from not just the dirty pool but also the salty ocean. Worse still, it would not remain clean for long. It was a foolish drop that boasted about its purity; its time had not come. The cycle continued.

The elders sat on one side facing the front door of the house on the south. There was Okaanya, there was Sindani, there was Wabomba, there was Wanjala and Kisiang'ani; all ready to persuade Mukesi undergo the rite. Sindani was the first to speak,

"Son, our people say a tree with sweet fruits shows the signs at a tender age. And you have shown all the good signs up to now. We're surprised at your recent behaviour. Is it fear? Do you fear lukembe? A son is the elephants thigh, he shouldn't fear. This is our kimila-tradition. We teach you the ways of the sons of Mwambu. We show you how to live with both enemies and friends. We teach you how to be a man. It's compulsory for every son to face the knife or be banished from our society..."

"Yes...yes..." Kisiang'ani affirmed. The others nodded their approval.

"If that thing of yours is not cut, you'll never stand before a gathering of men and say anything," proceeded Sindani. His tone was reproachful.

"Why?" Mukesi asked.

"Don't ask," thundered Okaanya, "too many questions spoil everything."

"Get cut and we shall answer your questions," asserted Sindani.

"Unless you tell me why I must get circumcised, I'll not accept it," asserted Mukesi.

"Foolish boy you'll never get a child!" Growled Okaanya.

"Lies, Pusi has a son," replied Mukesi.

"You'll never get a girl here," warned Wabomba.

"Oh, I don't need to marry a daughter of Mwambu."

"You must!" Barked Kisiang'ani.

"You'll never get a decent burial," Sindani warned.

"Once dead, you can burn me if you wish," Mukesi blurted.

Kisiang'ani rose and slapped him hard. The boy staggered back and collapsed in Sindani's arms.

"Thanks!" The boy shouted.

"You must respect elders!" Kisiang'ani roared bracing for violence.

"No, no, no, In-Law," intervened Sindani, "you like war and it doesn't solve problems!"

The elders averted a storm. Mukesi heaved under strong swipes of anger.

"In-Law, our people say, 'a man who wants peace adds his staff in the hearthstones,'" asserted Sindani.

"And the stubborn elephant doesn't nurture his task," rattled Okaanya's voice.

The situation subsided. Sindani resorted to the use of questions to see what the matter was.

"Why do you hate being cut at home?" He asked.

"They smear you with flour," Mukesi replied.

"I must smear you with it," Kisiang'ani snarled.

"You look like a ghost."

"And I must smear you with cow dung from the rumen on the eve of the day."

"And march nude like a mad man for twenty kilometers," Mukesi said.

"That's culture," Wanjala blurted.

"To chop off my things?" Mukesi barked.

"It never happens," Sindani defended.

"Dad, do you recall Matumbai's son?"

"I stopped arguing with you sometime back!"

"And do you disinfect knives, or you want to transmit HIV AIDS?" Mukesi went on.

"That's an *American Idea of Denying us Sex*," Wanjala joked.

"You are ignorant," Mukesi asserted.

"Shut up, even learned people obey customs!" Kisiang'ani roared and stood up.

Five elders fell on him to prevent assault.

"Culture is manmade and it can be unmade by man," Mukesi asserted.

"You've got to get circumcised, you fool!" Kisiang'ani threw Wanjala away and hurled his staff at the boy. He dodged and it missed him by a whisk. Mukesi retreated and fled from the scene.

In a few moments, Mukesi's rebellion was on the lips of every Okorian. Even children knew that he had refused to clang bells. Wherever was it heard that a son of Mwambu had rejected custom and demanded to go to the wood like bamia! The scheduled date for his initiation came and passed; Mukesi remained adamant.

The wind blew in breaks, relieving the earth of the heat of the scotching sun. The speed of the wind swayed the mahogany and the Elgon teak on Mount Masaba. These were easy times; these were hard times. In a distance, Mukesi saw a whirlwind. It whirled the dust onto his trousers and sprayed it on his cottage.

"Damn vandal!"

He cursed the wind. It had just destroyed the poultry house the previous day. He stood up and flounced to Katami's house in search of his surviving chicken after the disaster.

Although it was the eve of Christmas, initiation songs could be heard all over Okoro. Mukesi was astonished by Okorians. They could not sing any religious song to prepare for the birth of the Messiah.

A radio in Katami's house said it was ten mid morning. The front door of the hut was ajar though oppressed by deadly silence. The weaver birds that often sang romantic songs were missing on the compound today. Two hens raced by. They confronted each other and fought. The darker pecked the white one in the eye and crushed it. The victim shrieked and fled. An eagle swept by and soared high at an acute angle with the casualty's chick in its claws.

"You!" Mukesi shouted at the eagle. All was fruitless. A deep voice sneezed and coughed. Mukesi's heart palpitated. Around the village went circumcision songs.

They sang about Mukesi, Kisiang'ani's son who was so learned that he demanded to go to the wood. The singers condemned him as a coward softened by western education.

Mukesi was infuriated. He vouched to deal with the master. He flounced past Katami's house. The door creaked and a voice startled him,

"What brings you here!" It was Kisiang'ani.

"I'm looking for my chicken," Mukesi replied.

"You've come to spy what I tell my wife?"

"It was….an eagle…"

"Has your mother sent you?"

"No!"

"Do you see the embarrassment you've brought me?"

"I'll go to the wood."

"Numskull! Don't you hear my name in those songs?"

"A ha!" Mukesi chuckled.

"Scoundrel! Don't show me your rotten teeth." He boiled with anger.

"Father of a scoundrel is the worst scoundrel!" Mukesi replied. He took off. Kisiang'ani pursued him.

He ascended the anthill, fled down and took the main route to the farm. It was irksome to run through the star grass on the farm. Thrice he fell, picked himself up and sprinted, Kisiang'ani groaning behind him. Confusion reigned on the compound. Sitawa and Katami yelled, each imploring the combatants to stop.

"Run brother!" Wekhanya shrieked at Mukesi. Mukesi realized it would turn out to be the worst day of his life. Vengeance rang in him. He held his father responsible for the anger that had ripen in his heart. He had agonized enough under his tyrannical rule and would not let it go.

Now he wanted to stop and confront him but he feared to tarnish his name. Kisiang'ani flung a staff. It whizzed by and just missed his head. Mukesi reached a Mango tree and grasping the branches, swung and disappeared into the leaves. Kisiang'ani cast tens of stones onto the tree. Hastily, Mukesi swung from branch to branch amidst showers of stones.

Under the tree, Kisiang'ani paced up and down with fury. His chest was broad and naked.

"Descend and fight me if you're a man! Brat!" He growled.

"I won't!" Mukesi screamed amidst sobs. Kisiang'ani stepped forward, picked some soil clods and hurled them at the boy. The clods struck him in the ribs, shattered the skin and sprayed into his eyes. Mukesi groaned. He raved and writhed. The villages gathered along the fence to watch the unfolding drama. It was a rare offer they could not pass. Sitawa stood near her husband making entreaties with all the strength he could gather.

Mukesi restrained his temper as much as he could. A piece of wood whizzed and crushed his temple. A streak of pain ripped his nerves and blood splashed on his chest. He moaned and whined. His mind went round and round. His thoughts got muddled. He almost lost consciousness. He glanced at the ground and there glared his adversary challenging him to a fight. He let go his grip on the branches of the tree and landed on him. The two strong men grappled; their muscles twitched like fighting bulls. The older tried to sweep the younger to the ground but the latter retaliated so fiercely; the fight was at equilibrium: two Buchachas in confrontation.

There was a stalemate. Sindani rushed at the scene to separate them but the grip was too strong to untie. Mukesi disentangled himself and let go his right, left: one, two, three, four. He hit him at a close range. The flailing fists thudded from the loins, guts, mouth and forehead. They landed with the thump of a sandbag, *no*, an empty box. Sindani tried to calm the young man but stray blows caught his eyes. More blows ruptured Kisiang'ani's nose and blood trickled on his naked chest. The boy shrieked like a lunatic, plunged in a trance and ran home. Reja and Okaanya rushed at the scene to assist Kisiang'ani. It was too late.

Mukesi was beyond despair. He fell in love with violence and embraced ruin. He raved, picked a sword and swore to bring Katami's life to an end. The jittery audience at the fence diverted their attention into action to bar the hero from committing a crime. He stormed into the house and emerged with a cow hide strap. He darted towards her hut and fished her out.

Reja followed but the boy was too fast for him. Katami's shrill voice rend the air as a rain of straps consumed her feeble trunk. Her first born, Wamalwa received some straps too. Reja with other villagers advanced. Katami shrieked; blood painted her body. Wanjala attacked but a whiz of the strap scared him. More villagers advanced like the waves of the seas; he threatened them with his sword. They besieged him but every direction he moved cleared a broad highway, enough for the sea whale to slip away. A hamlet never misses a daring soul. Wanjala attacked and almost caught the knife. But his gods had gone for a swan. Mukesi swung back and let go his right foot. A kick landed on Wanjala's mouth and send him flying into the compost pit. His hand sent jets of blood.

Reja lunged forward. He encountered a fist that nearly smashed his eye balls. Omalabe tried his luck but the sword missed his eye by an inch. They retreated; the way was now clear. It was without star grass to stumble him. It had neither hillocks nor rugged potholes. He schemed his flight in a second. He sped towards the Eastern side of the hedge, hoisted his body over it and crashed on the main path to Okoro.

A few cowards tried to pursue him but his speed was too much for them. Dust rose as he disappeared into oblivion. Clouds above bulged to block the sun. The villagers shook their heads; a son had committed an abomination. By bush telegraph, it was conveyed to Butilu in Cheleba. The old lady had no other person to blame except Sitawa.

"She's training an army to frustrate Katami!" She had screamed

The villagers swore unanimously never to give Mukesi a girl for marriage. They advised Kisiang'ani to rent a house at Lwanda and settle the younger family. He heeded their advice. However, when Okaanya exhorted him to curse Mukesi, he reflected for five minutes and tears flooded his cheeks.

"Are you a man?" Okaanya asked.

"No, he is my son," He asserted.

"How can you be beaten by a boy you lay a woman to sire?"

Kisiang'ani never spoke another word to him.

Chapter Twenty Three

A unique boy he had grown to become. He was somewhat emotional but endowed with intellectual abilities. He was a loner with a super memory but shabby of airs. The female teachers of Okoro Primary School abhorred his carelessness. His tattered pair of shorts, stained shirt, unkempt hair and jigger stricken toes nauseated them. Whenever his peers asked him where the jiggers had originated, Wekhanya would say they had come from Wele to punish the home for their sin.

Sitting in the class this day, Wekhanya reflected about many issues. He could not explain why his parents could not buy him school uniform. His father's separation from his mother agonized his soul. He knew he could not request his mother to buy him even a pen; she struggled a lot to pay Masika's fees. The thought of Masika, however, consoled him. He remained the only solace in the crucible of affliction. Masika had passed his primary exams. He had taken the first position in Okoro division and secured a place in Lenana School.

It was a performance; Omumia's son had never exhibited since the inception of Okoro primary school. Many a boy who had looked down on Wekhanya now envied him. There were boys like Oriama who were not only contemptuous but also spiteful at other tribes. But Lenana as he had heard was not a school one found in a village like Okoro but the capital city, where even the head teacher of Okoro Primary School confessed never to have stepped.

A black ant bit him. It detracted his jumble of thought. He hoisted his puny body, pressed his hands in the pockets and itched the bitter part. The fact of sitting on the dusty floor haunted him but he had no option. Fated to be a son of Mwambu, Wekhanya had no right to secure a place on any desk. The boy had suffered this since his enrolment in Okoro primary school.

They had been called names having transferred from Lwanda primary school to Okoro. Masika had been denied a chance in the examination class and Wekhanya given a floor in class five. The whole family had suffered hostility. The local community, had a dislike for these sons of Mwambu. Consequently, Wekhanya with his siblings were called emoit, a local name for Satan.

In the class, girls sat fronting him on the dusty floor. They stretched their feet with backs leaning against the wall. The majority of boys sat on the desks. The prefect, tall dark boy roamed from one end to the other caning noise makers and teasing emoit. He came to him and stared at his face. Wekhanya was busy extracting plaque from his teeth.

"Emoit!" He roared, "don't stare at me. Your mouth stinks!" He thundered and pushed his mouth away. Wekhanya's soul sizzled with violence. He wanted to fight him but he feared his physical size. Oriama was fierce, older and massive. Some of his classmates were Mukesi's age mates but were still in primary school.

What upset him most this time were the jiggers. They embarrassed and humiliated him. They eroded all his self-esteem. Pupils hummed around him. Some laughed and others giggled; some tickled and other pinched. Caro, a pretty girl, giggled and pointed a finger at him. Wekhanya faltered and checked his fly. Oh, his penis peeped out of the tattered shorts. Oriama rose and swaggered to where he was. He frowned at Wekhanya.

"Emoit!" He growled.

"What?" Wekhanya asked.

"Jiggers!" Oriama thundered, gesturing at his feet.

"Ugh, leave me alone," the boy protested.

"You've infected the class with jiggers!" Oriama continued.

"So?"

"Don't say that emoit! I'll get your foot and remove those jiggers!" Oriama insisted and bent to pick his right foot.

He jabbed his nails in the wounded sole. Yellow pus oozed from the wound. Oriama released him. Wekhanya broke down, hemmed in by children with complaining faces, "Emoit lo!"

They lamented about the devils that had brought jiggers from Lwanda primary school. They swore to tell the head teacher to expel them from Okoro. It was sheer fib; Lwanda had no jiggers. The sandy and loamy soils of Lwanda could not provide suitable conditions to nourish the vermin. The parasites had been left in the home by relatives who had come from Cheleba to condemn Mukesi's rebellion.

They had stayed for weeks cursing and disowning the boy. Kisiang'ani had refused to say a word. How he had desired to warn them against careless use of the tongue.

He was too proud to confess but he knew what it meant for a parent to open his mouth to curse. Masika and Wekhanya were confounded at their partial judgment. As eye witnesses, they had seen Mukesi's provocation. How could they forget the stones that had ripped his temple? As if that could not hurt them sufficiently, they had infected the compound with jiggers.

The home was rife with vermin. They invaded everywhere. Katami's sons were bitten from toes, fingers, heels, shins and penises. Wekhanya pitied Watila, the second born when Kisiang'ani discovered a jigger on his penis. He pushed the foreskin backwards to dislodge the vermin. He inserted the sisal thorn and the boy screamed in terror. Blood spurt and oozed along his thighs to the ground. Watila had a foretaste of circumcision. Wekhanya had pleaded with his father to suffocate the jigger with paraffin; he had obeyed him.

Wallowing in embarrassment, Wekhanya limped towards a tree behind the classroom and sat down to wipe the pus in the sole of his foot. He felt rejected. He was rubbish disposed in a compost pit, he was shit to be ejected from a pit latrine. A pang of self-pity ripped through his soul. Wekhanya regretted why he was born.

His puny stomach rumbled. He was hungry. The thought of hunger took him back to a few years ago when famine lay siege to Okoro. It was a time when adults ran around shouting, "Ford Kenya, Simba! Haki na Ukweli, Ford Asili." It was hard for Wekhanya to explain. All he heard was the president's perpetual condemnation of the 'noise makers'.

As the noise proceeded, cassava became the staple food in Okoro. Wondering-Jew and other weeds like MacDonald's eye were its sole accompaniment. Kisiang'ani degenerated into semi-lunacy. He could pluck green maize on the farm, uproot cassava on the farm and snatch plates on the rack to exchange them for liquor. The mania pursued him to the present. These reprehensible acts embittered Wekhanya.

At the political scene was the normal blame game. State house accused vidole mbilis (pressure for multiparty democracy) for sabotaging the government to the International Mother and Father.

There was subsequent cessation of foreign aid. This coupled with massive looting of public coffers resulted in crumbling of industries. Okoro felt the pinch.

The bell rang. It was lunch time. Wekhanya picked his way behind the school pit latrine and hobbled his way home. Few pupils overtook him.

"Look, he's limping," one of them shouted.

"His toes are….re...fat," said another.

"He has jiggers," said yet another.

"I'll beat you!" Wekhanya snarled.

The children scampered down the slope like chicken escaping the claws of an eagle. Wekhanya became downcast. A crowd of boys and girls trailed behind him. His ear could perceive Oriama's voice admonishing, insulting and molesting.

"Tell him to remove jiggers!" He could hear him roaring at Wamalwa.

The words cut through his heart and his thoughts became morbid.

Wekhanya hobbled on. He reached the junction and left the route to Lwanda. As he picked the narrow path home, a tipsy man caught his sight. He had unkempt hair. His hands gripped the distended belly firmly. His pair of trousers were dilapidated and dusty. With hands still at the tummy he sang a dismal tune :

Nalila Kisiang'ani nalila	*I weep Kisiang'ani I weep*
Nalila Kisiang'ani nalila	*I weep Kisiang'ani I weep*
Nalila Kisiang'ani nalila	*I weep Kisiang'ani I weep*
Nalila Kisiang'ani nalila	*I weep Kisiang'ani I weep*

Although the tune was sorrowful, the dance was extremely humourous. He thumped his feet; he stopped. He thumped them again and staggered in Wekhanya's direction. The red patches at the knees, the black pullover and broad face convinced Wekhanya that the comedian was his father. So shamefaced he was that he hated him. Shamelessly, he thumped forward and mingled in the crowd of pupils. Oriama then got a chance to tease,

"Who is this drunkard?"

"He is a teacher," two boys replied.

"I don't know him," said Oriama in pretence, "Wekhanya, who is he?"

"He is Wekhanya's father," the children said innocently.

Wekhanya loathed his father. He wanted to denounce him. He did not see himself as a person any longer. Who was a person without reputation.

"Why is father always shaming us?" The boy asked himself. Kisiang'ani changed his song and danced gyrating his waist.

Onulile rarao kumwena,oo!	*You have taken your father's groin*
Onulile rarao	*You've taken your father's wife*
Nanuumbolela chisoni mukholo	*Who has ashamed me in the clan?*
Omwana wange Mukesi	*My son Mukesi*
Anulile sese kumwena,oo.	*Has taken away my wife*

The dance intensified into a frenzy. His waist vibrated fast, his hand at the belly. Something tripped from the belly and children flew into peals of laughter. Wekhanya stole a glance from a distance. He was horrified to see big cassava tuber. The cassava farm had lost peace; his shebeen queen in Okoro was going to celebrate. She received plates, cups, knives, kettles, clothes and shoes. Everything fetched a price on the local brew markets of Okoro: women, girls, mud blocks and even staffs.

"Oh, chang'aa!" Wekhanya exclaimed, "who the hell gave birth to you? A Wanangali that turned our home into a desolate place!" He turned to the song. The message was wrapped in a taboo language. He meant Mukesi had snatched Katami from him. What a false accusation!

The boy limped home, his heart apprehensive of what was imminent. Although they had met, he knew he would return and pick a quarrel with him. He went round the bend and came into the compound. He went straight for the door of their hut. Alas! It lay supine on the floor. He could see everything in the hut from the entrance. He saw the dilapidated suitcase, wooden box, rickety bed, flimsy table and little oil lamp. That was an augury of the real menace to come.

He tottered to the cupboard, and brought out a plate of cassava mingled with soup of wandering Jew. It was the staple food since the advent of multi-party democracy in the nation. Wekhanya devoured it, spitting stabs. Some tubers had a bitter taste and they made him feel nauseated. All of a sudden, a feeling of personal danger fell on him. He deserted his meal on the table and stole out. Her late sister's grave caught his sight and widened the scope of sorrow.

"Had she been permitted to live, she would have fulfilled his purpose on Earth,' Wekhanya shook his head. A song detracted his flow of thought:

You reject your father	*Oloba rarao*
You reject your father	*Oloba rarao*
The boy with bad manners	*Omwana wembelekeu*

Is indeed, Wekhanya.   *Ewe Wekhanya.*

The boy was shocked. The mention of his name stirred him into a rage. Had Kisiang'ani not shamed him enough? Why did he follow him to obliterate the remnant of self-esteem in his soul? He moved a few paces ahead and the seasoned oral artist came right into his vision. With a bottle in his hands, he skipped two strides forward, tightened his grip on the bottle and performed a frisky kamabeka dance. On perceiving his scanty audience, the artist repeated his stanza passionately to elicit response. In spite of the foolish gimmicks, Wekhanya unearthed exceptional creativity in his father.

The man seemed to launch his creative impulse somewhere in a vacuum to extract a work of art with style and message relevant to the social situation. He played around with words and the sound of his cords to produce a moving piece. His creative works drove the informal audience to tears as they dug down his downcast soul, unraveling past bitterness, fanning past wounds and complaining over them. Tears could be seen streaming down his cheeks at the climax of his performance, his improvised drum at the most appropriate rhythm of the song.

While sober, he refused to sing. He could only flatter African pop artist like Franco and Pepe Kale in Zaire, Chico Chikaya in West Africa and Yvonne Machaka in South Africa.

Perhaps it was not wrong to say that Kisiang'ani was a mentally gifted man whose environment was too wanting to empower him climb the stair case to his praxis. Although his anger outbursts made him as choleric as Buchacha, his continuous fits of depression assigned him melancholy temperament.

Wekhanya was touched by Kisiang'ani's predicament. He saw him as a man of talent but incapable of utilizing it well. If he only channeled his emotions and fancy to the entertainment industry, he would be a great man.

Otherwise, he saw his father as an ineffective teacher. Did he know that it was a Thursday? Was his Head Teacher aware of his absence? How could a teacher at lower primary, master of all, miss a class to uproot cassava to exchange for Chang'aa. Who was a teacher? A good example in everything; a mason of the foundation of development.

What values was his father inculcating among children in Okoro? Wekhanya had asked his father,

"Dad, what example are you giving this village?" Kisiang'ani stopped his song and gazed at his innocent son. How could he explain for him to understand. He scratched himself.

He placed the palm of his right hand on his cheek and wrecked his brains. His innocent children failed to understand him. They lacked the wisdom and discernment to see through his predicament. Who among the sons of Mwambu had successfully endured the aunt's lamentation? What about a curse? Could Wekhanya understand this? Could the boy elaborate the consequences of breaking a marriage vows? Did he understand how it felt to be pampered by a pretty house girl as your wife scorned you? Kisiang'ani wondered whether his son could unravel the puzzle underlying his anguish. Resolving that the boy was a mere fool, he decided to give him a physical treat.

"Be off you rat!" He croaked.

"Why did you break our door," the boy shrilled.

"I'll castrate you!" The man roared.

He flounced ahead and picked a hoe with a short wooden handle. Wekhanya sprang up and ran. He gathered all energies and pursued him. They ascended an ant-hill and descended over the little grave. They sprinted through the star grass and picked the main path to the Sindani's. Kisiang'ani stumbled over a cassava stump and flat he went to the ground. The boy sped into Sindani's compound. He thanked his swift limps.

Kisiang'ani rose again, panting like a buffalo. He picked his hoe, raised it high and swung after the boy. It was such a demonic speed that within five seconds, the hoe was above his head. The gods seemed to have let go Wekhanya's luck. A star grass caught his leg. He tumbled in a pot hole, rolled twice and using somersault stood and sped on. He heaved. He panted. He saw the hoe above his forehead, the man swearing to chop him. He then shrieked at the top of his lungs. He saw doom, darkness and death.

But why would he live anyway? Had he ever lived since he was born? He was born in death and he died every day. Life to him was death and perhaps by dying he would live.

"Swerve!" a thought came to him. He swerved northwards. Kisiang'ani tried to turn but crashed in a sisal hedge as the boy fled through the coffee farm to Reja's.

"Catch...the...brat!" Kisiang'ani shouted at Reja.

Reja emerged and tried to intercept the boy. Wekhanya thrust a crumb of cassava that had by chance remained in his hand. It smashed on his nose and sprayed into his eyes. With a groan, Reja collapsed in his tattered shirt to cleanse his eyes.

"Your brats resemble you!" Reja roared, "they're all rascals like you!"

It created a chance for the triumphant flight of 'the brat'.

He skidded under the lantana hedge, hopped onto the main path and sped to school. He raised dust as he gathered his energies on his race to salvation. He did not feel the hunger; at least he was alive...

Chapter Twenty Four

"**I**s this the boy you chased?" The man asked pointing at Wekhanya.

"Yes, how did you know?" Kisiang'ani affirmed, astounded.

"I knew at the instant that you chased not just a child but a uncircumcised boy," the man boasted.

"Omukuka (ancestor) Wekhombe, how did you know?"

"My heart got bruised, I lost peace. I consulted ancestors and they told me to come here."

"What do you mean, Omukuka?" Kisiang'ani asked mesmerized.

"I'm saying your ancestors need something done."

"Like?"

"Welcome them home."

Wekhombe spoke authoritatively as the true seer of Wele. He pinched his snuff into the nose and proceeded with his magical instruction. He apologized for delaying to respond to a case he had diagnosed a couple of years before. He insisted that he had tried to resist this mission but three of Kisiang'ani's ancestors: Buchacha, Puraimu and Milisio had compelled him to come. Buchacha, he insisted was the most persistent. He had spoken to him that very afternoon while Kisiang'ani was chasing the boy.

Kisiang'ani listened with all keenness to every word that dropped from the seer's mouth. He analyzed them one by one and related it to the impropriety of his conduct that afternoon. There before his eyes stood the solution to his predicament. He pardoned the failings of his children from Mukesi to Wekhanya.

He saw Wekhombe as his protection against all the enemies of life. He now had a spiritual insight into his problem. Why would all his children including Rachel and Wekhanya despise him? A sorcerer might have done something.

Kisiang'ani regretted having ignored Sindani's advice to seek help in Ukambani, a land renowned for its astute diviners. Here was a mother whose sons were free from detrimental effects of adultery and theft. She encouraged men to work hard and dig their own wells to enjoy their own water. If you violated her rules and dipped your stick in somebody's well, it stuck in it in as long as the owner wished. Words were spoken about the power of these seers. They could command a thief's hand to recede into the stomach. If you stole his cock he could command it to crow from your stomach.

"Your neighbor," Wekhombe whispered.

"What?" Kisiang'ani almost shouted.

"Don't shout. What bites you stays in your clothes."

"Please repeat what you've just said."

"Your neighbours…picked your hair," Wekhombe said, pointing at the Sindani's.

"Sure," Kisiang'ani sighed.

"Do you see that murembe tree?" He asked. His finger gestured at Sindani's farm.

"Yes."

"The witch has raised a serpent under the tree."

"What for?" Kisiang'ani wondered.

"To lay on your hair and your children's."

"Then?"

"You rave mad," Wekhombe blurted.

"What can I do then?"

"I should insert talisman in you."

"I see."

"Hang a protective charm around your neck."

"Yes."

"Erect a shrine in your home to welcome your ancestors."

"Will you need something to grease your palm."

"A miller eats in the grind mill. I told you the first time we met."

"All right."

"I forgot something…"

"Huh huh?"

"No, I'll tell you later," he said as an afterthought.

"Tell me."

"Bakuka have refused," he snarled as he left the home.

Chapter Twenty Five

Superstition was on every lip in Okoro. It formed the core of each soul. The poor attributed all misconduct to bad spirits. The sons of Mwambu believed in one Creator whom they called Wele Khakaba– the generous giver of heaven. Wele spoke through Bakuka, the ancestors, who in turn sent the message through abang'osi- seers to the people. The seers foretold the future, initiated people in the vocation and handled other mysterious challenges in the spiritual realm.

They also believed in the existence of evil spirits called bisieno. In Okoro, these wicked spirits were called Kamaembe, literal translation, Mangoes. These lethal spirits were hoarded by malicious people called balosi- witches. Balosi were trained by their fathers from childhood into mastery of the craft.

Among the most dreaded witch in Okoro was the man Sindani. Grapevine had it that in his giant Murembe tree flourished a gigantic snake that determined the destiny of many in the village. It was also said that he possessed a mystic staff with powers that squeezed out the spirit of anybody it was pointed at. Indeed as Kisiang'ani came to know, Sindani had lost his two sons mysteriously.

Wekhombe's implication of the man as a root cause of his predicament was only a confirmation of his fears. Throughout Okoro, he was renowned as a master shooter of spells and destroyer of marriages. He then rested his faith in Wekhombe who complied to execute his mission with infinite relish.

The sun was struggling to emerge from oppressive clouds that roofed the plains of Okoro. A vast blanket of mist slithered from Mount Masaba and crawled in the flat plain of Okoro. It obstructed sight, impeded movement and waned activity. In the misty home, Wekhombe slaughtered the first prescription of his cure: a she goat. He skinned it and roast the meat. The doctor with his patient feasted on the meat; he spared a few scrapes for erecting the shrine to conjure up the ancestors. Part of the liver was stuck on a sharp stick and stabbed at the heart of the compound. Wekhombe then erected a shrine in Katami's house.

It was a pyramidal structure made of papyrus reeds. At the centre of it was a dark basket containing a buffalo's tail, three cowries, and a long calabash with pebbles. Wekhombe explained how his patient was to use the medicine. Kisiang'ani had to rattle the calabash in the morning and evening as a thank offering to the ancestors. He would also rattle it when he got depressed.

"And when you shake the chisasi- the gourd, listen. The ancestors speak!" Wekhombe advised. He demonstrated.

"We're here…" voices whispered from the cowrie shells.

"You see, those are bakuka," Wekhombe said gaily.

"I see," Kisiang'ani replied full of joy.

"Now bring your sons to get the talisman!" The seer ordered.

Kisiang'ani rushed outside to usher in his offspring. Unfortunately, he found Wekhanya detaching the piece of liver from the stick at the centre of the home. The boy did not see why a good source of protein was idling there.

"You fool, trouble maker, devil take you!" Kisiang'ani roared and picked a stone to fling at the boy.

"Hark!" The boy cursed and skipped into the banana plantation. He missed the protective charm. The rest were rounded up: Wamalwa, Wataka, Khaemba, Rachel, Katami,

Wanyonyi were incised and insured against bisieno. He then rummaged through his bag and brought out a thin leather string that he secure tied around Kisiang'ani's neck. He whipped out his flywhisk, waggled it above the patient's head and muttered some magical incantations. He reinforced it by spraying jets of saliva on him. He whipped out his holy water from the bag and sprinkled it on his patient. He pondered for awhile and then asserted that there was one ritual he had not performed because one bull was missing. Kisiang'ani had presented two goat, and one fat bull.

"You haven't brought a brown bull, you see," he complained.

"Money's a big problem my friend," the patient pleaded.

"I'm not your friend," the man changed, "I am Omukuka."

"I'm sorry, Omukuka, I'll settle the debt later."

"Then I can't complete my assignment."

"Haven't you finished?"

"No, I haven't initiated you to become omung'osi."

"So what next?"

"You pay, I finish. If I disobey ancestors, they'll finish me, you see!" He chuckled.

"Give me some days," the patient pleaded.

"All right, where're my things?"

"Which...?"

"Didn't I tell you?"

"There's something you promised to tell me on the material day."

"Haya, I must depart with everything that was within my sight during the ritual."

"What do you mean?" Sitawa asked sharply.

"I mean you served me on those dishes," he pointed at Sitawa's best utensils, "pack them for me! I listened to the gramophone, pack it now!"

"Ei?" Kisiang'ani doubted.

"Do it if you want to live tomorrow," the man warned calmly. Kisiang'ani gazed at his weird airs and gave in.

"I slept in those blankets, pack them! That bicycle carried the bread I ate, I go with it!"

Wekhombe counted and counted. Kisiang'ani secretly prayed that the man did not point at any of his wives especially Katami. He gathered everything the seer gestured at from the rags, hoes, knives, including the clothes his children wore while undergoing the surgery. Wekhanya got dumbfounded when the man pointed at the shutter on the pit latrine. Wataka and Rachel could not suppress their laughter.

Kisiang'ani sounded a tough warning to all his children because any disobedience would be punished by death. Wekhombe lumbered away, the bicycle looted and loaded.

Twenty Six

After one month, Masika tumbled in Okoro from school. He had been sent home for fees. Looking at the boy keenly, it was not just school fees he needed. From his head to the toes, his attire had a lot to desire.

Masika studied at his father and pitied him. He was physically emaciated, materially poor and 'mentally beheaded'. He could not comment on the spiritual; the rest was history. Even the sweet music of his home that he had cherished like chicken had been replaced by a parochial rattle- a calabash with pebbles. Masika could not see how this half seer could pay fees; he was in his own world.

The boy turned to music for solace. He sang Reggae and Lucky Dube became his idol.

"I am a prisone aa a a a...a.a...a," he could sing with passion. As Wekhanya observed, his brother would soon be a prisoner like his father; singing a lot but making no use of the talent for any gain. Masika got disappointed. The bicycle had gone, the lambs had waned, one brown bull had gone and he could not plough with one bull. The gramophone was missing; the economic status of the home had flopped.

He shuddered at the circumstances and hugged the wish to die early. His father was degenerating; his spirits were irrevocable. He had lost a sound manner of looking at things. In Masika's view, he was quite unhinged. Twice he had observed him come home, march into Katami's house, and rattle calabashes like the Kenya ape man at Fort Tenan

"Hell!" Masika cursed with confidence. The change irritated him. He had been content with a drunkard. He would not adjust to a Kenya ape man? The boy was getting disillusioned. On the fourth day at home, he accosted him,

"Father, I've been sent home for fees," he asserted as Kisiang'ani was leaving the shrine.

Kisiang'ani was tipsy but sober enough to think.

"Sitawa! Sitawa!" He called his wife.

"Eeee!"

"We must sell a piece of land for our son to learn!" He asserted.

"We won't," Sitawa refused.

"We must!"

"Our farm isn't enough inheritance for our sons," Sitawa said.

"There's no land inheritance in this home."

"Noah, what'll they inherit?"

"Education!"

"But…"

"No arguments. Our sons are bright. Masika will go all the way to university."

"But there're no jobs for the learned nowadays. Graduates are tarmacking."

"Sitawa, there're no tarmac roads in Okoro. Say they're potholing or murruming, a ha!"

Sitawa laughed too. Masika became hopeful but an inexplicable feeling of doubt conquered his heart.

"But there're jobs for those who pass," Kisiang'ani persisted.

"We must give our children education from Wataka, Wamalwa to Rachel and Wekhanya- the trouble maker, a ha! Even that one is thick, upstairs!" He chortled. Masika got shocked at those chortles.

He returned to his shrine; the soul of his creative works. Here he composed and sang moving songs while rattling his percussion instrument. Wekhanya who had observed his father throughout from the pre to post Wekhombe era, doubted the seers therapy. It was ineffective if not a fiasco. Masika declared it a fraud. It had inflated Kisiang'ani's melancholy, bloated his self-pity and soured his despondency. He sang more sentimentally, he danced more vigorously and bartered everything for chang'aa. He stopped singing and dashed out,

"Sitawa," He called.

"Eeee!"

"Do you remember the dance we attended?"

"Huh," Sitawa hummed with embarrassment.

"I wanted you to recall Chuma, our bouncer."

"What about him?"

"He told me that whoever beats his father, his son will beat him."

Sitawa did not say a word. Her husband looked tormented by many things from the past.

His eyes had beads of tears.

Masika and Wekhanya got startled. Their father carried generations of burdens on his heart. His confession gave him temporary relieve. Nonetheless, it gave Wekhanya food for thought. Did his father mean that Mukesi's rebellion was predetermined? He saw it as a wrong bearing of things. Mukesi's defiance was a normal human reaction against tyranny. He wished to know the whole story about his conflict with the grandfather but he understood the arrogance of elders among the son's of Mwambu could provoke resistance.

The boy grew to learn the consequences of creating a hostile environment for the growth of a human being. The seed of violence is sown and groomed to suit in the hostile surroundings. It comes naturally to survive in the environment; that's why he had cast a stone at Reja and sped away without penitence. He felt guilty.

Secondly, the boy learned that beer, was a traitor. He could reveal your secrets to the enemy. They were embarrassed to understand that their good mother had once attended a night dance with a boyfriend. It reminded Wekhanya a story Sitawa had told him,

"Long long time ago, there lived a beautiful girl called Mila. Mila looked down on many suitors who came to ask for her hand in marriage.

With her father, they called suitors names. They called some poor and others ugly. His father's chief aim was to sell his daughter at an expensive price to grow rich in goats, sheep and cattle.

One day as they were doing their normal duties, a handsome young man appeared in the village. Bubulo, for that was the village's name, had become famous owing to the presence of a the beautiful maiden. He said he had trekked all the way from Mwombe, a world of yards away to come and betroth Mila.

Muliongo, Mila's father, was extremely elated. After a customary interrogations it dawned on him that Tatabasiani, the prospective son in-law was not only wealthy but also descended from the wealthiest family in Mwombe.

Marriage negotiations had begun and in three days, Muliongo had married his daughter to the handsome man in the richest clan of his people. The wedding had been as pompous as need be.

Two years after her marriage, Mila could not be spotted, in weddings, at the well or anywhere both in Bubulo and

Mwombe. Moons became seasons; no one set an eye on the beauty of Bubulo.

A wife belonged to society; Mila's beauty was society's beauty. Although she was not their spouse, her beauty was food for their eyes. They also hoped that her beautiful daughter would marry their sons.

Whenever they accosted her husband about the subject, he would only reply that Mila had gone to visit his family in Butilu. It made them all edgy.

It then happened that Mila's father arranged for a feast to celebrate a bumper harvest of millet. He prepared busaa and invited most of his relatives. They ate, ate and ate. They drank, drank and drank. The son in-law was excited. People began boasting about their achievements. He decided to boast too.

"Give me the Litungu!" Tatabasiani ordered his father in-law.

Muliungo gave him, the traditional guitar. He began singing:

Mayi wa Mila solila Milaakobole Tatabasiani
Litonda liaMila nanavilakhwitungu, Tatabasiani.
Papa wa Mila Solila Mila akobole Tatabasiani
Litondo lia Mila nanavila khwitungu Tatabasiani.

Mila's mother, weep until Mila resurrects
Mila's father weep until Mila resurrects
I have knitted her navel on my guitar

Mila's relatives weep for Mila to come back to life
Mila's people why can't you weep for her to resurrect?
Her navel have I knitted on my guitar.

Tipsy as he was, Tatabasiani released all his secrets to his enemies. It was terribly shocking for Muliungo to discover that the man was not only an ogre but had also eaten the jewel of his life. The women wept as the men locked him from inside. They set the hut ablaze and Tatabasiani was reduced to ashes. That is what beer can do," Sitawa had finished the story.

With cogent reasons, Kisiang'ani had convinced Sitawa to sell a piece of land for Masika to resume his studies. The selling price was thirty thousand shillings but the man paid ten thousand in cash. Kisiang'ani received the cash, hands shaking. Pressing the wad of notes in his trouser pockets, he admonished Masika for idling and singing around instead of preparing for departure. Masika put on hastily and accompanied his tipsy father to Okoro market. They boarded a matatu to Bangamek. Kisiang'ani then led his son to Blue Waves Bar and Restaurant.

"One beer and one Coke!" He ordered the waiter in a gruff voice.

The waiter responded quickly. After five minutes, another order came,

"Ten beers!" Kisiang'ani roared, "two fantas for my son!"

Masika refused to eat. He could not feast now and 'fast' in future. It was a moment to sacrifice, it was a moment to fast. He commiserated over his father.

"Please father, may I have my fees?" Masika requested.

Darkness closed in on them.

"It was my farm remember, no orders," he warned.

He frisked his pockets and pulled out a few leafs of notes. When Masika counted, it was five thousand.

"Lo! Five thousand only...?" He cried, "The fees balance is twenty two thousand!"

"Ugh! That's rude," blurted Kisiang'ani, "a good son should be grateful for the little he receives."

Kisiang'ani swaggered away from Blue Waves. Masika's eyes followed him. He saw him enter Kingeti Bar and Restaurant. Never say die, Masika had to hang on life. He boarded the bus to Nairobi.

Sitawa with her children at home were cock-sure that the father had taken Masika to school. The night was dark and frogs could be heard croaking from a distance. The geckos sang and crickets creeked. At ungodly hours of the night, a hoarse voice of a man rend the air,

"Bananas! Bananas! Bananas!"

The voice woke the children up in the house and then disappeared into the banana plantation again. The props fell and stems fell; the man harvested them. Kisiang'ani strutted into the house heavy laden with bananas on his shoulder. He boiled them without hulling. He picked a steel basin, emptied five litres of Kerosene in it and set it ablaze. The flames attacked the fuel with a boom and whirled all directions.

"Chicken! Chicken! Chicken!" He shouted. He pranced along the floor and caught a hen. The hen squeaked as he hurled it into the dancing flames. The hen flew across the flames. He grabbed it and flung it to the heart of the flame with dramatic violence. The whiff of smouldering feathers filled the sitting room as the delicious meal edged towards seasoning.

"You want to finish Mukesi's chicken," Sitawa mumbled from the bed.

"Look, do you wish me dead? You can't even sympathize?"

"What for?"

"I tumbled in a deep pit at Okoro Primary."

"Oh, I'm sorry, how did you come to that?"

"I had just left Wambilianga's Bar at the market. I picked a short cut through the school when I saw myself descending down down down…in…the dark."

"Ei! then…."

"I found myself at the bottom with bruised knees."

"Why do you walk at night..."

"Listen first. Something rattled under my feet."

"What?"

"A snake!"

"Oh, mother!"

"It had coiled itself in a corner. It began recoiling upon sensing me."

"Uuuuuwi," Sitawa screamed, "what did you do?"

"I thank Bakuka for strength. I threw my arms at the sides and climbed."

"So you escaped the bite?"

"Can't you hear my voice? A man is a man!" He boasted, "I only left my shoes there."

"We'll send someone tomorrow," Sitawa suggested.

"Wekhanya, the trouble maker, ha, ha, ha!" He chortled.

Chapter Twenty Seven

If the minds of people are locked up in caves of obscurity. If their eyes never see beyond their circumference. If their souls are bound to their narrow way of life and their attitudes impenetrable to new ideas. Then they embrace ethnicity, kiss nepotism and court anarchy.

Races and tribes like parents and relatives are predetermined in life. They are gifts the Creator appropriates as He wills. They are statuses we are ascribed to and it hurts to segregate any person basing on them. Should there be any culture or religion that advocated such prejudices, it was at Mukesi's warpath.

People are people had become his saying. They all suffered the same diseases, they all felt the need for security, they all dreaded poverty and all had red blood in their arteries. When it came to Africa, Mukesi believed that they all worshipped the Creator though with a different name. The sons of Mwambu called him Wele, sons of Ramogi, Nyasaye, sons of Gikuyu, Ngai and Bayobos, Asis. Consequently, he did not see why he would start hating Wanjiko just because she called her Wele, Ngai.

Mukesi viewed this as the summit of retrogration. It had caused holocausts in Zaire, Somalia, Rwanda and Burundi. Who could understand and measure the bitterness he had for it. Who could gauge the depth that the axe had scooped in his soul except himself, having witnessed Maruti, Sindani's son, shot in the cold blood.

He had seen wiry men that Saturday. They had worn tattered masks, and shorts. They were raiding and torching all houses belonging to other tribes. Bangamek was a Kalenjin word and hence they wanted to repossess the district and send all the sons of Mwambu packing. They had passed Reja's home, Masengo's and reached Okaanya's home. The first two villagers owned nothing and so there was nothing to steal. They tried to round up Okaanya's cattle but they sped in all directions. What a mystery! They moved on to Wabomba's home. He escaped. They pursued him. They ran round and round ducking bananas and trees.

The ruffians finally caught him, tied him on a banana stem and shot him thrice on the stomach. The booms of the killer had ripped the air and Wabomba had gone leaving a crowd of orphans. The brutes had then crossed the river and emerged through the Kisiang'ani's. With his father, Mukesi had hidden in the cave behind the kitchen. Indeed they would have never lived to see the sun again. Showers of bullets had sprayed the home. The metals had jerked red sparks on the powerful rock. They had left with three bulls.

At the Sindani's, Maruti, his third borne had refused to let go the cattle. He had argued with them; they had sprayed twelve bullets on his chest. In Lwanda, eight sons of Mwambu had walked into the gang. The boys were naked, going to be circumcised; the ruffians had charged with machetes and beheaded them. They had collapsed dead, emitting urine and blood from the same spot.

These were just but few of the dangerous benefits of declining national integration and exalting tribalism, segregating others and cherishing one's own; elevating yours on the staircase of worth and casting your neighbor's in the gutter. On the outside they hollered our culture our pride: in the heart posed the stench of ethnocentrism.

To his acquaintances Mukesi said, "It's good to love your people but it's also good to know that Kenya has many other peoples."

Following his expulsion at home, Mukesi had wandered on God's earth and ended up at his friend's home in Naivasha. He worked as a tout then a watchman. He had spurned the temptations and perils of the night and then started taking up building contracts in town. Mujengo, as they called it, was paying but unreliable. He had then left for Kabati to work on a horticultural farm. He had ascended to the post of the clerk but sacked for being so bookish. Mukesi had fallen in love with novels.

On his desk, you did not miss a copy of *Weep Not Child* or *Petals of Blood*. In the house, his peers confronted volumes of *Great Expectations, Oliver Twist* and *Othello*.

He loved Dickens right from his biography to his works. He failed to understand how a man could have a poor father like him and still rise to a celebrity status. It inspired him.

As he sat in his room this afternoon, his muse was lively. He gazed at the beautiful flowers of Naivasha and became poetic. He launched himself somewhere in oblivion and wrote a poem about Dickens.

Release him, release him,
He who watered the seedling of the new genre,
He who tended the garden of English prose;

Release him, silent cemetery:
Westminster Abbey,

Release him to minister to Mystery of Edwin Drood,
He desperately needs the expertise of his hands.

Release him,
He whose works traverse generations:
Hard times, Bleak house, Great Expectations;
A dexterous spider, a restless ant.

We miss you, Dickens
At the Poet's Corner
I bitterly mourn but
though you died, you live.

Mukesi read through his poem. He was tremendously pleased with himself. 'I'm a writer,' he thought. 'You're a general worker,' another thought struck him. He insisted that he was a writer but the education system had not given him an opportunity to exploit his talent. The 8-4-4 system had starved his artistic impulse by accessing him to only one novel at high school.

Nonetheless, Mukesi encouraged himself that although he looked seventy at thirty five years of age, his aspirations were as tender as puberty. He longed to become a prolific writer, the first ever from the caves of Okoro. Obviously, he would take journalism and his life with Wanjiko would be exemplary.

Now that noun took a special place on the menu of Mukesi's memory. Whenever he picked a mouse and double clicked on the icon, 'Wanjiko,' the contents were mesmerizing: Age, thirty six; height, four feet six; complexion, brown; waist, plump and massive; calves, fat; waist, Luhya taste; hair, wigged and heart, refined. She was not uncultivated.

She was a general worker in Agenda Flower Company limited but carried herself with dignity. Her skirt was neither too high nor too low. She cherished romance and music, the virtues she found in Mukesi. She also found him progressive but she almost hated him when he revealed that he was not circumcised.

She had taken three days to explain the importance of circumcision. It's hygienic reasons and reduction of chances for contracting HIV. On the third day, he got persuaded. During one of his leaves, she had taken him to hospital and out of her money had him circumcised. These are some of the incidences that strengthened their cord of love.

She remained his intimate friend and they shared everything. She even persuaded Mukesi to attend church services. The first time in two decades, Mukesi stepped in church. He began learning a lot about the character of God. Mukesi did not see the stereotypes people created around her tribe in her. Secretly, he vowed he would hold dedicated her love and make it historic that his final romantic pledge was uttered to a heart so dear to assist him carry his miseries. It was his nature not to 'mix' ladies. His darling yearned for deep kisses but he avoided them; he hated pre-marital sex.

Someone knocked at the door of his room and Wanjiko strolled in.

"Hi dear."

"Hi, sweety."

Mukesi raised his head from the voluminous piles of books. Clad in a purple pair of shorts and green singlet, Mukesi was studying *A Tale of Two Cities*. He cried with Dr Manette and sneered at Stryver. The entry of his fiancée charmed his soul. Her cooing voice alone was a spice of their affair that was two years of age. It was a nicety wanting in the daughters of Okoro. The few he had come across were abrasive and hostile. This had impeded him from making head way in love. But the daughters of Mumbi were very feminine in body and soul. Some as he came to learn, stuck to the Western movies to learn the current trends of dress and speech. Swarms of bees, they had learnt, never flew towards raw flowers but fragrant ones.

And Mukesi exulted in his broad mind. It had given him a beautiful wife. He admired the way she pronounced those romantic niceties: my dear, dearest dear, my darling, dearest darling. They always inspired him to love.

Mukesi showed him an armchair and she slumped in it utterly disgusted by his romantic drought.

"I have missed you," she cooed.

"I have likewise missed you," he replied.

"I'm scared by what's happening."

"What?"

"Persistent rapes on the farm."

"Someone raped?"

"My friend Caro."

"You mean to say…?"

"You men are beasts, very weak!"

"No, maniacs. Not all men are weak, dear."

Mukesi served her with cakes.

"Even, you," Wanjiko pointed a finger at him.

"It's you ladies who can't bear with a man's attraction."

They laughed it off and munched their cakes. Wanjiko turned as loquacious as was her custom. She found it so pleasurable to be in presence of this man whose origin was alien to hers. She stole a glance at him: streamlined face, muscular arms, broad chest and dark complexion. Although insolent sometimes, that pondering look made him the handsomest man to have ever proposed to her. Whenever he smiled to her, she melted into waters for him to drink. But he refused to drink. The tribal qualms remained trillions of miles away. The untidy room, the haphazardly arranged table, she could not see. She was ready to pick the ripe fruit of pleasure, love, yes; romance…

"When…will…you….marry….me?" She asked, drunk.

"We should see your parents first," Mukesi replied.

"We don't need to. People just get married."

"No, darling, we have to."

"Why, my dearest…..?" She whispered.

"My conscience demands so."

"My love, don't be a perfectionist," she cooed.

"You've got to wait a bit, I've got no money."

"Sweetie, who told you I came for money?"

"You guys love it," blurted Mukesi.

"Oh, avoid those stereotypes, sweetie, Ngai! oh!" She broke down.

"I meant ladies not you…"

She wept the pint.

Mukesi was touched; he had hurt his darling. He raised her to her feet and kissed her. Wanjiko passed her hands around his waist and caressed him. She reciprocated the kiss, her tongue stirring his. Their hearts drummed in each other dispelling loneliness. There was something that exhorted him to undress her. His mind was intact; Wanjiko dead in his arms. He extricated himself from her and lay her on the bed. He had to see her father first.

Chapter Twenty Eight

She was the soul of discretion and the balm of his soul. She was a beauty and his only beloved. He missed her with the click of each second and he had to marry her to avoid an illicit liaison.

They therefore left for Karatina in the forenoon to obtain parental blessing for their marriage. Mukesi, though resolute, was apprehensive about the visit. Ethnicity and bride price were a bitter reality. At the core of his soul sizzled a spring of passion for Wanjiko; however, he was not at all prepared to succumb to the parochial demands of custom.

Mukesi had gathered sufficient information about Karega wa Mwangi, his prospective father in-law. He was among the pioneer graduates from Ukere university in Masolo and was so proud of it. He was a snob in the superlative and at friends and relatives he scoffed. University, Mukesi had not reached but in the name of Sitawa he swore never to be intimidated.

In spite of his little education, Mukesi had supervised graduates in flower farms. He had seen graduates who could not take a girl out owing to the poverty of their situation. There were those with money but could not plan their finances to live a life befitting a graduate. The young man had grown to learn that it was one thing to be a scholar and another to be wise.

It is this that provoked him to dislike Karega. He had battered Wanjiko. He had almost squeezed life out of her just because she had not made it to university. His darling had always recounted the experience with the bitterness of gall. Her father had expected a B+ from her but her brains could only manage a C plain. That is how Wanjiko had fled to Naivasha where she lived with her uncle.

Mukesi therefore had to prepare for fireworks. If her father had nearly killed her over poor performance then he would not condone his daughter's presence in the home with an alien man. He fondled his wrist pocket just to confirm all the necessities of his expedition were in the right place.

They alighted at Karatina and Wanjiko paved the way. They plodded their way through the thick mud stumbling and floundering. His thoughts were morbid over the subject. From his youth, he hated autocracy. It was his philosophy of life. You could harass Lot Mukesi, Noah Mukesi or James Mukesi from elsewhere but Cecil Buchacha Mukesi of Okoro, no Sir.

Wanjiko walked ahead of him. He gazed at her from the tip to the heel. Her beautiful waist swayed to the pace of her strides. He felt big.

"That's Mugumo tree," Wanjiko pointed.

"I see, we call it Kumukhuyu," Mukesi replied.

"Kumu…kuyu," Wanjiko tried to pronounce it.

They laughed and hugged each other. "Hey, I realize we are both Bantus" Wanjiku remarked. "I will only add a 'ku' to my mother tongue 'mukuyu' They burst out laughing. Embracing the fact that they are not so different after all.

"Darling, ever heard about its mystery?" She pressed on.

"Oh, only read about it in *River Between*."

"Books, books!" She sneered, "Everything to you is books."

"That's the way. You're as you are because of the knowledge you have."

"So?"

"So they're sources of knowledge and we've to chop, sweetie."

"Darling you'll make me sit and read when we get married," she cooed.

"Of course our house must have a library."

"Oh, thanks!" She heaved and patted him. She hugged him.

"Let's move, sweetie," he directed.

"But Ngugi isn't ashamed to tell us about female circumcision," She asserted.

"It's a reality. Literature must mirror society."

"I'm happy, FGM is banned," she said

"Darling, you can't end a cultural practice by a declaration."

"Ngai, no…"

"They'll still practice it in the privacy of their huts, will you go raising skirts to check?"

"Then how can they change?"

"Change them spiritually. Religion changes people distinctly."

"Muriega," a hoarse voice greeted.

"Turieega, muno" Wanjiko replied.

The man introduced himself as Muthuri and proceeded in kikuyu. Mukesi got alienated from the conversation. On realizing this, Wanjiko replied to all his utterances in Swahili. Muthuri got annoyed. He muttered a few rude words and swaggered away.

"Scram, " Mukesi barked at him. Muthuri glared at him.

"Muruya, where are you taking our sister?" Muthuri burst out. Mukesi calmed and fondled his coat. Muthuri wanted to attack but he regarded his enemy's bold glance and despaired.

They strolled along the narrow path westwards, went around the bend and picked main route that led them eastward into Wanjiko home. The road was enclosed in trimmed hedges of cypress, roses, Kei apple entwined in one another to form a beautiful live fence. It was a so magnificent sight that Mukesi got scared. It was as top-notch as his intended. He encouraged himself.

He looked a hundred yards ahead and saw a high purple gate between two high pines. Adjacent to it was a massive whelp tethered by chains. At the slightest sense of a human being, the whelp barked fervently at thirst for war. Its guttural barks sent jitters in Mukesi. He patted his coat.

He had seen these hounds in Naivasha but this was one of its kind. It had very long canines, rotund neck and blood shot eyes. And its thunderous bark drove you to short call. The beast's barks bruised his heart.

A thick fog descended into the compound. The high pines and eucalyptus filtered the light of the sun; the home became dull. The day frowned. He saw the house. It matched the beautiful enclosure. On seeing Wanjiko, the janitor unlocked the magnificent gate; they entered. The wall was white, the roof was tile and the plan was intricate. Mukesi had no words to describe such a plan. A dark blue Benz rested in the shed adjacent to the entrance. They strolled on well-trimmed Kikuyu grass to the entrance. It was serene and tense.

Wanjiko pressed the bell baton. The door skidded ajar. To his amazement, there was no human being as they entered. Mukesi strutted in with audacious airs to face the object of his apprehension.

The room was spacious and ventilated. Its enormous windows were clad in dark curtains. The grey paint and dim light transformed it into a cave. The colour Television on the table was a mere mockery to grief stricken crew. The full extent of the room was past its blossom. The floor complained of negligence. For decades it had neither swum nor bathed, leaving it under control of grime. A stench of urine from the toilets resisted human habitation. Mukesi gathered himself. He overcame the anxiety that had beset him.

The visit was not impromptu; they had sent word. A door grumbled and griped. Another one creaked and lamented. A tall dark man emerged from the corridor leading into the other rooms to the East. Karega wa Mwangi came in. He was a grey haired man; a balding man. His tummy shielded the upper part of his groin. His frail feet dragged his heavy trunk and he staggered with a hippo's gait. It was his grimace that exuded his insolence to any observer.

The old man slumped on the sofa and it complained of overloading. He opened his blood shot eyes and in a single breath infected the room with a whiff of a queer lager. There he was, the man to whose children was an infested hut they dared not visit, a hyena of a man who had hunted a lifetime of idle booty.

"Wi mwega, Shiko," he greeted.

"Di wega muno," Wanjiko replied.

He did the same to elicit some Kikuyu from Mukesi but his attempt hit the wall. Karega never was so astonished in his life. How could a Kenyan fail to understand the language of Gikuyu and Mumbi? 'Worse still, the 'illiterate' man was his prospective son in-law. Absurd….Absurd...' He thought. An incredulous smile spread on his lips.

He reclined on his sofa and reflected. His temple wrinkled into corrugated folds. From the outset, he never liked foreigners. These were the irimu his parents used to narrate in stories. To bring a foreigner was to contaminate the blood of the tribe. Some of these tribes were cannibals and would bring mediocrity in the tribe.

He regretted his decision to have expelled her from home. Now she was a fugitive. From a fugitive she had then degenerated into a dissolute bitch, never good for anything. She was a wreck of Volkswagen whose reparation costs exceeded the buying price of a brand new one; a confused thing, a street girl whose father had rejected and landed in the hands of the destitute; the gutters…and… tears glistened on his eyes.

Karega who had always been dispassionate and strutting around with a business air conceived an instinctive delicacy of pity for his daughter. But the milk was already spilt. He had one option left: to extricate the bugger from his daughter. He raised up his eyes and growled,

"Why didn't you tell me that you were bringing me this kihii?"

"Fafa, he's circumcised," Wanjiko replied.

"Fool! How did you know?" Karega thundered.

Mukesi now prepared to broach his subject,

"Mzee…," he began.

"Hey! Don't call me mzee!" He interrupted.

"Tell me your tribe first before you say anything!" The old man roared.

"All right, I'm a son of Mwambu from…"

"And where's your father! I can't negotiate with a lad!" He interrupted.

"I didn't come here to be growled at!" Mukesi warned, "I simply came to let you know as any gentleman would that I'm taking your daughter for marriage and to be told how much bride price you'll need. Don't you see any sense in that?"

"Of course, there's dowry to pay," he sneered, "a hefty one especially for the uncircumcised like you."

"Dad, people are people," asserted Mukesi.

"Don't teach me! No….No…a million times! I graduated from Ukere university 34 years ago with honours in cultural studies. I'm not a destitute like you!" He roared at Mukesi with a glare of Mathathi and Demi.

The harangue stung Mukesi to his bones. He heaved with fury; his hands trembled.

"Wanjiko," the man continued, "are men over in our land? What prompts you to bring this thing in our home?" He pointed his staff at 'the thing' his lips elongating and parting and pouting to expose his rotten teeth. His eyes sternly scanned the object of his utterance with despise.

All of a sudden, an emaciated old woman in a floral dress hobbled into the sizzling room. Wanjiko was tense, listening to the insults that tumbled from her father's mouth. Perhaps he thought she was a pit latrine to accept all diarrhoea and dysentery without question. He was mistaken. She wasn't a mere stooge for every choice to be made for her. There were many sons of Mumbi, richer and handsomer; but Mukesi was the man she could love forever.

Karega was wasting his sugar.

"How are you, Wanjiko," the old woman greeted.

"Fine."

"How are you Son In-Law?" She greeted in Swahili.

"That one can't marry my daughter!" Karega thundered at her.

Mukesi lost all his patience. He had only heard about negative ethnicity; he came face to face with it. He could now see why his darling had run away. No one chose to have low IQ. No one chose to be a Kikuyu, a Luhya or a Luo. Why would he be condemned just because he spoke another language? A tear dropped from his eye. Wanjiko wiped it.

"Tell me the bride price!" Mukesi shouted.

"Do you have money? You're too poor to marry my daughter."

"Is that the bride price?" Mukesi blurted. He patted his coat.

"You have the pride of a beggar!" The old man roared and sneered.

"Man, you're wasting my time!"

"Seven hundred thousand!" The man declared, hand on the table.

"Plus twenty thousand, the breast she suckled," The old woman added.

"I'll pay fifty thousand in installments," asserted Mukesi.

"Dog, be off!" Karega thundered.

"I'm not a dog!" Mukesi whispered overcome with fury. He lunged forward and gripped his throat. A struggle ensued. The old woman simply watched. Mukesi punched the old man's nose. He tried to yell but he grabbed his mouth, smothering him. He collapsed on the floor, shuddering. He farted. He peed. Blood oozed from his nose.

"Don't call people dogs..." He whispered "and if you scream I slaughter you..." He raised his forearm to strike but Wanjiko grabbed it. She told him to escape; Karega owned a gun. They darted out.

"They have killed me!" Karega screamed.

The two scampered towards the gate. The janitor let the mastiff free and it charged at them with insatiable voracity. Mukesi whisked his sword from the coat and in a flash struck. The hound fell in two equal halves. They tumbled and swirled on the ground emitting funny noises. They charged on.

He plotted his flight. The gun she had hinted was meant to kill him. The janitor tried to resist but when he saw Mukesi lift the bloody weapon, he surrendered. Wanjiko threw away her high heeled shoes and ran barefoot. She had been a long distance runner in high school and was ready to follow in his steps to the last destination. Anxiety assailed them. They jumped over the hedge into the main farm. As soon as Wanjiko joined him, a bullet zoomed by; a boom succeeded.

Mukesi hoisted her onto his bull shoulder and fled in a zigzag motion. Gathering strength, he skipped over gullies and furrows; dodging trees and ducking star grass. Twice he stumbled crashed to a near fall but he braked and ran on. He panted. He sweated. A few more booms. He fell flat on the ground. She lay safe on her shoulder. They rolled onto a furrow and waited.

"I'll die with you….," she whispered.

"Thanks, my love," he whispered back.

They reached a fence of wire mesh.

"Thank God, over this lies the highway," she said.

A few noises reached them from the home.

In a flash, Mukesi cut the wire net. He kicked the wound with his shoe; a big door showed up. They dashed out to the highway. Mukesi kissed her and they embraced. There they were; abandoned junks, marginal lands that God denied the right to the water of life. They were unlearned professors and orphans with affluent parents. They had no other option but to become one to combat rejection.

"I have no father," Wanjiko said crying.

"Here I am," Mukesi replied.

Chapter Twenty Nine

A fuzzy sense of despair assailed him in spells. He feared he would die of want. He was a dishevelled old man; a withering man with a balding head. The thought that he could sleep and sink forever, sowed jitters in his soul. The immense family and approaching retirement lowered his spirits. Kisiang'ani unwillingly accepted that his second marriage had changed his life for the worst.

Polygamy had sowed the seed of strife and intensified contentions. His decision to favour the second wife had fanned jealousy and violence. He had deserted Sitawa to fend for herself as he nourished his queen. The subsequent fights and quarrels had pushed him into drinking to confront them. Flat in his dirty blankets, Kisiang'ani refused to imagine his age. Being a proprietor of a maiden so young, the pretty agemate of his son, he could not afford to age. He mused over it and smiled. Nonetheless, nature's leveller was a fact he could not deny. He would reach him anytime and demand his breath.

If he indeed came, what account would he give to his Maker? How had he served him? There were a world of myths about life after death. Some said you had to cross a river while others talked of angels carrying the righteous and demons smothering the wicked. He dreaded both. Life was sweeter on earth than elsewhere. Kisiang'ani did not want to die.

Frankly speaking, his shift to polygamy had not been as palatable as he had imagined. It had been excellence of failure if not confusion and vandalism. Even now to be honest,

Katami's conduct was suspicious. Her soul had turned fragile; and fidelity, shattered.

As he reflected in bed, Kisiang'ani was unconscious of time. Although he saw the rays of the sun through the window, he was unaware of the exact time. Could it be a morning or an evening? He wondered. He had slept the whole day and now hang-over beset him at painful intervals. In spite of his hangovers, he was sure of the absence of his wife Katami.

His favourite wife, the strut of his falling life, was changing for the worst. He noticed change even in the 'game of life'. She was unusually tired 'and that water, water...that never was…' Kisiang'ani thought. He hauled his body and turned the other side.

He had heard of her loitering in Okoro, Lwanda and Masolo. Was he becoming senile? He wondered. Old or young, Kisiang'ani could not understand the bug that itched some women not unless they got scratched by men other than their husbands.

He coughed and then thought about retirement. It was an ogre that scared many teachers in Okoro. Thirteen years beyond retirement age- owing to foul play- Kisiang'ani still desired to teach and earn a salary. He still needed it to pursue his self actualization. Like Kisiang'ani, many teachers in Okoro vowed to smite it from teachers terms of service. It deterred them from becoming what they wanted to become.

Kisiang'ani remembered Mr Masinde, a respected head teacher who had fainted in the office after receiving his retirement letter. It was a grievous matter and soon it would knock at Kisiang'ani's door.

In all these hard circumstances, one thing gave him a reason to smile: Masika's progress in school. His son gave him a reason to live. He had passed his exam and qualified to go to university. Wekhanya who had joined Friends Kiboko would pass too. Rachel had not merited University but could take any diploma course. Wataka and Watila were all doing well in class.

Kisiang'ani rose on his two feet and put on his creased, dark pants, withering grey shirt and tyre sandals. He paced to the front of his house and surveyed the lawn in apprehension. His head reeled. He knitted his brows to curb the twilight of the setting sun. Arms akimbo, he surveyed Katami's kitchen and saw a few feathers of weaver birds. His children had lunched on game. He staggered away; he had to drink something to keep his low spirits at bay.

His home was as patent as a clutter of stools in the slums of Mathare. The shattered door gawked at him with horrible misery. It was fed up with constant cyclones of apartheid. It was a featherless hen whose chicks shrieked desperately in the cold. If houses revolted then Sitawa's had sufficient reasons to: it had been segregated against long enough.

Kisiang'ani was a miserable bee of a man that had erected a lifetime of crashing combs. Even his pants cried for his service. The underwear protruded through two sizable holes at the buttocks. His hair was a contracted hedgehog exposed to danger.

He ploughed his way through the coffee trees and picked the narrow path to Sindani's. The orb of the sun sunk behind Tororo plug and darkness besieged Okoro. Up ahead of him, a reptile sang a sad tune. 'A gecko,' the man thought.

A short call pressed him. The pressure escalated to the climax and before he reached out for the zip, the force overcame the decrepit brake and the contents sprinkled on his thighs. His finger searched over the zip but lo! The outfit had no zip; it was closely knitted. He fumbled with his belt and the hustle ripped it into two. The left part of the belt tumbled on the ground as he sprinkled on the grass adjacent to him.

"It's yesterday's liquor," he thought. His trousers needed improvisation. He harvested a sisal blade and split it into thin straps. He sorted out one and passing it cautiously through the loops, he strung his pants tight.

Kisiang'ani patted the pockets of his withering pants. A wad of notes weighed it down. With the scarcity of the month of May, his appearance at the Sindani's was the advent of a sailing boat to drowning men in lake Masolo. Under Sindani's family tree sat gaunt faces, thin trunks and subdued voices. There was a bunch of delinquents whose natures were being refined in the blazing furnace of life. Here, lust was manufactured, hatred was hatched and vengeance carried out. Women were gambled and sex sold. Countless lives had been butchered and homes torn asunder in this gathering.

The hungry eyes all turned at him. Had he not been at the bank the previous day?

"Welcome teacher," Masengo said gaily.

There was Okaanya, there was Pusi, there was Reja and many others whose major preoccupation was the siphon. He shook their hands except Reja who was too tipsy to raise his forearm. He gawked at Kisiang'ani with blood shot eyes, grunted and continued shaking his siphon.

Kisiang'ani did not bother him. Reja had been his comrade in the pot for nearly three decades. He was hefty and muscular. Ugly of face and elephant of gait, Reja was a popular man in Okoro. He was deeply in love with the pot, hence a buoyant bachelour at fifty eight years of age. He lay any woman he found accommodating anywhere, anytime. A wife would curtail this freedom. Consequently, he was a father of many and parent to none.

The siphons shook. Kisiang'ani ordered for more liquor and it was poured into the central pot. Warm water was added. He whipped out his straw, flung it to expel any dust and plunged it into the pot.

"Thank you Omukinyikewi," Sindani appreciated.

"Not at all," Kisiang'ani mumbled

"But where's your cook!" Okaanya blurted.

"Who?"

"Katami."

"I don't know,"

"Hide a patient and we shall hear mourning in your hut," Okaanya warned.

"Is she bad?" Sindani asked.

"She's a people's wife nowadays! She helps many men," Okaanya roared. His voice was hoarse.

"A he he hewa!" Reja rumbled in a wicked laughter.

"Musinde (uncircumcised), why're you laughing?" Okaanya asked.

"If you dip a finger in beer, does it decrease?"

"No," snarled Masengo.

"If you pierce a small hole on the riverbed, will the hole remain?" Reja asked.

"No," replied Masengo.

"But a short man can't measure for us the height of a firewood rack." Okaanya snarled.

"Yes, these bamia eat our wives!" Sindani remarked.

"Where did you see Katami," Kisiang'ani asked him.

"Lusese's shop at Lwanda," Okaanya reported.

"Wallahi, I've also seen her there," Masengo swore.

Kisiang'ani swallowed a lump. His appetite was deteriorating.

"How do you know women who're unfaithful? I've observed something…"

He asked Sindani but Okaanya interrupted,

"Just cry but do not throw the skirt beyond the thighs."

"But the woman is selling his things! She must be announced!" Masengo roared.

"True, what bothers you hurts you." Sindani asserted.

Kisiang'ani's taste for the drink took to its noble heels and he stood up. That the soft bosom of his dearest wife was heaving under the chest of another man, that her sweet sighs were pulsating under the weight of a smart fool in Lwanda ripped his sick heart with a lethal exuberance.

Katami of all the people, the woman who possessed the real warehouse of his manhood. The woman whose warmth gave him a reason to live? No, such a woman could not turn against him. He felt cheated. Such decadence was intolerable among the sons of Mwambu. A woman only disclosed her contents to the husband and shut the lid tight after service. Hers was perhaps, the culture of Masolo.

He cleared his throat of a knot of phlegm and lumbered through the shrubs home. He ploughed his way back, his mind burrowing the rotting heap that his soul secured. It hurtled through the potholes of life in which he had stumbled, confronted the immense storms of shame and touched the irreparable wound he had sustained in polygamy. What he had heard at Sindani's was a tormenting discourse which ushered him in the stinking mire of violence. He had to take action.

Chapter Thirty

Katami was now a pretty mellow of a woman. Her unending duties and jealousy from her ex-mistress did not bar her from blossoming into the charming creature she was. Her plumpish rump, round calves and pointed breasts killed men in Okoro.

At thirty one years of age, she had had four births in Kisiang'ani's house, all of which had brought forth sons for him to behold. It was yet another cause of his ceaseless depression. He had desired to sire daughters with her; not callous boys who would batter him like Mukesi.

This was something Katami could not control. He had scolded her after the birth of Watila but she had frowned and kept quiet. Children to her were blessings from Katonda and it was His preserve to give a boy or a girl. It was therefore blasphemy to question the creator. Her husband's condition of late worried her. He seemed more engrossed in the bottle than anything else. Whenever he appeared, he was so emasculated that he could not turn to her. His providence waned too. Communication wilted and her marriage was as dreary as a funeral.

In all these, he pointed a finger of blame at Bakora, the embattled ruler of Masolo. His regime committed mass atrocities. Katami sometimes asked why Katonda permitted such people to live. He had converted her land into a patient suffering from an incurable syndrome. In her heart, she carried immortal hatred for Bakora, which was ignited whenever Kisiang'ani tried to frustrate her.

Looking at her sixteen years in exile, a snob would assume that Katami had never had ambitions. Katami had aspired to learn and pursue a bachelors in English in Ukere University. Then she would have chosen a handsome man from among her own people for marriage. He would have been young of course 'to play the game' satisfactorily. But as time unfolded her fate, she only sat to witness the triumph of reality over dreams.

She came to learn that for children in countries like Masolo, it was good to have dreams but you needed violence and masculinity to make them real. Logically, men stood a better chance. Education, which is another ladder to rise in society, was impaired by atrocity. One option remained for the girl: the tenderness of her looks. There she was.

Sixteen years along the way had opened her eyes to the bitter realities. As she grew to understand the ins and outs of marriage, she yearned for breathing space. The high expectations she had brought in were shattered in the gutter. Her predicament was further magnified by the culture of the people of Okoro. It was completely at variant to her people's way of life in Masolo.

In Okoro she saw children who could not stand above their base natures. She saw fathers who neglected the hoe, fathers who stripped naked and sauntered in front of their children. Sometimes Kisiang'ani would put on her skirt and run in the compound shouting. It hurt her; she was tired of living with a mad man.

Among her people in Binala, a father was a father and when he spoke, a child did not answer back. A son would not fidget at his command, let alone laying his hand on him. But what did she see in Okoro? A son not only beat the father but also assaulted his wife.

What a hell of a marriage! She regretted her decision to marry him. She never knew they were such uncultured animals in human bodies. Here were children to whom decorum was the devil. Intelligent they were but decency called for more. It did not matter what a father did in Masolo. Even if he came home with a girl and caressed her before children, he remained a father and would only be punished by custom through elders of the clan; not violence instigated by a son.

Katami was at the precipice of her marriage. She was not ready to live a wingless life. She was still young and needed a gentle touch, a fondle and a kiss from a strong man. She consulted her cousin Betty who lived in Lwanda.

"My man is fake nowadays," she said.

"When a cooking stick is worn out, what do you do?" Betty replied.

"You look for a new one," Katami said.

"You see, you've got the answer."

"I can't do that," refused Katami, "I'll become pregnant."

"Tell him to use socks."

"What's that?" She asked with surprise.

"Don't be ignorant!" Snarled Betty, "it's called kondomu."

"How did you know all this?"

"We're refugees, cousin. We have to survive but we must not die of Slim."

"Does the thing cure Slim?" Katami asked innocently.

"It collects all his waters."

They laughed.

"Will you enjoy anything then?"

"Yeeees, oh my sister!"

They chortled.

"I thought slim is a disease of white people," asserted Katami.

"Oh, no!" She whispered, "my friends….have died of it. Even that Kizinga, the head master of Okoro died of it…."

"How did you know?"

"He wooed me but when we went to bed, he had a lot of wounds all over…oh…sister." She broke down. "He tried to rape me and I …I…overpowered him!"

"Oh! Katonda webale!" Katami exclaimed.

"That's why I insist, cousin, use the socks."

The words pricked her because she had spent with Lusese a number of times without using a condom. After the lecture, she proceeded to Lusese's. She never needed to buy a condom because he was a thriving shop keeper at Lwanda.

Lusese was a robust man; young in years but mature in womanizing. He was a monument of generosity and a pillar of selfishness. Katami visited him when her husband was absent especially pay day because he seldom returned home.

It was then that Okaanya appeared at the shop to buy nails to repair his poultry house.

"What has brought you to the rich man's place?" Okaanya asked.

"Lusese is my step sister's uncle's cousin," Katami replied. Okaanya went home. His seven decade experience on earth could not permit him to believe Katami's words. He would not dispute the fact that kinship was revered among his people. No one would be condemned for paying a courtesy call on a relative regardless of age and sex.

But those bedroom eyes he observed between them had defied kinship. He even saw Lusese pass his hand on her breast. "What Sisieno of a kinsman was that!" He cursed, spat and vowed to tell Kisiang'ani. 'I found them almost ready for action,' he thought, 'how can a man caress someone's wife in an open shop? What is happening to our children today? Sex was sacred in our days. It was only done in a locked hut under a hide or blanket!' That was Friday.

On Saturday evening, Katami sauntered her way home. She was worried over Okaanya's presence at the shop. She had been caught pants down. Lusese had just moved his hand from her skirt to the bosom in a gesture of love when 'the devil' appeared. She also knew her sons had not eaten, given that Sitawa was her arch rival.

As she paced into the home, everything was silent. The voluble weaver birds peered into the distance under a poetic depression. Perhaps they were preparing to write a sonnet about the fate of the Kisiang'anis.

The sun was going to bed and darkness spilling in. She cast a glance far ahead and saw a tipsy man throwing the soles of his feet haphazardly to evade the wet grass. He appeared to be in the worst of his spirits. His haggard appearance was a molehill of excrement to her. She was clad in a mid skirt. Her juicy thighs and calves were on show. Her fingernails and toe nails were polished with colour. Her hair was well set and feet shod in scarlet open shoes.

Her husband entered the bedroom as she entered the kitchen. Her four sons squatted around the hearthstones in their futile attempt to prepare food. Their father, like all circumcised men, would not step in the kitchen.

Wataka with his brothers had been forced to loiter on the farm, pluck wandering Jew and boil it for supper. He would not go to maimukhulu (step-mother) Sitawa and borrow; he was aware of the friction that existed between the two houses. As the first born son in her mother's womb, he gathered all experience within his reach to save, Mutiti, the youngest son from starvation.

He climbed on eucalyptus tree and laid traps in the nests. The snares had caught five birds which he had roast for the boy. The toddler had devoured the meat and uttered syllables of praise to the tipsy father who was singing to abate his depression. Mutiti had thanked his father for providing a delicious meal.

"Mama, where have you been?" Wataka asked.

"Mumiiiiiiiiiii!" Mutiti cried staggering to the mother.

"Don't ask stupid question!" Katami screamed at Wataka.

"We've suffered. The child had no food and..."

"Marry your wife and watch her!" She blurted.

Wataka got hurt. He broke down and trudged away. He put his hands on his head and wept. His mother had always been compassionate. He could not tell what had changed her over night. It is him who knew the toil they had gone through during her absence. Would it be wrong to ask after chewing tens of raw mangoes?

In the house lay Kisiang'ani, his ear cocked following everything as it occurred. He was scheming the best solution. The magnitude of betrayal ripped through him and he felt like hewing her into piles of meat. He could not believe that the little 'thing' he had picked from the rubbish pit of Masolo to save from misery could do this to him.

"The girl who made me reject Waliaula's advice has now turned against my love! Surely, he who rejects advice takes the path of death," Kisiang'ani thought.

Someone tapped his back.

"Supper is ready," Katami announced.

"Where were you last night?" Kisiang'ani mumbled from the blankets.

"I went to see Betty and…"

"I'm not a kid!" The man said and grabbed her neck.

He shoved her to the floor and punched her. The blows thudded from head to groin. She shrieked but punches muffled her shrieks.

Wataka, Wamalwa and Watila screamed and threw everything they could at their father. A tumult rose in the house.

"How can you take your hole around to be scratched by any dog?" He roared.

Katami screamed bitterly. He lunged forward and jabbed his nails in her back. She winced. He realized the weapon was weak. He lowered his jaw on her back and sank his canines in her flesh. Katami screamed and bent wherever his mouth went. Kisiang'ani severed chunks of meat from her back, thighs and breasts. She yelled at each significant bite.

"Let me go back home! Let me gooooooooo!" Katami wailed. He kicked her groin; she collapsed on the Radio.

"You'll buy a new Radio!" He growled.

Wekhanya and Masika arrived at the scene but the man had locked the door from inside.

"I'll stone you if you touch mummy again!" Wekhanya dared him.

"Stupid boy!" Kisiang'ani shouted, opened the door and tried to grab him. They ran away and Katami got a chance to escape. She left the following day poorer than she had come.

Chapter Thirty One

ukesi fabricated oceans of streams and converted hillocks into mountains of stress. He walked with a crumpled brow, brooding over a wasted past, which was the haunting demon of his life. From his supervisory duties on the farm to the bedroom of his dear wife, he remained sad, sulky and dreary. Wanjiko pressed all the buttons at her disposal at least to eject a morsel of glee but her attempts sunk into the abyss of defeat.

And the more he persisted, the further he shrunk from her as though she were an inanimate or ferocious wild game. Not a glance, not a syllable did he spare for her. Her heart got imprisoned in the cell of loneliness and uncertainty. She who had no father and mother where did destiny want to take his only father?

Wanjiko longed for that time when her lover would break forth from the tomb of loneliness and reach out for her. Of course they had had their share of matrimonial friction but at the centre of her heart lay his sweetness. She understood clearly that no bolt fitted in with a nut without the crushing friction of the spanner. This is what she had suffered once when he had descended an electric slap on her to wane his belligerence.

Had she not carried paraffin and added it in water? Would they have mixed? Were the sons of Mumbi not matriarchal? Were the sons of Mwambu not patriarchal? She had to relinquish some aspects of her people. The headstrong nature of Mumbi could not be tolerated by Mwambu. Then had she submitted and their succeeding nights had been turbulent fountains of honeymoon.

But something had snapped in his soul immediately Brutus, the new source man, stepped on the farm. Her sweet husband slunk back to languish in melancholy thoughts. He recoiled and slept in his own blanket as though she were infected with a deadly disease. He shunned everyone and went about like one accursed by God. He fanatically stuck to his reading table. As long as he had a pen, a novel, a note book and a thermos of coffee within his reach, then he had all he needed.

Such was the wicked mania that was making a hazardous headway into her dear marriage. His aloofness provoked his acquaintances to equally avoid him and he remained an island of sorrow. Mukesi would lodge at statehouse without regaining his spirits. Even placates and entreaties he objected. His happy feelings were withering and irascible feelings sprouting whenever he stirred from the long melancholy spells. Wanjiko became jittery. Her future became dim. Should fate shatter her man into pieces, would she return to the man who had disowned her?

Something struck her mind. Their only son, two years of age, was in great measure deprived the comfort and advantage of the rural environment. The playing space, the social warmth, the mother tongue-rich in proverbs, narratives and riddles, and other aspects typical of African culture.

Generally, Wanjiko blamed her husband as the worst enemy of himself. These disappointments that had long deprived her the power to work, his constant shifts from the summit of joy to the depths of sorrow owed to his seldom venture in truths that lay beyond the five senses. Religion, like curses and witchcraft were trifles that did not affect him in his cloud of conceit. Her attempts to take him to the church met with boorish remarks. The trio were remnant features of the dark ages that a high born lady like Wanjiko ought not entertain.

In his opinion, the superstitious in themselves were an alien species of humankind and they put society in a horrible mess. They were hence unhinged if not lunatic. Yet in all these, misfortune attended his progress; it crushed his destiny into crumbs of misery. Wanjiko understood the dark powers that subdued the universe. As a true daughter of Mumbi, she had an inherent belief in the manipulation of life by the unseen. Only the ignorant questioned it. It was want of insight to think that an acrobat had drills to perfect the magic of sitting on sharp nails. Absurd. They were powers of the dark world who defied the good God and came on earth to twist the destiny of man. It is this that prompted her to carry out morning prayers whenever she discovered that her husband was at the precipice of death. Consequently, he would feel his burden lifted and breath a word if not a phrase of thanks to her.

It was after those words this morning that Wanjiko with rekindled hopes decided to valiantly plead her cause with charm.

"My dearest dear, what will become of me without you?" She began by throwing her thin forearm around the neck and spraying thousands of kisses on his mouth.

"Forgive me dear, lord on the throne of my heart," she said in torrents of tears, "should it be my former belligerence, dear; should it be the brutality of my father that causes you this pain, should it be my supposition that you're unfaithful; should it be the insolent Brutus, dear, forgive me, forgive them and let it gooooooo!" She cried in the fullness of her heart and lay on his bosom. Her hands secured his back and her tears bathed his big chest. She was a starving hyena, a restless solicitor of the moisture of life whose sole spring was the rejected son of Mwambu.

The heart of stone melted into the water and his conscience reproached him for his previous indifference towards his dear wife. The flood of remorse in his soul wrecked his self importance as he stooped to kiss the uncertainty out of her breast. They cuddled and the size of the resultant tension started claiming their muscles.

"It's Brutus, that good for nothing…, my love," Mukesi wept like a baby. She wiped his tears.

"Forget about him, hold him not in your heart." Wanjiko entreated him. She kissed him. After a lapse of five minutes, his face glowed with the expression of eternal joy. Then had Wanjiko realized the true role of a wife: the mother of her children and mother of her husband.

The punctual messenger of time had risen and splashed beams of light over Brutus' assets when Mukesi left his wife for his work. Brutus was a fat man of monster height and exactly white complexion. Although he was a Boer, he had had decades of residence in England.

Born on the lap of opulence and baptized in avarice, Brutus was a man of little cultivation. His soul neither knew protocol nor courtesy. In his opinion, all Africans were stupid owing to their low material condition. It was very alarming to Mukesi that a people who professed high degrees of civilization should exhibit such low manners. Bloated in his pride, the man tramped over his management. He insulted and abused his laborers, ignorant of the fact that Kenya was thirty seven years of age.

Mukesi was tired of intimidation. He saw it as violation of the principles of administration for a leader to be foul mouthed. He had confronted such autocrats. He arrived in this meeting, which Brutus himself had scheduled in his luxurious home on the East of the farm. As Mukesi fumbled with the door to enter, Brutus who was cheerfully explaining something changed in a second. He put on a grimace. His mouth twisted; his colour tended towards red.

"Good morning, Mr Brutus," Mukesi broke the silence.

"Stupid man!" Brutus thundered and rose to his feet, "why do you come late!"

"I had issues to settle with my wife, sir."

"Stupid! Did you come here to screw your wife or work?"

"I'm not stupid!" Mukesi snarled.

"This's my farm and everybody else is stupid!" He roared, "you can go and fuck your miserable wife elsewhere."

"What's wrong with you," Mukesi tried to complain but a bitter bomb reached him.

"You are sacked!"

Mukesi roved round and round. Dozen upon dozen did he roar, 'brute' 'fool' 'beast' with fists clenched and face contorted. Brutus was not the kind of man who went back on his word. He had said it.

"How I loathe the wretch!" Mukesi muttered and picked his way beside the greenhouses on the flower farm. 'Perhaps there was no wretched man on earth like Brutus,' he thought as he entered the room to unfold the news to Wanjiko.

The idea of returning to the deserted cave of Okoro was exceedingly repugnant to him but he set manfully forward on the journey to Okoro to face the uncertain future. The past skirmishes notwithstanding, there was nothing to look to but submission like the prodigal son, to kneel before his withering father in penitence. Perhaps then would his lost vision regenerate to leave alone these scurrilous remarks of Brutus, these meagre wages of Brutus and climb the staircase to the summit of his becoming. For a man must of necessity go somewhere.

PART FIVE:

THE END

Chapter Thirty Two

Okoro was shrouded in a haze and clad in a dismal air. Dew hung idly on the miserable grass. A bored serpent of smoke meandered from Sitawa's house above the three men to oblivion. In front of Sitawa's house stood a rickety table surrounded by Kisiang'ani, Masika and Wekhanya.

The morning sunlight was creeping into Okoro under a sizable strain by the solid mist that rendered it bereft of joy. Kisiang'ani was now thin and haggard. He was a wizened old man, a man enfeebled by dissipation and emaciated by domestic misfortunes. His flimsy air was a standing testimony of the families he carried on his back rather than the number of years he had walked on Wele's earth. He fended for Mukesi's, Sitawa's and Katami's family.

Kisiang'ani was never in funds but in the bottle to pluck up his descending spirits. He had tried again and again to relinquish this besetting sin but it had gained quickly on him to the current state of infirmity. Those who have followed the track of his history will confidently agree that Kisiang'ani was a crestfallen man. He was a mixture of conformity and deviation to the norms of his people, a man who had obeyed and offended tradition at the same time. He was the best example of offendobey or Afrowest, the muddle, which manifested culture and alienation simultaneously.

He was an uprooted tree and a dislocated animal in the puzzle of identity crisis whose blood and breed risked extinction in the haze of modernity. His dilemma owed to the alien waves that tossed him haphazardly. His home was a monument of genius and a pillar of debauchery, an epitome of eminence and a factory of mediocrity. It was a woman whose appearance beckoned admiration but the heart solicited extreme hatred and repulsion.

Kisiang'ani was not an apathetic man but he had his own way of loving children such that few appreciated. He would rather not manifest it for them to live. This morning, he evinced an unusual attachment to conversation, a change that surprised Wekhanya.

He was clad in his tattered baggy pair of trousers with two holes at the seat; a long sleeved shirt worn out at the cuffs. His feet were shod in tyre sandals. His hair was white, the hair of wisdom- and his beard was clean shaven. It exaggerated his dark complexion.

With a snuff in his right and cupped left palm, he was today a loquacious father. His sons cocked their ears to listen with pleasure. Though emaciated, he was wise, albeit disappointed he was knowledgeable and though poor, he was enlightened, having waded through the turbulent pools of life for tens of seasons.

He unlocked his closed heart in a sage air and rolled into his listeners experiences of unrivalled insight.

"I expect better of you sons," he pressed a pinch of snuff in his nose and continued, "in our times we talked in proverbs but where are they now? Today we tell people frankly because we have a civilized government to protect us from the evil men we rebuke. Sons, I'm elated by your work. You are the reasons for my living. I'm glad you have maintained a brilliant record of work at school, which is the true initiation nowadays. Circumcision today is passing your exams. Forget about what Sindani still does in this bottomless pit of ignorance. This owes to your good luck, to have had responsible parents who went farther to sacrifice their pleasures to educate you. You were very lucky in this cave to have such parents. You have an educated mother and an educated father; they both know the benefits of education."

"You aren't like me sons. My father was a beast. He was a father by default. His advice was animus, his chiding a strap and punishment a spear. I didn't have a benevolent father but a lone wolf; a spendthrift who simply disposed land to buy Marijuana and beer for his consumption, leaving mother alone to strive and provide for the family."

"'Lazy woman!' He would shout whenever she asked for food. It was hers to strike the hoe on the farm from which she was thwarted without his blessing. From the diminishing farm and wanderings, she gathered pumpkin leaves, she gathered enderema, she gathered lifwafwa, which we ate to grow up. If he would not provide food, would he provide fees? Education was confusion from the colonialist. He completely refused to pay my school fees."

"Nevertheless, I did not give up. I did not fold my hands on my chest and weep. I tightened my grip on life. I rose up as a man and obtained contracts in Chebyuk. I leased land, ploughed it and grew onions, which I sold to pay fees. I competed with your mother till she married me as an achiever. Sons, you have seen how much she has assisted me. That's why it'll be great embarrassment for you to go to university only to return and marry illiterate girls. I'll resurrect from the grave and separate you! You don't have to marry a graduate, but a wife should do something....all right?"

"Yes father," they affirmed.

"But life is not," he proceeded, "an expansive haven of peace. Sometimes she will take you to the clouds and other times sink you into the abyss. She may woo you to kick her but then retaliate with an electric one. However, in all this, the successful is the enduring and persistent one. He enjoys the palace and endures the wilderness. But he who puts his hands on his head and starts crying, 'Father! Mother!' And wait for manna from heaven becomes destitute and leaves nothing on earth when he dies."

"Sons, this far I have brought you, you have no reason to masquerade as beggars whether I die now or tomorrow. Everything is possible to those who put Wele first and cling to their objects of pursuit."

"Yes, be focused on that object. Gather your shattered pieces. Be a self-possessed man, controlling your base natures like anger, greed and boasting, lest you lose everything altogether. Watch your chance, watch your ambition. Guard it, for that's the talent Wele will want you to give an account of."

Kisiang'ani sneezed and drew his dirty rag to wipe his nose. Wekhanya gazed at him with a deprecating smile. 'Who was he to bay about such ideals anyway?' Masika glanced at him with a reproachful face. It restrained him from distorting the river of wisdom, which flooded into them. Wekhanya's hate for dissipation clouded his judgment. Kisiang'ani was the most qualified to highlight the demerits of dissipation.

"Do not plunge into extremes. It's not the preserve of an achiever. Keep somewhere in the middle. Balance your pursuits to yield an all round person. So that when you look at yourself, you'll behold the beautiful rose of diligence but your uncertain future is the bitter consequence of the same. Keep simple of attire. Boast not, you never know whom you're telling your good plans. The world has many enemies of progress."

"Be more selective in your choice of friends. Bad friends will show you the home of the harlot and the brewing ground of beer. Sons, they showed me how to take it and as I enjoyed my freedom, I got enslaved. Children, I got enslaved to a lover who kills her man before his time."

"I take it but don't taste it. I know its awful consequences. Make do with what you have. Riches will never come; the sun will never stop to wait for you. Buy a goat instead of a radio, a heifer instead of television and a piece of land instead of a car. As time flies, the former appreciates but the latter depreciates in worth."

"The pen is your hoe and the book your farm. It is the best inheritance you can give to my grandchildren. Use knowledge to get what you need but do not kneel before it. It is Wele, the giver of all who deserves your knee. That spirit of worship in the Ababulo blood should be nurtured. I too loved prayer but the rigors of life…" He stopped to clear his throat of a knot of phlegm and looking at Wekhanya, he said, "Son, I give you a cane to lead the family to its destiny. If a rascal hurts you, only use the fist; avoid a weapon," Wekhanya nodded. He turned to Masika, "You now become my first born, son. Guide your brothers well. Always reconcile them so that your unity may lead your generation onto a bright, future dais of glory. If destiny gives you something small, share with your siblings. But do not neglect yourself. That's wicked generosity."

Kisiang'ani rose his eyes and gazed farther in the north. With a magnanimous air, he glanced at the dilapidated man coming towards them. He thought sentimentally about him. Mukesi, the first fruit of his life, had never been successful. His anger had provoked him to disown him.

'Did I really curse my son? No, I didn't speak an ill word against him. The cycle has to end.' His visage tightened in penitence for the past errors and sins. Mukesi's attempts to succeed had been a fiasco. He had returned to a life of porridge in Okoro with his dear wife, Wanjiko. Kisiang'ani candidly confessed that had she been a daughter of Sela, she wouldn't have stood his poverty. Wanjiko had passed the test of true love. How erroneous the stereotypes were. He had heard rumor about greed among her people; what gluttony did he see in her?

Kisiang'ani had forgiven his son on the day of his arrival and hoped things would work well for him. Mukesi reached where they were, his features contorted by extreme dejection. The poverty of his attire expressed the urgency with which his soul needed repair. The visage carried the sulkiness of a frail mongrel.

"How are you son?" Kisiang'ani greeted.

"I'm alive."

"Welcome," Masika said.

"Thanks! I'm shocked at Kizinga's death," Mukesi's said.

"Sure? Is that man dead?" Asked Kisiang'ani anxiously.

"Yesterday."

"On my way to Bangamek, I got the report of his illness."

"That plague will finish people," Masika said.

"It's their immorality. However much you tell them!" Wekhanya barked.

"No, go slow, slow, that's life son," Kisiang'ani said.

"AIDS can strike anybody," Mukesi said.

"No it's for those who're immoral," Wekhanya snarled.

"You're still young," Mukesi persisted.

"And it's bad because the majority of those who die are important to our society." Kisiang'ani asserted, "we have to guard our passions," he stood up. He had had his say.

He now desired to have a good time with his peers somewhere in Okoro. Wekhanya was confounded at the manner in which their father had imparted into them the history of his life. He now understood the cruel treatment he had been subjected to in the home. His father who had never known what a father's affection was had no option but shift the same to his offspring.

Kisiang'ani picked his way through the coffee, roamed through the pot holes and tuft grasses in search of the lord of his soul in Okoro. He was one lord who remained the bane of his soul in Okoro, a sovereign who contributed millions of bricks to build an Okoro worse than useless. You did not need to mention him for the women of Okoro knew him as the root of their men's impotence. But Kisiang'ani embraced him even now as he ploughed his way to hell knows where, he had flung his antennae ahead to seek him out.

In his soliloquies, he reproached himself that he had made him deprive his children the discipline precursor to a bright future. Nonetheless, he hurled the 'hell' of self search away. It was sugar wasted to brood over a lost past. He could not mitigate in any other way the blunders he had committed. All that remained was to wait for the evil angel who had swept his ancestors away. He had swept Kizinga and Kisiang'ani was not sure of the following day. This thought made him fear. He feared the angel; he feared his creator. What account would he give Wele? How would he account for his life?

He shuffled on with a light gait of a praying mantis. He was a loner as he was accustomed to nowadays. He was avoided in every waking moment of his life. He was a white man whose children had learnt in big schools so it rendered him without a friend in Okoro. A few that came his way were insincere. But Kisiang'ani was a social animal; his social instincts craved their warmth. His feet led him all the way to one enemy of progress in Okoro.

She was the Chief General Staff of the vicious army that plotted to destroy anyone who laboured to uplift Okoro above its misery. The number of those she had led into the world yonder through her schemes was as countless as her singed hair.

Chang'aa, for that was her name, was a giantess of a decade's experience in widowhood. Conversely, she was always in the family way. Her bass voice and crumpled face hinted about her hellish tricks to bury Okoro deeper in abyss.

"'That Kizinga was a man,' Kisiang'ani thought as he approached Chang'aa's home, 'yes a man who made my sons go places…always in suits…I must attend his funeral…is it today?...yes, I'm a great man too...with bright sons…a ha ha!...but it's strangers who pay their fees…no…but they're…my sons…a, ha!...where are my suits?...A ha…I pawned them for beer…Anyway it's that good or nothing Repa…I wish I bought her the blankets!..And that padre Waliaula…no…it's my father! Oh dad…I confess the wrongs I committed against you…forgive me!'"

Tears of remorse filled his eyes and the path around him was prevailed by Mauka's presence. The air swirled and spun. There before his eyes he stood clad in his leopard skin, unkempt hair with a spear in his right hand. Kisiang'ani rested his eyes on his and Mauka beckoned him gaily.

He rose from his delirium; he had collapsed and swooned. He was not the kind that got intimidated by swoons.

There he was at the heart of creatures whose hearts yearned for divine renovation, huddled around the pot. This pot with its clients was very important in Okoro. It was a battleground for chitchats and the belligerents, and a downward spiral of gossip that resulted in dreadful consequences. It was a fireside for the sons of Mwambu who shivered in the icy cold of crumbling marriages. It was a mine from which the wimps extracted courage to face the rigors of life. It was a spring of novels and a theatre for comedies and tragedies. Summarily, it was the arena of rebuke, a house of criticism and a ruination of many a home.

Here the miserable obtained temporal hope, acts of chicanery were considered and jealousies implemented. With timid friendliness, Kisiang'ani shook the hands of his comrades and was offered a seat near the pot of life. The hut was murky. It was crammed with shabby men engrossed in the simple operation of shaking and sucking the siphon. He whisked out the siphon from his walking staff, jerked it to shake off any intruder and plunged it in the pot at the centre. The pot was coated with a generation of soot and dust. It resembled the one he had spotted on the farm loaded with remains of Reja's father.

"Bamia, ugh!" Kisiang'ani thought, "they exhume the dead!" He sucked on. It brought him to Kizinga.

Is that man dead? He asked himself.

It ripped through his soul and left him broken. He realized how helpless he was before death. The drink warmed his guts. It calmed his mind; his anxiety abated. He then thought with a touch of sourness over his family's progress. Its big size drained the tiniest ray of hope from him.

'Now that I…am going to retire…who'll…take care of them? Who'll take them to school?....and Mukesi? Who'll cater for his higher education? No…let me go… My ancestors…take…my life…!' He was ambushed by storms of despair and defeatism. They bloated his soul like a balloon and threatened to blast it. He needed a supernatural hand to relieve him. The worldly strain overloaded him.

"That Kizinga was a great man," somebody shouted with a booming bass.

"In…deed," Kisiang'ani affirmed with a titter.

"Great indeed!" Okaanya shouted, "great in eating our daughters," He spat on the muggy floor. All the men chortled save for Kisiang'ani.

"But he was always smart," Kisiang'ani said.

"Now look at him!" Sindani thundered, "looks are for women! A man is what he does!"

"That's true!" Okaanya blurted, "unless Kisiang'ani tells his sons to forget suits and work, they'll be poor! Should it not happen, you'll circumcise me again."

"But my sons eat books," Kisiang'ani said, calmly.

"Cowdung, they're bullshit," Sindani thundered with venom, "they know much but do nothing." He cleared his throat of a knot of phlegm and spat on the floor.

"Get out of here you fool!" Reja roared.

"Go and drink on the table of the rich," snarled Masengo, "the rich who send their children to university."

"Cains!" Kisiang'ani shouted fearfully.

"Get out!" Okaanya snarled.

"That's why you spoiled your sons by taking them to the wood," Sindani asserted.

"Who?" Kisiang'ani asked.

"Wekhanya and Masika," the men chimed simultaneously.

"Go! Go and sit with those who have!" Sindani growled at him.

Kisiang'ani resisted. With Reja, Sindani pushed him out. He paced out of the hut, timid, as was his custom of late. He had nurtured a mania of evading brawls to extend his lifespan.

There he was, rejected because the creator had denied him daft offspring. The cold air outside woke him from the somniferous effect of the drink and he saw Chang'aa sitting in front of her hut. On seeing him, a constrained smirk appeared on her visage. She then flew into a mechanical laughter.

"Come here," she called, "I'll give you free drink." She rose and hurried into the hut.

"Leave those fools alone!" she went on, "don't sit with failures like those," she said with eyes that carried a fabricated expression of sympathy.

"Thanks," replied Kisiang'ani, "I'll kindly welcome your generosity." He staggered towards her, completely green about the seething envy in her breast. Like his male allies in the hut, Chang'aa was aggravated by his acid emphasis on the sons progress. She had schemed a way out

Kisiang'ani's desire to quench his thirst could not permit him to examine her shrewd smiles. She emerged from the hut with a cup of drink and handed it to him.

"Thank you," Kisiang'ani said. He grabbed the cup and gulped the drink down his throat. It flowed down his guts and warmed them. He swallowed more gulps and his face got twisted by the heavy weight of his eyes. As he stared at his queen for a second helping, a sharp twinge of pain ripped through his intestines. Kisiang'ani assumed that it was the effect the sweet potatoes he had eaten the previous day. The pain whirled and escalated in him. He abandoned his cup and stood on his feet. He staggered in puzzlement out of Chang'aa's compound and ploughed his way through the high grass on his way home. Throes of pain seared his stomach with sparks of burning coal.

He tried to imagine the cause. The cold reality struck him. Chang'aa had wreaked vengeance for all the Cains of Okoro. It was clear to him that the academic excellence of his sons had precipitated floods of jealousy that was beyond human resistance. A streak of pain stung him, a clap of thunder succeeded. It poured on him in sheets. He pressed a pinch of snuff in his nostrils and sneezed to lessen the pain but he coughed, retched and collapsed in the wet grass.

The storm raged. The big cock of the sky crowed over him. It unleashed dreadful sparks and earth shaking thunderbolts that soaked his clothes in dirty pools of water. He vomited in vain attempt to expel a minute chip that stuck in his throat. He cleared his throat of phlegm and spat repeatedly. The chip could not move. He peered at his spittle; he could not see in the dark.

Kisiang'ani shivered in the cold. His teeth chattered and skin puckered. He was alone in the bush. He swallowed and the fluid crawled down his guts corroding tissues, ripping organs; pulverizing them into naught. He groaned. A hillock of pain lanced in him. It rolled round and round from the throat, twitching and crushing his guts to the rear.

Periodic spasms interrupted the uniform current, and jabbed him at crotchet pace. As the current approached his hind quarters, the gate gave way and jets of fluid splashed out. Kisiang'ani twitched and rolled in frenzy as rumbling sounds of defeacation exploded in the wet grass. The twitches, dwindles and jerks rolled him back and forth. He gaped his eyes but saw nothing. It was extremely dark.

He had curled like a serpent in a small depression on an anthill. The fluid gushed out of the bubbling spring in the parting of his bottoms to ease the burden of anguish in his diminished tummy. He writhed and groaned. He called the names of his sons; he called the names of ancestors. Getting no response, he shut his eyes. Insects, birds and reptiles sang around him. The geckos led the song, the crickets attacked it and owls added the Isukuti beat to sustain his heartbeat.

A knot of pain crashed down his guts. It burst out from his behind with a deadly sting. A light liquid flowed easily and continuously. He gathered all his energy to open his eyes and look at his hind quarters but failed. He stretched his hand and touched the fluid. He gawked at it with his fainting vision. He saw blood. He closed his eyes again and before him stood his aunt Repa.

"So you have grown rich and despised the breast that fed you? I toiled with Sifuna for ten moons! I bore him! He gave you a job! Now you deny me a mere blanket to cover my thighs? I'll show you the spot through which Sifuna came!"

"You can't force me to give you things!" Kisiang'ani shouted.

"uuuuuuuuuuwi! Look at this ogre!" The woman screamed and raved mad. She threw her skirt onto the ground. She raised her blouse and exposed her groin. She bent once, twice and thrice; her bottoms expanding and contracting at him. He picked a spear and raced her around the home. The neighbours intervened.

A wave of rejection swept over his freezing members. There were blinding flashes, thunder rumbled and it poured on him. The trees around him danced to soothe his fainting pulse. On the solitary anthill, he huddled, alone. He had toiled alone his way up, he had lived alone in Okoro, away from his kinsmen, now he wrestled alone with peril.

The sharp spasms intensified again. He choked with bile and vomited. His mouth was the bitterness of gall. He gathered his energy to open his eyes. He failed. He roused his arm to feel his surroundings. Lo, he was beyond apoplexy. He perceived nothing but darkness. He could hear voices. Voices. He strutted past Chang'aa and swaggered down a highway to a new world.

Chapter Thirty Three

This is the moment poverty and idiocy become bliss on this deviant earth. Only the wise endorse the bitter truth that thorns also flourish on a beautiful rose. Subsequently, the poor man is saved from many problems that a rich man encounters. It is during such moments that a blessing becomes a curse and the blessed man will penitently denounce his blessings and blame his creator for holding back his curses.

This is how Noah Kisiang'ani Mauka, in this infamous cave had been condemned to live a dissipated life, leave a scanty history and heart breaking reputation. The way he died was shameful yet his roses rather thorns betrayed him.

He was picked on the summit of the anthill the following morning amid groans, wails and shrieks and carried home. His members were smeared by an awful concoction of spittle, excrement, blood and mud. His scanty attire emitted a jumbled stench of busaa, shit and bile. His face was contorted by permanent ridges of his unwillingness to die. His peers tiptoed around him with headshakes, chorus of sobs and streams of tears. They were not sorrowed by his fate but their addiction to the Mistress of Okoro.

Okoro was drained in floods of wails, which escalated to its fringes in due course, and hundreds milled into the compound to mourn their teacher. Screams poured in thousands of litres. A hero had fallen. A prominent man had been cut off by the foul schemes of a villain. Okorians compelled everything to put on the garment of gloom. But the weaverbirds were cheerful in their ignorance of loss and they sang as though a season of plenty awaited Okoro. They tossed in frenzy from tree to tree while dodging the angry stones from bereaved villagers.

Many words were said. Chang'aa was among the mourners, deeply aggrieved by the departure of her client. There was Okaanya, Sindani, Masengo and Reja too. Amidst the torrents of tears, many voted the deceased as the epitome of innocence and discretion. He had lived a life that was above reproach and there was not a single learning like him in Okoro.

"The storm killed him," a voice whispered, "no, it must be ekidada, don't you see diarrhoea?" said yet another.

In the far distance was Sitawa, deeply immersed in the intensity of her loss: shrieking, wailing, tapping her thighs, patting her breasts and threatening to tear her attire asunder. She emitted throaty groans that strongly exhibited the sincerity of her loss. She insulted the villain and blatantly refused to be comforted.

"We were with him at Chang'aa's home," asserted Masengo

"Shhhhh…shhhhhh," He was silenced by Okaanya and Sindani.

"It's the storm that killed him!" Sindani diverted the topic, "you know there is another type of Chang'aa called Lifuro…he…he …don't joke with you."

"Yes once you take her," interrupted Sindani, "the body repels cold water. It's worse if you have not eaten as Omukinyikewi does!"

"We're not here to blame our brother!" Khaemba said, "we're here to condole the bereaved and wish our brother a nice journey to the land of the ancestors."

Masika, Wekhanya and Mukesi saw their father's corpse in the living room with extreme shock. Even Mukesi, who rarely manifested feelings, broke down and whimpered like Wanjiko. Masika gave a chest bursting heave and tears jetted out of his eyes.

Wekhanya was too astonished to shed a tear. To come to the belief that he who had spoken candidly about his past twenty four hours ago had returned home forever was impossible. He was dismayed beyond despair, the land where tears were an alien species and lunacy the first born son. His heart coagulated into a diamond. He uttered no cry. He roamed the compound back and forth like one in a delirium. He moped in solitude, at the fringes of human intercourse and went along shaking like a solitary banana stem in a cyclone.

Wekhanya tried to understand his father's decision to impart in them the scanty history of his life and unravel the puzzle of his sudden departure.

But professional mourners like Chang'aa refused to conceal their feelings and darted in frenzy; singing dirges and uttering heart rending shrieks. They pointed their fingers of calumny at the young man, Wekhanya. He seemed to lack a grain of feeling that distinguished people from beasts.

Wekhanya surveyed the corpse in the sitting room once more. There were signs of diarrhioea, spittle and abdominal swelling. He desired to know the person who had killed his father.

Meanwhile, word had reached Cheleba and Kisiang'ani's relatives descended the mountain with cascading fury. They poured in the home with noonday sun. They were armed not with food but shrieks; not with money but yells. There was no etiquette. They arrived with a thunderbolt of hullabaloo. Did they not love Kisiang'ani? Had he not been a teacher? He would feed them to prove his generosity.

There ensued a mighty roar of noise and bustle; kicking of utensils, flying of stones and jerry cans, screeching of tables and benches and any other customary confusion. Emotions flared. Young men plunged in a trance, clad in traditional warrior costumes shrieking and stabbing the ground with spears. There were voices and noises with notes and tones that ignited sorrow and scepticism. Their faces had never looked so tight, their eyes had never looked so bright; their bodies had never looked so ill, their souls had never exhibited such ebullience. They ran back and forth assessing the material condition of the home.

They poured profusely, they gushed generously as a sign of their love for Kisiang'ani. They were old men and old women, children and adults laden with tears and misery. Repa, Maratani, Reja and Livuva sauntered around the home, sad but with bright eyes.

As the din settled down, a guttural wail rend the air. Every one turned to look. The man had cast away the shirt and his bony trunk greeted the mourners. He stormed into the living room where the corpse was lain. He touched it and emerged holding his spiked staff high. He sang a poignant tune.

U wi!	*U wi!*
U wi !	*U wi!*
U wi !	*U wi!*
U wi !	*U wi !*

Mukhwasi wanje	*My brother in-law!*
Mukhwasi wanje	*My brother in-law!*
Wandekhela engunyi	*You've deserted me in anguish*
Wandekhela binanio	*You've abandoned me in torment.*

He danced round and round, stopped and wiped his face with a rag. He greeted everyone. Wekhanya identified him as Maurice Binyasio, his distant paternal uncle. But, his presence did not carry much gravity like that of Maratani's. He could not be taken lightly. He was known as far as Bangamek as a seasoned officiator of Kumuse. It was a ceremony that marked the final farewell to the deceased on the third day after burial.

As a literature student in Milenia university, Wekhanya was delighted because it would be an opportunity for him to witness the ritual that was only observed as an honour to an elderly person in death. He knew it was a ring meeting, a privilege reserved for people with grand children.

Kumuse was the only ceremony among the sons of Mwambu revered beyond circumcision for boys but Wekhanya doubted its feasibility since his father had been a rebel to the norms of his people. Wekhanya himself had been taken to the wood (hospital) for circumcision. This was alien to tradition and hateful to Maratani's prophetic spirit. Already, he had twice complained about the offhand treatment the Kisiang'anis were giving him. Omukambisi was an important guest who would not taste vegetables in a teacher's home.

This coupled with alien religious surroundings in the home were provoking him to offer a substandard service on the material day as a warning to his people. He had to purge down alien values. Omukambisi was sometimes requested by relations of the family to reprimand some people in the family. Some members in the Kisiang'anis had to brace for criticism or even curses.

The Kisiang'anis had to look, ransack every nook, to find food for the crowds. Binyasio stirred from his seat and growled, "Me, I have cried more than anybody else. I want food! My brother in-law was a very good friend to me! He bought me a glass of Chang'aa whenever we met! I want food, not weeds!" He screamed and pranced around the home. He assumed the reins.

"Wanjala!" He called, "Cut that tree down and light the fire of tears!" Wanjala began his work as the self proclaimed head swaggered into the cattle shed. He released the muscular bull, Tope and called three men to assist slaughter it.

"No, no, no, that's our only bull...," cried Sitawa.

"We can't shame Omukambisi!" Binyasio shouted.

"True! We can't!" Blurted Wanjala.

"A woman owns nothing in this home!" Wafula declared. Sitawa shrank and proceeded with her food search. Masika had to forego a semester's fees to meet the cost of the ceremony. Fifty thousand shillings was pumped into food and Binyasio was sent to buy and grind two bags of maize. One bag was ridden into the compound and the other spotted near Okoro Primary being shifted to the Binyasios.

The huge eucalyptus at the centre of the compound was brought down with a mighty crash and strong men reduced it into a rack of firewood. The bull was slaughtered; Wanjala and Wafula flitted back and forth with bright eyes carrying huge chunks of meat into Katami's house.

In one of these exhilarating trips, Wanjala passed, stooped like a hunch back and loaded with the ugly head of Tope. As he hurtled away, he stumbled to a near fall and the scene afforded many a hearty laughter. Over the night, old men rested by the fire of tears, telling oral narratives to condole the bereaved while roasting chicken. Many chicken had to be roast to display the deceased's largesse.

"Nandakaywa, the monster, swallowed all the people in the village and left one courageous young man who had built a fort to protect his only sister," Maratani began. They were sitting around the fire of tears. He pushed a log into the fire and proceeded,

"Mwambu, the young man had violent dogs that barked like thunder whenever the ogre tried to attack. The three dogs, however, protected them on condition that they tasted the food before any human being did. They would not fidget at the enemy if this was disobeyed. Mwambu obeyed this instruction and they lived very long."

"One day, Mwambu told his sister that he would travel to a far place for one moon. He therefore told Sela to do as he had always done to be protected from Nandakaywa. The first two days after his departure, Sela obeyed the instruction to the letter. On the third day, she ate the food and then gave it to the dogs. They refused to eat."

"Nandakaywa stormed the fort. Sela raised her pretty face and saw a tall fat beast with three mouths. He had one round eye at the forehead. His hairy body shook with fury. He roared and picked Sela."

"Dogs, bite him!" Sela cried but it was too late. The dogs huddled at the gate sadly. He seized her and swallowed her."

"When Mwambu returned, he called his sister but there was no response. He ransacked every corner of the fort; his dear sister had been swallowed by the ogre. Mwambu set off to look for Nandakaywa. He had swallowed Mwambu's friends, parents and ancestors. He picked the moon spear, the sun spear and the lightning spear; he walked all the way to the ogre's home."

"Mwambu reached there at sun-up and found young ogres at the gate. He bet they were Nandakaywa's children."

"Where is your father?" He asked.

"On the farm," replied the ogre.

"Call him, I want Sela!" He ordered

The young ogre climbed a tree and called in a song:

E papa E papa	*Father! Father!*
Omwene Sela echile	*Sela's owner has come*
Namuendebe kaloba	*He refused to sit*
Namuekindi kaloba	*He refused another seat*
Balikenye yoo yekamayeye.	*He wants your honourable seat.*

Nandakaywa heard his son sing and commanded one of his slave ogres to go and check what was amiss at home. Meanwhile, Mwambu speared the son with the moon spear. He fell dead."

"When the slave ogre reached home, he got an opportunity to steal the labourer's beer in the house. On seeing corpses of the master's sons, he thought they were tipsy and chortled,

"A, ha, ha, ha! These Nandakaywa's are very drunk today! Have you finished the beer?" He greedily ran to steal the beer and Mwambu found an opportunity to kill him."

"Mwambu ordered other sons to call the father in futility. They sang the song, he speared them; they sang the song, he speared them. The slave ogres came, they got diverted by the beer; he killed them."

"Finally, Nandakaywa decided to come. The thump of his feet was the rumble of thunder. *Bwu, bwu, bwu, bwu* thudded his feet. Rutia…tia…tia…Rutia…tia…tia flew the sparks from his mouth. He opened his three mouths and growled at Mwambu. The young man did not get scared."

"I want Sela!" He ordered.

The sparks were the only response he got from the ogre, "Rutia…tia…tia…tia!"

"Mwambu whipped out the moon spear and threw. The ogre opened his mouth and swallowed it. He cast the sun spear. The ogre swallowed it but it blew out one mouth. Mwambu now whipped out the lightning spear."

"No...no...no!" Cried Nandakaywa, "Cut this small toe and take all your people."

"Mwambu cut the smallest toe of his right foot and the whole village came out. He greeted them very happily and they unanimously made him the chief. That's the end of the story."

Maratani received nods of appreciation from the young men.

"You're our future, sons," Maratani said, "Nandakaywa has eaten Kisiang'ani and Wekhanya must be Mwambu!"

The following day saw the rise of acts of vandalism. Mukesi's goat vanished and bananas were harvested haphazardly. Masika decided to warn his relatives. It was a short speech,

"Kinsmen, you're all welcome," he had begun, "allow me to say something inconsistent to your wish. Our home is under new dispensation. A phase of suffering has ended. Okorians, let us learn from that and change our lives. Death is inevitable but the way you die matters. I'm tired of Chang'aa in Okoro!"

Chang'aa who was sleeping on a mat at the entrance of Sitawa's house stirred up but her friends pinned her down.

"It has caused great harm. This home would have been a palace but for Chang'aa. Okoro would have had good roads, educated sons and daughters. We should be ashamed to boast of only two in public universities."

"Ugh! Sit down!" Maratani growled.

"Ugh! What's this baby trying to tell us?" Mamai asked.

"I respect elders," proceeded Masika in Maratani's direction, "but we can't lead the clan by hate, curses and witchcraft!"

Silence ambled over the gathering.

"How many among you visited our father when he struggled with the curses one of you cast on him?"

Anxiety set in.

"Boy, sit down!" Blurted Maratani.

"You vowed never to see father till death. Are you happy now?" Masika asked the old man. His chin shook with anger.

"And you hated him because he loved mother," Masika continued, "we should stop our pretence and be honest."

Maratani cleared his throat of phlegm and staggered to the dead man's room.

Chapter Thirty Four

"From dust we came and to dust we return," Padre Waliaula's ageing voice rend the air. He was a withering man with scanty singed fibres of hair. His face was so wrinkled that Sitawa could not place his identity. They had neither met in church nor market since the flop of the marriage.

His black Bible with a metallic zipper rested on the long table fronting a brown coffin in the south. Around it were Sitawa with her offspring. Beyond the small tent were thousands of people. They had all gathered to witness the last send off of Noah Mauka Kisiang'ani who had toiled on Wele's earth between 1930 and 2001.

In front of Sitawa's house were dying fires of tears that ejected dark clouds of smoke. It rose a few feet high to engulf the clergy. They had come from the church, which Kisiang'ani had loved and hated; it was Anglican Church Okoro.

Here and there, the kinsmen continued with guttural shrieks. Repa was among them. Chang'aa sat with amazing piety nodding at each word the clergy spoke. If Repa had got the remotest hint of her scheme, she would have deposited her only coin on the credit side of her account for she was gratefully wronged. Indeed she would have patted Chang'aa's back; her wicked design had succeeded with landslide triumph.

Waliaula proceeded with his message,

"It's below the pass mark of life to disobey the principles of the God whose spirit we use, whose air we breathe; whose water we drink and whose light we use daily via his faithful creature of the sky," the laity clapped.

"That's now a man of God," Maratani said and struck his staff on the ground.

"Yet man born of woman has few days to live on earth and that's why it's crucial, brothers to mend our ways. Looking at Genesis chapter six, God has given man one hundred and twenty years to mend his ways."

"And now about the deceased, I declare him a righteous man! His registration number is 666 and he wedded in 1976. He even served as the church Secretary for two years; he left it because he was a very busy man. See, children, will you emulate him? Will you wed?" He gazed at Mukesi and continued…

"And as our Lord put it, a good tree is known by its fruit. Look at his children! Can an evil man educate his children to University?"

"No!" Binyasio shouted.

"Thank you bro," said Waliaula in Binyasio's direction, "I therefore believe that God has placed his soul in eternal peace."

"Amen!" the crowd applauded.

"What did that kid tell us last night," grumbled Maratani, "his mother's but…," he spat with obscenities. Some women complained of taboo. Waliaula led a hymn of praise as the last offering to the deceased was collected.

All the teachers made a special contribution; a wad of notes plunged in the offertory bag. The bag moved round from hand to hand until it reached the pew. The clergy had to bless it before going forth to the widow for summing up. The total sum of the offering in Sitawa's hands was seven hundred shillings in coins. Not even the head teacher of the new Okoro Sec school had given a note. Nay, Wekhanya had given a twenty shilling note!

But Noah was no longer part of the earthly sins. He had left the living and joined his ancestors. The small hillock of red earth in front of Sitawa's house was the eternal evidence of this. A cross was made and driven at the head with a lamp adjacent to it in the first three days. Maratani maintained that Bakuka stuck around the grave at this time hence the need for light. In his view, relatives had to surrender their hair to be shaved to receive their blessing. It was a way to appease them.

In the view of Masika, Wekhanya and Wanjiko, Maratani's suggestion was idolatry. They incited their siblings to refuse the shaving. The old man wanted to use force but Mukesi warned him.

"Blasphemy!" Maratani cursed. *How could a young boy protest against Omukambisi?* He shook his head and vouched to deliver a substandard message. This was his day.

Khusena Kumuse (walking the arena) was adhered to with intense obedience and what was said in the meeting considered law. Maratani therefore walked out of the house clad in a cloak made from a cap of cowries and a flywhisk for giving blessings. On his wrists and arms were special bracelets of two types made from elephant tasks. He was now a spirit, ready to pounce on the prevailing vices in Okoro.

The kinsmen believed that Maratani was appointed by Wele Khakaba as an intermediary with sons of Mwambu. How blessed they were to have such a man from their clan. His presence on the third day after burial was a great privilege. He was a master of the history of the tribe and a stock pile of wisdom. His availability would assist in peaceful distribution of Kisiang'ani's wealth. The men had sat on stools facing north and women on mats opposite men with feet stretched.

In some cases, a woman was not supposed to cough. She would be greeted by a practical curse from Omukambisi. Maratani walked with his flywhisk, the length of space between the men and women without swallowing saliva. He would do this throughout because his words were indisputable; he would rather spit it. Masika and Wekhanya looked at him with jitters.

"Death began long ago," he began, "but it's not the end of life. You don't need to lose your grip on what you're doing sons. Be men. Be strong. That's why you came naked alone as a man to face the knife."

"And if you went to the wood, that's the rebellion we denounce!" Wekhanya sneered.

"Elijah Wanameme came and went. Wanameme who broke the whiteman's flagpole in Malakisi and shat on it, Wanameme who shot a ball skywards and it did not return to earth. Death fell him to the grave. Masinde Mulilo came and went, Maina Wanalukale came and went. Maina, the great hero disappeared to the other Mountain where live our people, he came and went. Mango came and went-yes Mango, the warrior who killed the flying snake and became the first man to be circumcised among our people! He came and went to the land of our ancestors. Think of Wasike Wa Musungu. He rose in Malakisi, played litungu well, but he went; Wambilianga wa Muganda came…."

"And went," the audience finished.

"Yes," he resumed, "who was Kisiang'ani not to die? He has joined our ancestors. He has joined Buchacha, his brave great grand father who never spared a Muyobo."

"He has joined Puraimu, he has joined Kurima, he has joined Milisio, pooh! Death has been there since we came from Misri. We came and lived in the place where the sun sets…yes…there," he pointed at Masolo, "and Mwambu our ancestor gave birth to Mukisu, Mubukusu and Murakoli. The three sons faced the knife on same ground and that's why we are called baluhya- those who belong to the same Luhya (ground of circumcision)."

"Murakoli was very obedient to Mwambu and Sela. Mubukusu was fairly respectful but Mukisu was rebellious. Sons, respect your parents. Honour your mother, now she's a widow. Some of you did not respect your father but now respect Sitawa. Even you Wataka. Although our people say a step-mother is not a mother, they also say a man who doesn't respect his mother won't respect someone's mother."

"And who in this world will sit back and watch his mother being despised? Mukisu was cursed; don't you see them fighting in Masolo? Murakoli was told to rule with kings owing to his loyalty. Don't you see them always close to the presidency in Kenya? And Mubukusu was told, 'You'll prosper by the grip of the hoe and the wheeze of the cowhide strap. You'll always oppose your enemies and succeed!' Didn't you see Mulilo in opposition at independence? And now Wamalwa. Wamalwa who takes lunch with white people and speaks through the nose. Wamalwa insults you and you laugh. Wamalwa will defeat his opponents!"

"Sons, respect is something number one. When you meet a man, your father's age, say, 'how are you, papa.' Your mother's age, say, 'how are you, mama.' Not the animals we have seen in this funeral. You have rejected customs and embraced a bad culture without understanding them well."

"A female monitor lizard told her male counterpart to ask where he did not understand. Children, follow her example. Ask and learn. And some of you have a lot of anger." He raised his flywhisk and fixed his gaze at Mukesi.

"The elephant who likes fighting does not nurture his task. The man who loves peace throws his staff on the blazing hearth. Kisiang'ani was just as rebellious and ignorant. You're going the same direction. The water in the clouds laughs at the water in the dirty pool. It forgets it's still water; only it's time hasn't come. Had he obeyed our customs, he would have learnt that beer has made the tethered cow to dance. He did not learn this wisdom and he went, to show us that unless a toddler stumbles he can't fear to walk alone. Children, is sense getting into your heads?"

The siblings did not fidget. Maratani waved his flywhisk in Masika's direction and continued,

"The world is a rim. Many seasons I've lived on earth and if you don't heed my advice, we shall see. You shan't go far! Heed the advice of those older than you. The pot that cooks bitter vegetables doesn't lose the bitter taste."

"Your customs save you! Your work saves you! If you put on suits, deep your hands in pockets and expect to prosper; forget! A blessing is better than beauty! A woman is not a face; neither is she clothes! Some of you have brought a brown girl here with bad blood. She paints nails instead of working…and…"

Maratani faltered to see the worst moment of his five decade career. Mukesi, Wekhanya and Masika rose and swaggered out of the arena. What profanity! Sitawa was edgy as Maratani made some incoherent verbal fragments.

"A thief dog knows itself." He asserted, "The sun will not set with you still alive."

"Don't curse my grand children!" Butilu screamed.

"The sun will not set tomorrow with these rebels alive," He repeated.

"Let's wait and see!" Masika declared.

The sun shone bright and warm as it strolled to Masolo. The birds sang and insects hummed. The flowers sparkled in the evening twilight as a whirlwind swept by to mark the last cycle of Kisiang'ani's life.